GW00643212

A Roman Affair

Book 3: The Hotel Baron Series

MARY OLDHAM

Copyright © 2022 Mary Oldham
First Printing 2022

All rights reserved. This book or any portion thereof may not be reproduced or used in any manner whatsoever without the express written permission of the publisher except for the use of brief quotations in a book review.

ISBN: 979-8-9859324-0-9 Kindle
ISBN: 979-8-9859324-1-6 ebook
ISBN: 979-8-9859324-2-3 Paperback

Any references to historical events, real people, or real places are used fictitiously. Names, characters, and places are products of the author's imagination.

Story Editor: Sue Grimshaw
Grammatical Editor: Arleigh Rodgers
Cover Art: Lynn Andreozzi
Interior Book Design: Teri Barnett/Indie Book Designer
Author Photo: Tanith Yates

Printed in United States of America
By-Creek-Ity Publishing
Portland, Oregon

www.maryoldham.com

To Sue Grimshaw. You are the dream maker, thank you for always being next to me in this journey and encouraging me when I have those nagging doubts. Thank you for loving Maria and Spencer.

CONTENTS

CHAPTER ONE

The limousine door opened, and Maria Medici stepped under the warm breezeway of the Stark International Hotel Portland, Oregon. It wasn't her first time in America, but it was her first time in Portland, and she felt uneasy. She didn't want to look as nervous as she felt. Her half-brother, Alex, had invited her and the other hotel managers to Portland for the fiftieth-anniversary celebration. One thing she knew—the Stark Corporation liked to celebrate everything. But, in her beloved Roma, fifty years was a blink of the eye. Fifty years was nothing. Two thousand years—now that was something.

She had tried to get out of flying to Portland, but Alex wouldn't let her. He thought it was time for her to meet her sister, Rebecca. Of course, that was if Rebecca agreed to meet her. All in all, she'd have preferred to stay in her beloved Roma with her new fiancé, Pablo Tino. They had a wedding to plan, and she had a dress to buy. And for the first time in her life, the price wasn't an issue. She had more money than she knew what to do with, thanks to the trust fund her father had set up for her and the profit-sharing her brother had insisted on for the last couple of years. Maria Medici was a wealthy woman.

She had invited Pablo to come with her, but he was busy back in Roma with his own business. Then again, he didn't know she was more than a hotel manager. She was a Stark— even if she was still trying to figure out the world and her place

1

in it, being the product of an affair between Garrison Stark and her Italian mother, who had died giving birth to her.

Being a hotelier was in her blood. And damn it, if Alex wasn't trying to get her to embrace her heritage. She still hadn't worked out how she would tell Pablo. He loved her, so it shouldn't matter, but she still hadn't come clean, as the Americans would say, with the information. It would be all right. It had to be.

Removing her oversized Gucci sunglasses as she walked through the lobby of the elegant hotel, she made her way to the front desk, oblivious to the adoring stares of every male in the encompassing space. She was exotic and looked like a young Sophia Loren. Not that she discounted the blessings of her looks, but there was more to her than just a pretty face.

Still, you might be able to take the girl out of Italy, but you couldn't take Italy out of this girl. She looked every inch of her Italian heritage, wearing a tailored black business suit with her signature stilettos. She strode indifferently, resembling a model straight off a runway in Milan. Her carriage and posture announced that she was something more than extraordinary.

"Welcome, Ms. Medici," a young man offered, brightly smiling at her as if she was a movie star as she approached the tall mahogany desk.

"How did you know who I am?" she asked, feeling a bit paranoid.

"The driver let us know you were on your way. I hope you had a good journey," the clerk replied nervously.

He looked as uncomfortable as she felt. She nodded. "Yes, *prego*. Thank you for asking."

Clearing his throat, he continued, "Mr. and Mrs. Alexander Stark would like you to dine with them this evening in their suite at seven if you aren't too tired from the journey."

Maria glanced at the ornate wall clock over his shoulder. It was already after five. She was tired and jetlagged, not at all ready to face her brother and sister-in-law, but she was looking forward to seeing her niece, Lexy. She would make it.

"*Si, grazie.* I mean, yes, that will be fine, thank you," she muttered in brash English, as she accepted the key card he handed her to the executive suite. She wondered how all the other VIPs with the Stark Corporation felt about being ousted from the suite for her arrival. Well, sometimes family had its perks. She liked this one.

Without another word, she made her way across the lobby to the elevators as a bellman with her luggage struggled to keep pace with her. She heard him behind her and finally slowed to accommodate him. Holding the elevator for the young man, she noticed the broad smile he was giving her. Rolling her eyes, she wondered what was wrong with these doe-eyed American men. This kind of effusive reaction was the same as she got when she visited New York several months earlier. Americans needed to retain their emotions. They needed to act more aloof, more European.

The executive suite was on the same floor as Alex and Daisy's private suite. She knew the corporate offices occupied several floors somewhere in the same building. Day after tomorrow, she would see them when she met with Alex in his office. He had a surprise for her hotel, something exciting he'd said, and she was not looking forward to hearing whatever that meant. She didn't like to be surprised. Americans seldom understood Roman or Italian culture.

The bellboy kept stealing sidelong glances at her as he carried her luggage down the long hall toward her suite. Without a doubt, he was trying to get up the courage to talk to her. If he did, she would reply in Italian. Slipping quickly into other languages usually helped her maintain distance from anyone she didn't like or want to engage. When you spoke five languages, that talent came in handy.

She was tired, felt the need for a cool bath, and inadvertently sighed, drawing the bellboy's attention. He was too damn observant.

"Ma'am, is there anything I can get you?" he asked, holding the door to her suite open for her.

"No, thank you," she said politely and held out a substantial-denomination American bill. She was over-tipping, but his smile at receiving the gratuity made her feel good. Let no one ever accuse Maria Medici of being cheap or not understanding every position in the hotel.

Stepping into her large suite, she was immediately drawn to the wall of windows. The suite was on the top floor, allowing for the windows to curve into the ceiling and expose a mass of blue sky set against the urban skyline of tall modern buildings. She could see the meandering Willamette River and several bridges. Aside from having a river running through its city, the cityscape was completely different from Roma's, which featured short, red tile-roofed buildings.

The suite itself was elegant, far more refined than Villa Roma. She explored each of the five rooms and noticed a bouquet of fresh flowers in each room, filling the entire space with a sweet aroma. A welcome basket of gourmet foods and good Italian wine was on the coffee table. Without a doubt, this was her sister-in-law Daisy's generosity at work. In the time she'd gotten to know the other woman, she'd come to like her. They weren't as close as sisters, but they were working toward being very good friends.

The corner bedroom had a view of the city. Maria had to admit that everything about the space, from the linens to the furnishings, was beautiful and perfect in every detail. It was hard to believe the hotels in Portland and Roma were in the same family. Then, realizing the metaphor for herself and her American brother, she smiled sadly. She was used to not quite fitting in but acting as if she did, even when it was pretty clear she had no business doing anything of the kind. People talked about going home on holidays and special occasions. She didn't know what that meant. She had an apartment, but Stark Corporation owned it. She had decorated her apartment herself, but most of the furniture had been second-hand and was thrown together. Maybe once she moved into Pablo's house, she would feel at home. At least, that was her hope and her dream.

Alex and Daisy were the only real family she had. Maria had been raised in an orphanage until she was ten, when the Medicis adopted her. They had taken care of her, and there had been love, especially from her father, Giuseppe. Unfortunately, they had been older when they adopted her and were both gone by the time she was twenty. Their home had been her home for a little over ten years, but when they died, Maria saw the enormous mortgage owed on the property, and she knew that there was no way she could pay. So in the end, she gave the only home she'd ever had back to the bank.

Pulling her cellphone from her Ferragamo handbag, she was about to dial number three on her speed dial (number one was her hotel, and number two was her brother Alex) when she remembered what time it was in Italy. Should she send a text? That would wake Pablo. If she knew one thing about her future husband it was that he did not like to be awakened in the middle of the night for anything, even for sex. The man enjoyed his sleep and did not like to be disturbed for annoyances. Sex and her phone call would fit into that category.

He was still a little angry at her for making this trip without him. Why did she need to go? Did she honestly think she'd keep this job after their marriage? It was very doubtful. Some duties came with being Countess Tino. Did she believe she could have a career and carry out her duties? He didn't think she could do it. She did, but for how long, she didn't know.

She decided on an email. Pablo always checked his email when he awoke each day.

Quickly, she sent him an email letting him know she had

arrived in Portland and loved him. He would scoff at that last part. He believed her, but he wasn't "mushy" as he had accused her of being. He was too much of a businessman: practical, and direct. He wanted to marry her. That was enough of a statement. That meant he had to love her. Or so he'd told her when he proposed.

After nine and a half hours on the plane, it felt good to finally arrive in Portland. She unpacked her bags, then she took a shower, wanting to redo her hair and makeup before facing Alex and Daisy. She stepped into the hall at three minutes after seven and headed for their suite. She'd dressed in a simple but elegant Dolce & Gabbana black sheath dress, with a chunky gold necklace and bracelets. Gold chandelier earrings framed her face. Her large emerald engagement ring added a bit of color to her monochromatic outfit. Unable to get her long, sable hair to lose its natural wave, she swept it into an elegant twist, secured with a gold clasp that matched the rest of her outfit.

Knocking on the door carefully to protect her perfectly manicured red nails, she was immediately greeted by her handsome brother, Alex, whose green eyes were so like her own. He held his oldest daughter, Alexandra, who was a little over a year old, in his arms.

"Look, Lexy," he said, smiling, "It's your Auntie Maria."

The child tucked her face against her father's chest and then seemed to change her mind about facing her aunt. Instead, she looked at Maria and then held out her arms. Maria leaned forward, kissed each of her brother's cheeks, and said, "Auntie Maria? No... no... I'm Zia Maria. It's Italian." He rolled his eyes as Maria reached for the child and handed him several wrapped packages containing gifts for her niece.

"Honey, Zia Maria has arrived, and she is bearing gifts," he called and put an arm around Maria's shoulders. "Nice to see you too, little sister."

"Maria!" Daisy called excitedly, heavily pregnant and hurrying to greet her. "Oh, I missed seeing you greet Lexy."

Maria looked at Daisy, her eyes settling on Daisy's extended stomach, and said, "How are you feeling?"

"Like a whale. I'm due in a few weeks, on June first," Daisy said, rubbing her large tummy. "Did Alex tell you? We are having another girl. We've decided to name her Lily."

"My brother has two daughters to raise. Good. He deserves it," Maria said, shaking her head.

"We want a couple more children, so he might have more daughters, or maybe a little Alex, which would be fun to see," Daisy said.

With Lexy still in her arms, Maria regarded the little girl and said, "Well, she is beautiful, like her mother. Let us hope Lily is as pretty. As for the others, I hope they are like Alex in every way. That should provide the right challenge for him."

"Oh please, one Alex is enough for any family. Don't get me wrong. I am more in love with him each day. I love his passion. I just don't think this family needs another one of him. I don't know if I could handle another of him," Daisy said as she lightly punched her husband's arm and received a kiss on the cheek.

Maria smiled and shook her head. Alex was passionate about his wife, his children, and his hotels. Maria didn't mind. It reminded her of herself.

"I hope this baby will have green eyes and be a beauty like her Aunt Maria and Aunt Rebecca," Daisy said, making Maria smile. She was related to these little girls. Momentarily, Maria was unable to speak. She had more connections—blood relatives. Now, if only she and her half-sister, Rebecca, had a relationship.

Daisy gave her a warm hug, and Maria tried not to overthink the moment, although, the hug from her sister-in-law and earlier from her brother felt good. Unaccustomed to having any kind of family for a long time, she often fought to contain her emotions when in the presence of Daisy and Alex.

"She does look like her mother, thank goodness," Alex replied, wrapping an arm around Daisy and kissing her cheek.

"Well, her eyes are all yours," Daisy announced, glancing up at her husband and then smiling toward Maria. "And yours. Green as emeralds."

Maria watched Alex and Daisy smile at each other and felt a tug at her heart. She loved Pablo like you loved a friend who was a lover, who knew you—but then Pablo didn't know everything that made her the woman she was. Would she and Pablo ever love each other as Daisy and Alex did? Probably not, but they were comfortable with each other, and that was something she hadn't had in life. His home would become her home. And wasn't it about time she had that? A real home?

After the Medicis had adopted her, she was sure her adoptive mother, who always seemed a little uncomfortable around Maria, would change her mind and return her to the orphanage. Then, Maria would learn how it felt to be dirty and hungry again. It was a feeling that you never forgot despite how desperately you wanted to ignore it. Maybe that was why Maria was a clean freak. Everything in her life, from her hotel to her appearance, was always neat and clean.

Lexy started to fuss, and Alex took her in his arms.

"Come here, my little darling," he said, and bent to kiss the baby's head.

Daisy led the way to a living room with the magnificent view of downtown Portland that Maria had in her suite. The long, open space was beautifully decorated in calming butter and cream silk tones.

Maria sat in one of the oversized couches as Alex walked to an elaborate bar and picked up a bottle of wine.

"A little something from home?" he asked. "I got it this morning. I was told it was good, a Brunello?"

"*Prego*, Brunello is always refreshing," Maria answered, watching as he expertly opened the bottle.

"How was your flight?" Daisy asked.

"Good. I enjoy the family plane, but I'm still a little tired," she replied, taking in every detail of the large suite. "I like this. It's so calming. The colors are soft, like the muted colors of Tuscany. Was that your intention?"

"No, but I think it has come together well. Part of Alex's request when I moved in was something peaceful. He wanted a calm space," she explained.

"You should see the bedroom. I let Daisy have free rein. It looks like the lobby of your hotel or a brothel," he said, with a wink toward his wife.

"You just likened Maria's hotel to a brothel," Daisy warned.

He smiled, shaking his head. "Villa Roma doesn't look like a brothel, but when we choose to update it, which is one of the things we'll talk about the day after tomorrow, I think we should make it a bit more subdued."

Maria raised her eyebrow, taking a sip of the excellent Brunello he'd handed her, but said nothing. They had never discussed redoing the color scheme of her hotel. The ease at which he'd suggested it now concerned her. Villa Roma was known for its bright red interior. To change it would be sacrilege. It is what returning guests knew and expected. She added another agenda item to her worry list.

Daisy picked up on her unease. "Alex, you're scaring her. I can see her tensing up. Knock it off."

"I'm not scaring her. I'm just thinking out loud. It makes sense to be proactive."

"He only scares me a little," Maria admitted. "I hate surprises."

"I want to know more about this man you're dating, this Pablo Tino," Alex said, sitting next to his wife and placing a hand on her knee.

"He's sweet, well-respected. He makes me happy, and we are engaged."

"What?" Alex said, looking shocked, while Daisy smiled and said, "Congratulations!"

Maria held up her hand to flash her engagement ring, a large, square-cut emerald surrounded by diamonds.

"He said it matches my eyes," Maria gushed as she looked down at the nine-carat stone and smiled.

"It is gorgeous," Daisy gushed as she reached for Maria's hand.

"Isn't he a bit old for you? What do we know about him?" Alex asked, wrinkling his brow as he scrutinized the ring.

"He is fifteen years older, but that is of no concern," Maria said dismissively. It had bothered her initially, but now she was used to it. Pablo was a widower, so it wasn't like he was some strange single man in his late forties who'd never been married. Thankfully, he didn't have any children, but she would probably have one or two because she had always wanted to be a mother. And she could give children the kind of home life she had always dreamed of while living in the orphanage—solid and loving, with a mother who cared.

"Do you love him?" Daisy asked.

"He is perfect for me," Maria replied. "And he is a count, so then I will be a countess. It is Italy, so it is in name only, but I will have a title."

"That isn't an answer," Alex said.

"It isn't the kind of love you two have," Maria admitted, "But, it is there. We are just different. I think Americans are very emotional. In Italy, we see it from all perspectives."

"You consider the business side of things," Daisy suggested.

"Yes, we are prudent," Maria answered, but she noticed that Daisy looked away and then gazed pointedly at Alex. Daisy no doubt wanted her sister-in-law to have the same kind of stupid crazy love she and Alex had. Well, Maria wasn't

Daisy, and she'd never been that sappy over a man. Alex and Daisy's love for each other was almost uncomfortable to watch. It had, at some times, made her a little sick to her stomach.

"Does he know about you, who you are?" Alex asked.

"Happily, no, he doesn't know that I'm the bastard child of Garrison Stark. I'll tell him eventually."

"You aren't the bastard child. Lovechild is much more accurate," Daisy said, herself an unacknowledged child of her father who had been having a long affair with her mother. "You'll be royalty. That is so exciting!"

"So, you haven't been exactly honest?" Alex asked. "There are secrets between you? What isn't he telling you? What has he hidden?"

Maria sighed. Alex picked interesting times to be the protective older brother.

"He thinks my parents were Giuseppe and Isabella Medici, which is the truth. They adopted me. They raised me. Everything I am happened because of them. They are the parents that mattered. Wouldn't you agree?"

"Maria, that is an essential part of the story. Let's not forget, you are a Stark. It is part of your heritage. The moment you decide to embrace it, doors will open. You've done a lot on your own, becoming the manager in Rome. If you let me tell the truth about your father, my father, you would be a partner, working with me, Rebecca, Adam, and Spencer. We are expanding. We need you. Adam is in Dubai, but I think he has some unfinished business in San Francisco and The Bay Shore hotel that might pull him stateside.

"Spencer has been touring our hotels around the world and wants to bring them all up to standard. Rebecca and her husband are on security detail. They want to change things up across the board. I need you."

"Has Spencer been sniffing around my hotel?" she asked.

"I know he visited it and made some observations a month or so ago," Alex answered vaguely.

"How dare he spy on my hotel? Why did he stay there and not introduce himself to me? Who does that?"

"Well—"

"Well, what? That is why you want to meet with me. You want to tell me what to change," Maria stated.

"Maria, that is exactly why I'd like to go public with you—so you have a voice."

"I have a voice. And it is deafening," she said, putting the glass down on the table.

"Well, it needs to be stronger. I want there to be an actual bite behind the bark. As it is, Spencer knows who you are, but it won't matter to him because you are a silent partner."

Maria narrowed her eyes as she said, "You told him? Why did you tell him something that was none of his business?"

"It kind of is his business. He'd like to work with you. He isn't going to go away," Alex said, letting out a sigh. "Remember what I told you? Three men—our father and my two uncles, one on my mom's side, one on my dad's—started this hotel corporation. By agreement, it passed to the next generation. Rebecca and I represent our father, Garrison Stark. Adam represents his father, Tobias Stark, who lives happily with his wife as a beach bum at our more tropical hotels. Robert Whitlow, my mother's brother, lives in Texas.

"It was never Robert's dream to be in hotels, but when my mother married my father, they all met, and the Starks saw the potential in him, and he was asked to try being a hotelier. He did it well, but we always knew his time at Stark Corporation had an expiration date. Uncle Robert is from Texas and has ranching and oil in his blood. He retired and started his second life back in Texas about ten years ago. He had enough money and a passion for ranching, which I think he is better suited for than a hotelier. Now, after a lot of cajoling and persistence, we got his son, Spencer, in the game. I'm happy for Spencer and happy for the help."

"He wants to play with my hotel," Maria snarled.

"You know, we share the ownership of some hotels, and others are owned outright by different members of the family. In this case, it is his prerogative to have a say in Villa Roma. He owns it. My visits were to be of help to him," Alex said. "But actually, it is part of his ownership in Stark Corporation."

Well, wasn't that just grand. An American from Texas owned her hotel.

CHAPTER TWO

S pencer Whitlow did not consider hiding in the shadows to be anything but watching from afar. He knew he needed to join the family, but the conversation he was catching snippets of was too good to interrupt. Instead, he leaned against the wall of the rooftop garden and listened to his cousin and his aunt.

"Alex has some explaining to do," his aunt said venomously, clutching her champagne glass and leaning against the rooftop garden wall, just a few feet from where Spencer stood.

They were gathered for the anniversary party on the top floor of the Stark International Hotel Portland. It was also the day after the mysterious Maria Medici had arrived and was making her presence known at the party.

"He's making a point," his cousin Rebecca replied as she and his aunt watched the other woman on the opposite side of the roof.

Maria Medici was the manager of the Stark International Hotel Villa Roma. Still, she was also the love child of Garrison Stark, Spencer's deceased Uncle Gary, and therefore, Rebecca's half-sister. Never before had Alex invited Maria to any event attended by Spencer's Aunt Victoria, Garrison's Widow. The women chatting just a few feet away thought it was rude to have Maria in attendance. Spencer thought it was game-changing. It had the potential to cause a huge scene. Someone might get physically injured. You could never tell with strong women.

Victoria and Rebecca were two of the strongest women he knew. He hoped that Alex would wait a few minutes because they could hurt him if he came over at the wrong time, and this needed to play out.

"Well, I'm still his mother. I don't appreciate it, and I intend on telling him so," Victoria Stark said as she set her champagne glass down hard enough to crack it.

"Do you think she looks like me?" Rebecca asked self-consciously. She was, until this evening, usually the most beautiful and best-dressed woman in the room.

"The last thing we need is a scene that could lead to a scandal. It was bad enough when Alex married one of his staff. The board was shocked."

Spencer knew that despite the fact they loved each other, there had been gossip when Alex had an affair with Daisy and then married her. And more gossip when their first child arrived seven months after their quick wedding.

"Mother, really."

Spencer remembered that Alex had threatened to fire anyone who said a bad word about Daisy. It was an overt abuse of power, but no one said a bad thing about Daisy.

"That woman doesn't have your refinement or class. She looks cheap," Aunt Vic observed.

Spencer did not think Maria looked cheap at all. In fact, she looked terrific in the champagne silk sheath with matching wrap and strappy sandals. Her Italian designer outfit probably cost a small fortune, but she was also sophisticated in a way you can't buy.

"Are you kidding? I wished I looked like her—so effortless, so beautiful. And her figure. Who has such a perfect figure? I bet she can eat anything and still not gain a pound, something about the Mediterranean diet," Rebecca said.

And the golden color set off her olive skin and telltale

emerald eyes that were so prominent among the Garrison Stark branch of the Stark family. She looked delicious.

"Come on, Mom, her outfit rocks. She has a perfect figure. She looks amazing."

"She looks cheap," Victoria repeated.

Rebecca was uncomfortably laughing when Spencer decided to join them. After the obligatory familiar kisses and hugs, Victoria asked, "Spencer, handsome as ever, where are your parents?"

"My mother is still getting ready, and your brother is drinking whiskey out of the minibar. Alex should rethink his policy of not billing relatives for their use of the amenities. You know how Dad hates these kinds of shindigs."

"Nice of you to join us from the shadows," Rebecca whispered with scorn.

"I think you get better looking each time I see you," Victoria said. "When you stand next to Alex, you give him a run for his money. I'm sure the board would agree. Maybe they picked the wrong heir to lead Stark International Hotels into the next generation."

"Aunt Vic, thanks, but you and I both know that Alex is an amazing leader," he said, looking to Rebecca.

She shrugged and added, "Mom is pissed at Alex, so he's no longer the most handsome man in the room or rooftop, as the case may be. So you may expect more flattery."

Spencer ran a hand through his wavy blond hair self-consciously. "Then I'd better enjoy this before your cousin, Adam, shows up. Women seem to like him too. I cannot compete with all these Stark men."

"He's not coming. He's stuck in Dubai," Rebecca said.

"Good, my chances are looking up," Spencer said.

"As if you've ever had problems getting women to follow you," Rebecca said.

"Thank you, cuz."

"Really, Spencer, how are you?" Rebecca asked seriously.

"I'm dealing with everything. I suppose after three years, it's about time I learned to live this new life," he said. He didn't want to think about Ruby tonight.

"Ruby would want you to live and be happy," she said.

"Maybe if I keep telling myself that, I'll believe it," he said. Ruby had been his other half for six years, but she hadn't remembered or known him for the last three. Nope, he would not go there.

"So what has the ruthless hotel baron done now?" he asked. "And where is Alex?"

"Well, he finally had a proper wedding to that Daisy," Victoria said. "Almost eloping when she was pregnant was one thing, but having the child with them as they walked down the aisle for their official wedding was quite shameful. The resulting photo was in *People* magazine. And now she is pregnant again."

"Quite pregnant from what I could see when I had lunch with them today," he said.

"Yes, my son obviously has no sense of control," Victoria quipped.

"Rumor is they want a third and possibly a fourth child too, so Daisy says that Alex likes to practice a lot," Rebecca said conspiratorially.

"Rebecca," Victoria admonished. "I would prefer not to discuss Alex's intimate life with Daisy. You sound vulgar. I won't hear it from my daughter."

"Just saying, Daisy is fertile, obviously—two years, two babies," Rebecca added, ignoring her mother. "Alex can't seem to keep his paws off her."

"Rebecca, that is enough!" Victoria admonished.

"That's why you're mad at him?" Spencer asked his Aunt. "He likes to touch his wife a lot? Isn't that a good thing?"

"You'd think Mom would like to know that her children's

spouses want to touch them. We haven't even started talking about my husband."

"Rebecca, stop talking," Victoria said. "I have raised over-sexed children. I won't have the paternal Stark crudeness rubbing off on my sweet Whitlow nephew."

"Thanks for reminding me. I've got to find Mitch and tell him I want sex later," Rebecca said, looking for her husband.

"Stop being so vulgar," Victoria said.

Rebecca grabbed Spencer's arm and led him a few steps away from their mother, who scowled at her a little more unpleasantly with each step Rebecca took.

"I don't know if you heard, but *she's* here. That is why Mom is all torqued," Rebecca whispered to Spencer.

"The Italian?" Spencer asked, glancing over his shoulder, pretending he hadn't already noticed her.

"Yeah, Alex invited her to this anniversary party because he invited a lot of the hotel managers. I think we were all surprised that she showed up. She sure isn't in hiding."

"But only a few of us know about her," Spencer said.

"Yeah, only the immediate family, but Mom is hell-bent on creating a scene just by how she is acting trying to prevent one."

"Where is the mystery lady?" Spencer asked.

"She's over by Luis. She's wearing a gold silk sheath dress."

Spencer didn't even need to ask his cousin. He already knew. He'd seen her the moment he'd stepped onto the rooftop. He'd seen her in Rome a month ago but didn't have the courage to talk to her then. He'd been kicking himself ever since. She was the most beautiful woman at this event, probably within a hundred miles of this event. He wanted to meet her. Hell, he wanted to touch her. How long had it been since he'd had those kinds of feelings about anyone but Ruby? Too long.

Soon enough, he'd be working with the mysterious Italian. His cousin had mentioned that she might not be as open to the idea as he thought she would be. He supposed he couldn't blame her. He hadn't been around for the last few years, and she'd had free rein to do what she wanted with his hotel. She'd done an excellent job. He didn't have any regrets, because his reasons for being absent were good, but they were his own. He doubted she would care if he told her. Well, his hands-off approach was about to be hands-on, and she would have to find a way to work with him.

"I've seen her, and I intend on introducing myself to her," he said. "Maybe you could make the introduction, considering she is your half-sister."

"I haven't even met her yet," Rebecca said.

"She's your sister," Spencer said, incredulously.

"Half-sister, and I don't know how I feel about it," Rebecca replied.

"She didn't ask to be born into this crazy family," Spencer countered. "Alex and Daisy like her a lot. They said she is brilliant and has a lovely way with Lexy. I watched her in action in Rome. She's amazing."

"Yeah, well, I like daffodils. But, that doesn't mean I want to give them free rein over every one of my flowerbeds."

"I'm going to meet her. I should have met her in Rome," Spencer said.

As he strode away, he looked over his shoulder and asked, "Aren't you coming?"

Rebecca had stepped back to her mother and shook her head. Ironically, he knew she'd like nothing better than to meet her sister. She was just scared. He knew a lot about fear. Life was too damn short to live in fear.

⋅⦿⋅⦾⋅

Maria saw Alex's mother and her sister on the opposite side of the garden. Maybe if she were a more evolved person, she could walk up to them and introduce herself. Well, that wasn't going to happen. She was pretty sure they'd like the earth to crack open and swallow her up.

Well, she had fulfilled her promise to Alex. She'd appeared at his party. Now, as soon as he or Daisy showed up, she was going back to her room, and once there, she'd order room service. Something American, like pizza or whatever they called pizza. It was laughable how different it was from the real stuff back home. Or maybe what they call a Caesar salad.

Her sparkling wine, not champagne from France, nor good prosecco from Italy, but some Napa Valley fake wine trying to be something it wasn't, was now drained from her glass. She hoped she wouldn't get a horrible headache from it. She'd need a second glass if she were going to stay much longer. She thought people looked stupid holding empty glasses at parties. They weren't fooling anyone.

"*Buona sera*, Maria."

"*Bonne soirée*, Luis," Maria said, slipping into French as the manager of Stark International Paris sidled up to her in his elegant yet nervous manner. They kissed each other's cheeks.

"How is Roma?" he asked, his hand immediately going up to straighten his tie after he gave his cuffs a pull.

"We are fine. I've decided to get married. That is my big news."

"Why are you doing that?" Luis asked, looking upset. "Who will I make love to when I visit Roma? I'm planning on visiting next month."

"Please do not remind me of our one night," Maria said, wanting to die of embarrassment. It had only happened once when she was lonely in Paris. After that, it hadn't mattered, and lots of alcohol had been involved. Enough alcohol that she had considered giving up drinking as penance. The actual sex had been okay, but nothing earth-shattering.

"What about our night in Paris? Can't we get together one last time for old times' sake?"

"Absolutely not. Really Luis? That was over a year ago. If it had meant anything to either of us, we'd have done it more often. Instead, you didn't call me for a whole week. You should have sent flowers and called me. No, I do not need to relive any of our past."

"I'm scared of you," Luis said. "You intimidate me. I thought you'd tell me to go to hell."

"Which is a good reason for us to never speak of it again."

Luis shrugged, defeated. "What is he like? Your fiancé?"

"His name is Count Pablo Tino."

"Wait, is he the man who supplies all the laundry, the linens, everything in Europe to our hotels? He is good-looking, but a bit older than you."

"Yes," she said knowingly.

"He's worth a fortune. Will you be a countess?"

"Yes," she said, showing him her engagement ring.

"Holy merde! That is a fucking rock."

"Yes, he is worth a lot. Not that I care," she observed dismissively. And she didn't, now that she was a wealthy woman in her own right.

"I heard a rumor that there are going to be some changes at your hotel. Are you leaving after you marry the count?"

"Of course not!" she said, horrified that Luis would know anything before she did.

"You probably don't need to work after you get married. However, Alex tells me the silent partner has decided to take an interest in your hotel."

"Spencer Whitlow?" Maria asked.

"Yes, Spencer. Do you know him?"

"No, I've never met him."

"Well, I've met him several times. In fact, he is looking at you now."

Maria jerked her head up in surprise and followed Luis's gaze.

A blonde man with a tan and an easy half-smile looked at them as if he knew they were talking about him.

"Merde, he saw us," Luis muttered.

"You should have told me not to look. Now he knows we were talking about him."

"Well," Luis said, "You're going to meet him soon. He's walking this way."

CHAPTER THREE

Maria was talking to that hound Luis, who managed the Paris hotel. Spencer didn't like the other man or his proximity to Maria. He felt the flagstones under his feet and could hear his shoes taking each step as he closed the distance to where Maria and Luis had stopped talking at his approach. He had her full attention. Maria was just as beautiful as he remembered from the brief moments he'd seen her at Villa Roma. He hadn't spoken to her then. Why? Had he been… shy? It had been a long time since he'd found another woman, other than his beloved Ruby, attractive. He was rusty.

"Hey, Luis," he said as nicely as he could to the other man, who reminded him of a ferret.

"Spencer," Luis said with a nod. "Have you met Maria Medici, the manager of the hotel in Rome?"

"No, but I have wanted to for a long time," Spencer said, as he extended his hand toward the emerald-eyed creature that was ethereally beautiful and staring him down as if she could turn him to stone like Medusa. She didn't like him. Obviously, his reputation had proceeded him.

"Spencer Whitlow, the other part of the family," he said, his hand extending further than it should in Maria's direction.

"*Prego,*" Maria said, giving his hand a wag versus a shake. She knew what he was up to with her hotel, and she was unhappy with him.

"I'm so glad to finally meet you," he said as she stared him down.

"You should have introduced yourself when you were in Roma," she said. "I understand you visited recently and spent some time at my hotel. We could have had an espresso or some prosecco."

She looked at him as if she hated him with every cell in her being. He would be taking over what had been her hotel to manage, so she was no doubt feeling insecure.

"I should have. I would have enjoyed an espresso or dinner, but every time I saw you, you were talking to staff or guests, and I didn't want to interrupt." And he hadn't exactly found his balls to initiate a conversation with the green-eyed beauty.

"I would have made time for you, Mr. Whitlow. I know who you are."

"We are practically family. Call me Spencer. And we will have our time to get to know each other."

Maria laughed at that as if it were the stupidest thing she'd ever heard. Spencer didn't know what to make of it. It wasn't funny, and he needed her.

"Hey, Luis, do you mind if I chat with Maria privately for a moment?" he asked.

Before Maria had a chance to complain, Luis trotted away like a downtrodden dog. That lack of backbone was why he would never be more than he was at Stark International Hotels.

"Was that necessary?" she asked. "Luis is a respected hotel manager that should not be dismissed."

"Notice how easily he obeyed. And, for what I had in mind, it was very necessary."

"What do you have in mind?" she challenged, her tone turning chillier.

"I wanted to talk privately with you, and what I wanted to say was none of Luis's business."

She nodded, so he continued.

"I want you to know I'm not here to undermine you or take Villa Roma away from you. I want us to work together, to have this project be ours. Does that make sense?" He asked, looking at the beautiful woman and wondering what she was thinking. Her beauty was a complication he'd always been aware of, but being so close to her, it had much more of an impact than he'd bargained. This could be a problem for which he didn't have an answer. He was out of practice.

She held up hand to display her engagement ring and said, "I haven't decided if I'm going to stay at Villa Roma for much longer. I'm engaged and will want to start my life with my husband. I've met many men like you before, Mr. Whitlow, and I just don't know if I want to prove myself to you. I've proven myself by how I run Villa Roma. That is enough. I'm tired, as you Americans say, of the bullshit."

It was clear that she didn't like him. So, he would need to backpedal, try a new approach, and hopefully find common ground.

"Wow, congratulations on the engagement. That is an impressive ring," he said, thinking that it matched her eyes but that her eyes were far more beautiful. "Please don't do anything before we get to Rome and look at the hotel together. I need you. It isn't bullshit. Quite the contrary; you're the expert on Villa Roma."

"Or maybe I just quit," Maria said, looking bored.

Spencer sighed and shook his head. That was all he needed. "Please, please don't. Don't make any quick decisions until we are back in Rome. Please?"

"I'll think about it, but I don't need to work, so I don't know if I will," Maria said dismissively. She glanced around the room, making it obvious that she wished their conversation was over. He felt like he was boring her. Spencer didn't know why she was so dismissive of him aside from the fact that he was finally getting back to work at his hotel—maybe she was intimidated knowing that. Or was it something else? Maybe she felt what he felt? Even if there were a trace of that attraction, that tension, he would be thrilled.

"I understand, and thank you for at least considering to help me. Is your fiancé here tonight? I'd like to meet him," Spencer said. He'd like to size him up, see how fabulous this guy was that he had captured this beautiful woman's heart. He also wondered what kind of idiot would let her out of his sight. If she were his, he'd be there, a protective and possessive arm around her waist, whispering naughty thoughts of what he planned to do to her later into her ear as they mingled around the hotel stiffs. You just didn't let a woman this beautiful or intelligent out of your sight.

"He is a very important businessman back in Roma, which is where he is currently," Maria stated.

"So he didn't want to come to the United States and protect you from all the men like me?" He should not have said that. The moment the words were out of his mouth, he regretted them. He was just out of practice with beautiful women, and this woman before him, well, she was intoxicating.

"Does Alex know what a rude individual you are, Mr. Whitlow, saying such inappropriate things to a business associate? You forget that we have a business relationship and that you should show me the same respect you would show a man in the same position. Something tells me that he wouldn't want you speaking to me this way. He is very protective of me."

"Yes, I'm aware of that. I'm very sorry that I offended you. Alex knows me very well, we are very close, and I wouldn't want to upset you," Spencer said, pointing to Alex and Daisy, who'd just set foot on the rooftop garden. They held hands, and Alex seemed aware of Daisy in a way that was both loving and protective of his very pregnant wife.

"But you did, Mr. Whitlow. You reminded me that I'm a woman who needs to be protected from men like you," Maria said. Her feistiness worked for her. "Why are you here? Why are you talking to me? Villa Roma is yours to do with what you want."

"I know you don't mean that. I know you love it, probably more than I do. I want you to help me. And yes, I'm here in Portland for this party and to have an executive meeting about our hotel tomorrow. Tonight is about celebrating and getting to know the others who are part of the Stark family. We are on the same team."

"Sure we are," she said, raising an eyebrow.

"I sincerely apologize for offending you. I didn't mean to put my foot in my mouth. It is just that I'm out of practice. I haven't been out much in the last three years, which I'm sure you can tell. So, let's try another approach. Here's an idea as to how to make it up to you. How would you like to meet your sister?"

CHAPTER FOUR

S pencer Whitlow couldn't have shocked Maria more if he'd asked her to set him on fire. That might have shocked her less.

"What?" she asked, not understanding the sudden change of subject matter.

"Well, Rebecca is over there, and she's shy about meeting you. She doesn't know what to say or do, or if you'll respond positively. She is completely freaked out because she thinks you are beautiful, but she also thinks you are intimidating. I can be the buffer to get you two women together. And if it goes badly, you can blame me. It would be my honor to be your scapegoat."

"I'll add it to the list of things I'm already blaming you for, Mr. Whitlow. It is already a long list. A very long list."

Spencer laughed, his handsome face dissolving into dimples, and Maria thought that even made him more handsome—not that she'd ever tell him. And damn it, why did he have to be cute? She didn't need her new boss to be cute. She did have a weakness for dimples. His blonde hair was wavy and unruly. Was it natural or bleached from the sun? She wondered how long it had been since he'd been to *barbiere*. Too long...in fact, if his hair was straight, she'd have thought it in need of a trim, but she liked it just the way it was. It was the perfect length. She wondered if the curls were as soft as they looked, and she thought of running her fingers through them...Damn him for being attractive. He was just a man. He was technically her boss and off-limits. Besides, she was engaged, and she shouldn't be thinking about things like this.

"I tell you what, let's make it interesting. Want to make a bet? Something that would matter to you?"

"I don't bet, Mr. Whitlow. I don't have to."

"Really?" Spencer asked, raising an eyebrow. "I bet I could make it interesting enough for you to change your mind."

Setting her glass down, she announced, "There is nothing you could do to get me to bet with you. So, I think it is time for me to leave before I toss my drink in your face."

"Your glass is empty. I wanted to tell you this earlier." As Maria wondered what this man was about, he added in a softer tone, "I like your accent. I like it very much."

She took in a deep breath and let it out slowly. Did Spencer have no shame? "Go to hell, Mr. Whitlow. If you keep talking to me about things like my accent, I'll have my brother beat you up. Maybe that will remind you that I'm a businesswoman who is engaged."

Unshaken, he continued, "Ah, my Maria, cut me some slack. I'm honest but not smooth, so hear me out. I'll make you a wager. By the time the stars are out and the dancing is in full swing, I will come up to you, ask you to dance, and you will accept because you will have decided that you like me just a little bit."

Humph, "his Maria"—why did she like the sound of that? He certainly was confident in himself, something that most Europeans were too, and Maria liked that. His aw-shucks-I'm-out-of-practice line was just that—a line.

Unnoticed to her, a band had started playing, and several people, including Luis, were dancing.

She laughed, amused that he wouldn't go away, and shook her head. Who did he think he was?

"What do I win if you're wrong? Because I already know you will lose," she asked, though feeling a bit unsure of her resolve.

"I'll become the silent partner again in your hotel, and you can oversee the remodel I have in mind. You can change it. Total freedom. What do you say? Do we have a bet?"

Despite herself, she smiled. "Sometimes, my English isn't so good. So let me repeat this back to you to make sure I have it right. If you win, I must dance with you, but if I win, you crawl back under some rock in your big, macho Texas? So, I don't have to see or deal with you again?"

"Yes, ma'am, mostly," he replied, drawing out his words. "Just so we are clear, I cannot guarantee that I won't visit Rome to see you sometime in the future."

"That's not what I want. I want you to go away forever." Maria was hoping her facial features were composed and conveyed this. Sadly, she wasn't feeling it. The idea of seeing him each day, working with him, had a slight appeal she had yet to figure out.

He smiled an "aw, shucks" crooked grin that she was starting to like a little too much. "You don't mean that. I'm really an okay guy. People actually like me."

"This conversation is the most ridiculous thing I've ever heard, and I don't believe you will, how do you say, 'keep your end' of any bargain we strike."

He shrugged. "The stakes are high for me, but I'd suggest you accept. It would appear you couldn't lose. I'm an excellent dancer."

Picking up a filled champagne glass from a waiter passing by, she took a sip and licked at the lingering bubbles on her lips, an overt delay tactic.

"I'd bet anything I have to see you do that again," he announced wolfishly.

"Goodnight, Mr. Whitlow. I'll see you tomorrow in Alex's office, unless you come to your senses before then and scurry away like the little vermin that you are," she said, feeling much less confident on the inside than she looked on the outside.

"May I ask a question?"

"What?" Maria asked.

"Why do you hate me so much? You don't even know me."

"You've been nowhere for the past three-and-a-half years I've managed the hotel, yet now you are here with all these ideas. You haven't asked me once about the hotel that I live and breathe every day. I am expected to accept everything you say when you know nothing. Maybe you've been to Roma once, that doesn't make you a Roman. It makes you an American who has big ideas, like the burger man who invented McDonald's. And just so we are clear, only Americans call it 'Rome'. It is *Roma* to those who know the city."

"That's a fair assessment. I'll leave you to enjoy your night, Ms. Medici," he said and turned his back on her before walking away.

It was hard not to throw her glass at his receding figure, but she didn't. His sudden dismissal of her was what she wanted, but Maria still was not happy. He made her feel edgy. She liked playing with him, much like a cat wanting to play with a mouse before killing it. Sport. Teasing. Challenge.

Deciding to ignore the arrogant Spencer, she mingled about and greeted other Stark staff. She was approached by several men for dances, all of whom she politely dismissed with a kind refusal. She knew her fiancé. He didn't like other men touching her. Dancing would be in that category. Her fiancé also would have disliked this event. He didn't like to mingle and make small talk. As he told Maria when she asked him to come with her, he was too busy with his work to help her with hers. She could respect that even if it hurt a little.

Pablo was born and raised with privilege to parents from the old country. Machismo was important to Italian men. Maria tried to allow him that, otherwise arguments would ensue, and that did not bode well for her. She wanted to have a family, something she longed for all her upbringing. Pablo would give her that.

It hadn't been easy, putting her progressive, independent thoughts on the back burner to make sure Pablo was happy. She had, though, because she knew what was at stake.

Eventually, she meandered back to her quiet space by the rail. A good place, she decided, to get lost in a crowd. The sun dropped behind a hill to the west, making the city lights come alive. In a few minutes, she could quietly slip away.

Damn Spencer Whitlow! He had found her weakness: family. Did she want to meet her sister? Yes. But it had to be on her terms, not terms arranged by Spencer Whitlow. Speaking of the devil, he was back. She could feel his presence before she saw him—or heard him for that matter.

"Ms. Medici?" She heard him say, but she was looking in the other direction and was in no mood to deal with his ridiculous bargains. What could she say to make him go away for good?

Turning, she was ready to attack but stopped short, her face breaking into an immediate smile. Spencer held Emily Wilder, her niece and Rebecca's daughter, in his arms.

"Hello," Maria managed, covering her surprise.

Spencer smiled because he knew what he was doing. "I wanted you to meet my little cousin, Emily. Emily, this is Maria."

"Hi, Maria," the little girl said with a sweet, shy smile.

"I helped her mother and daddy fall in love," Spencer said. At this announcement, the little girl looked up at him in awe and said, "Really?"

"Yes, true story," he replied, his voice sounding softer and more southern, laced with honey and molasses. "For your mom and dad, it was love at first sight. You could see the sparkle in your daddy's eyes. They just needed a little push to get them to realize it. I was the push."

Maria could think of nothing to say as she tried to commit

every detail of the child's face to memory. This was her niece. They shared the same blood, but she had no idea if she would ever even see the child again.

"Maria is so shocked, she can't say anything," he said to the little girl, his eyes mischievously twinkling as he set the little girl down.

"I... I... it's nice to meet you, Emily," she managed, taking in everything about the child, including the emerald eyes that were so close to her own. "I like your yellow dress. It is the color of my favorite rose."

"Thank you," the little girl answered shyly. "Mommy and I got it for the party. I like it a lot."

"It is very pretty on you. How old are you?" Maria asked, suddenly curious.

"Four. Your voice sounds funny," she replied, smiling up at Maria.

"That's because she's from Italy," Spencer said. "She has a funny accent."

"Where's Italy?" the child asked.

Maria answered, "Far away from here. It's in Europe. It's where pizza and spaghetti come from." She glanced toward Spencer and saw him nod in encouragement.

"I like pizza. I want to go to Italy," Emily said.

"Someday, you could come to visit me there. Anytime you want, and we can eat pizza," Maria offered.

"Really?" Emily asked, her face lighting up.

"Emily, there you are. I should have known you'd be with your uncle, The Troublemaker."

Before Maria could answer the little girl, her mother, Rebecca, joined them. Maria had no idea what to expect from the other woman.

"I was meeting Maria. She's from Italy." The little girl informed her mother. "She told me I could visit sometime, and we could eat pizza."

"That was very nice of her, but you're not going to Rome without me," Rebecca said, smiling down at her daughter. Then, her eyes hesitantly raised and met Maria's.

"Pardon my manners, ladies. Rebecca, this is Maria Medici, the manager of the Stark Hotel in Rome. Maria, this is my cousin, Rebecca Stark Wilder," Spencer said smoothly as each woman sized up the other. "She can be a pill. Actually, you both have your moments. It must run in the family."

"Thanks a lot, Spencer. You're just trouble." Rebecca turned to Maria. "It's nice to meet you," she offered and reached out her hand.

Maria grasped it and smiled. "*Grazie.* Your daughter, she's beautiful."

"Thank you. She's definitely a Stark. She has the green eyes to prove it." In Rebecca's words, Maria found acknowledgment. All of their father's children and grandchildren had unusual emerald eyes.

Spencer interjected, "I'll be going to Italy myself to work with Maria on a redesign of the interior of the hotel. Lots of exciting plans."

"Alex alluded to that," Rebecca replied, looking at Maria.

"I will hear all about it tomorrow morning," Maria added with a touch of skepticism in her tone. "I can barely contain my excitement."

"With Spencer, it's bound to be an adventure," Rebecca warned. "Don't hesitate to tell him he is being a jerk. I think he likes it when women are mean to him."

"Hey now, Maria and I don't know each other very well, don't be telling tales on your cousin, cousin."

"He's trouble with a capital T," Rebecca said, smiling for the first time. "I wouldn't trust him as far as I could throw him."

Maria nodded. "I believe you."

"Nice to have you both beat up on me. I would've thought it

was beneath ladies of your stature to do such a thing," Spencer quipped.

Both women laughed, easing the tension, then Rebecca looked down at Emily. "Well, we've had a great day, but it is way past someone's bedtime."

"I don't want to go yet. I'm just starting to have fun," Emily complained. "I haven't even touched Aunt Daisy's tummy yet. She said my new cousin was in there. It's a girl, and they are going to name her Lily."

"It was very nice to meet you both," Maria said, stealing another glance at her sister and niece. "I've wanted to meet you for a long time."

"Would you like to have afternoon tea tomorrow? The hotel is known for its afternoon tea, and we can get to know each other," Rebecca offered. "I understand if you are too busy…."

"Yes, yes, I want to come to tea," Maria said, trying not to sound too excited.

"Can I come?" Emily asked her mother.

"Another time, honey. I'll make a two-p.m. reservation. And maybe we'll have to visit Rome sometime soon, especially now that we know where Spencer will be," Rebecca offered tentatively. "We will want to make sure he is behaving himself."

"Really? Can we go to Rome?" Emily asked, her face lighting up with excitement.

"That would be wonderful. You're always welcome," Maria said and smiled humbly. Emily gave her a surprise hug, throwing her arms around Maria's waist. She bent down and gave the child a tight hug. "And we will eat pizza and spaghetti."

Rebecca seemed to remember Spencer at that moment and gave him a quick kiss on the cheek, and punched his arm hard. "Troublemaker," she scolded and gave one last smile to Maria before walking away with her daughter. "I'll see you at two tomorrow, Maria. I'm looking forward to it."

"Me too! Bye-bye, Emily," Maria said, watching them go.

Spencer's eyes never left Maria's as he took a step toward her. "Ms. Medici, may I have the pleasure of the next dance?"

Maria couldn't speak. Before she could react, he gently reached up and brushed a tear from her cheek. She grabbed his wrist with her fingers.

"Easy," he coaxed. "No damage to the makeup yet, but if you fight me, I make no guarantees. Take a deep breath. Good, now let it out."

She was so caught off guard that she did as she was told.

He stepped away from her a moment later and gave her a quick once over. "You look beautiful. Not a hair out of place. Now, how about that dance?"

Shrugging, she moved to the middle of the dance floor, leaving him to follow. The moon was full, illuminating the sky and shining down on the terrace. As she turned to face him under the veil of small white twinkle lights, the jazz band began a headily romantic rendition of "You're Looking at Me." But, feeling more than seeing, she knew the instant he wrapped her in his arms that theirs wouldn't be a dance of polite distance. Fitting snugly against him, she rested her head on his shoulder as they moved through the sea of dancing couples.

"How did you know?" she whispered in his ear.

"About you having not met your sister and niece?"

She leaned back, far enough to see into his eyes and count each long, blond eyelash that was a shade darker than the hair on his head.

"Yes."

Murmuring in her ear, he said, "Alex told me about you a while ago. And, just so you know, it's my very late wedding present to Alex and Daisy, making those introductions and getting past the awkwardness—but I did it for you."

She had no idea what to make of this man. Leaning against him, she whispered, "Thank you," and shut her eyes. The song ended, and another began. They stayed in each other's arms until the noise of the crowd dwindled.

She opened her heavy lids and noticed they were in a dark corner, away from what was left of the crowd.

Spencer Whitlow's face was close to hers. The tips of their noses were close to touching.

She whispered, "What are we doing over here?"

"I guess we just ended up over here," Spencer said.

"Take me back. People will talk."

"We only danced, my Maria. Your reputation is safe."

Startled by his use of "my Maria," she said, "Mr. Whitlow, I was not born yesterday. Don't make me angry."

"I'm sorry?" Spencer said innocently.

"Stop it. You are sorry for nothing," she said, pulling away from him, possibly a little slower than she should have.

He moved closer and kissed her quickly on the cheek, and asked, "Can't we at least be friends?"

"I'm engaged. Stop it!" she said, and shoved him hard as she stepped away from him.

"He isn't right for you," Spencer said, his hand still holding hers closely. "We both know it."

"How dare you?" Maria replied, trying to shake free of him. "You don't know him. He is perfect for me."

"He's not here, and he should be. He should be dancing with you. He should be kissing you. He should be whispering all the naughty things he is going to do to you when you are alone," he said. "You know I'm right, and you feel it too. I watched your eyes flutter as I kissed you. A happily engaged woman doesn't react that way."

"You are a beast! Have you no respect?" she whispered and stepped back, horrified that he could very well be right. She could still feel the place where his lips had touched her. This was trouble. Spencer was going to be trouble for her—sweet, torturous trouble.

"Now, kids, no fighting at the party," Alex said, stepping to Maria's rescue. He wrapped an arm around Maria's waist and pulled her away from Spencer.

"This animal tried to kiss me," Maria complained to her brother.

Spencer took a step back, raised his hands, and said, "I didn't try; I kissed you, but it was only on the cheek, so it wasn't as scandalous as it sounds."

"Jeez, you two. I was worried how you would get along. Spencer, leave her alone. Go chase someone else, but not my sister."

Spencer smiled and said, "I don't want to create a scene. She claims she's engaged. You didn't tell me that."

"It is none of your business, but it is another good reason to leave her alone. Oh yes, here's another—you are essentially her boss. And the most important reason, I repeat, she is my sister. My loyalty is to her. If she kills you, I'll help her hide your body."

Maria nodded and folded her arms over her chest.

"That hurts a little, Alex. I thought I was your favorite cousin," Spencer said, looking hurt.

"You're my favorite something, alright. Now, go to your room and get a good night's sleep. I need you fresh for tomorrow."

"Still like to control everything I see," Spencer said.

"Well, someone needs to have a level head."

"Meaning what?" Spencer asked.

"I'm protecting my sister from the resident wolf hunter. Kiss her again, and she will hurt you, or she'll ask me to do it," Alex said, holding up his hand.

"Are you sure I'm the wolf? She looks like she has no problem defending herself."

"Stop it, I mean. NOW," Alex said.

"Fine. I was just about to turn in," Spencer said, his eyes

resting on Maria again, making her feel somehow like she wanted to blush.

"Goodnight, Mr. Whitlow," she interjected, turned, and left. Behind her, she could hear Spencer laughing and Alex reprimanding his cousin.

CHAPTER FIVE

Maria needed a good power suit to bolster her confidence. Thoughts of Spencer Whitlow had led to a sleepless night of tossing and turning. He bothered her, and she was still unsure what to make of it—what to make of her body's reaction to that damn wavy blond hair and crooked smile. He made her forget she was a hotel manager, engaged, and utterly untouchable. They both needed to be reminded of all these things. Nevertheless, she intended to get things back on track today. He was her boss: nothing more, nothing less.

Maria contemplated this and settled on a dark navy Armani suit she'd bought in Florence three months earlier. It had a soft tie belt and a long pencil skirt. She paired it with three-inch Ferragamo heels as not to be too tall next to her brother and that sexy clueless jerk Spencer Whitlow.

This meeting would be terrible. She could feel it in her bones.

She applied her red Armani lipstick inside perfectly outlined lips and added just the right amount of brushed gold jewelry to set off her olive skin. Then she applied a spray of Bottega Veneta perfume with the subtle memory of leather, pink pepper, and bergamot to complete her appearance. Of course, she also was dealing with the memory of Spencer Whitlow, which was both pleasant and irritating.

The dance was more than just a dance. It was intimate. The

way he pressed every part of himself against her. So why didn't she move away? Maria hated to admit she liked it, liked him, and then he'd kissed her cheek. Did she want him to kiss her again? Did she want him to kiss her on the lips? Possibly... and that bothered her because she was wearing Pablo's ring. It was hard to admit this truth. Yes, she was slightly attracted to him. That didn't make her a bad person. It made her human. The attraction wasn't easily explained, it just was there. In the case of Spencer Whitlow, it was there.

Damn it. Throughout the rest of her life, she would have to face this kind of occasional attraction, only she would be married, so she'd better learn to deal with it now.

She would not tell Pablo. There was nothing to tell. Besides, he had a bit of a jealousy issue. Undoubtedly, Spencer and Pablo would meet, and wouldn't that be an exciting moment? Spencer would see that Pablo is fifteen years older than Maria. Pablo would not like that she was working for someone like Spencer, who was good-looking with a carefree "surfer on the beach" kind of attitude. The jealousy might appear. If Spencer said anything to Pablo about their first meeting... she shuddered thinking about the result.

After dining on what American's called croissants and coffee, but in actuality was a couple of subpar pastries and lightly flavored brown water, she headed to the corporate floor for her meeting with Alex and Spencer. She tried to put the night before out of her mind. If she thought too much about Spencer, her thoughts went to not only her frustration of almost wanting him but of the almost kiss. What had she been thinking? How could she let him get that close? Damn him! Maybe she could blame it on jetlag. Maybe she'd drunk too much inferior carbonated wine. Maybe she was just coming up with excuses that masked the truth. Spencer Whitlow gave flight to the hibernating butterflies in her stomach. He made her feel tingly in all her dark and quiet places. Once awakened, these tingly places demanded more attention. It was all bad, and she knew it. But she had to admit, she wanted to see him again. The tingles demanded it.

The receptionist on the fifteenth floor directed her to Alex's office. The door was open, and Alex greeted her before she could announce herself.

"Good morning," he said, looking happy, almost boyish. He was no longer bitter and slightly angry. Maria blamed Daisy. Since he'd married her, he'd lost his hard edge.

"That has yet to be determined," she replied.

Alex sighed and sat down, "I asked Spencer not to come until 9:30 because I needed to talk to you about something that has happened."

"My hotel?" she asked, immediately worried for her beloved baby. She hoped he wouldn't lecture her about how she and Spencer had interacted the night before. If anyone should be reprimanded, it should be Spencer.

"No," he said, looking more serious than she had seen him in the entire time she'd known him, which had been about four years. Whatever the news was, it had to be bad.

"What? You are scaring me."

"A journalist called me early this morning," he went on to name a prominent publishing house that she recognized although they were American. "They were at the party last night. It appears our secret is out. They asked for confirmation that you are my sister. They want to run a story online and in their magazine about the 'lovechild to an heiress' angle. The problem with publishing online is that they have one website for all their publications, twenty magazines and various news outlets, so the audience is vast. It reaches a large and diverse group and is popular both in America and Europe. It is like running the story on every news channel in the US and Europe. And, if they publish on a slow news day, other networks will pick up the story."

Maria's mouth felt dry, yet her palms were sweating.

"This isn't an issue for Rebecca or me. We've talked about it. We feel alright about the news becoming public. It won't be a problem for Adam or Spencer, either. It will be a problem for you if you let it. My mother is another story altogether. This will destroy her. Everything will come into question: her marriage, standing, reputation, and our father's reputation. It will all be examined, ripped apart, and put back together again. Damn, *Vanity Fair* will probably do another story. They love this kind of thing. And for some reason, they like to pick on our family."

Maria picked up where he had left off. "Everyone will know your mother's marriage wasn't happy all the time. They will know her husband cheated with some Italian whore, and a bastard child was the result."

"Maria, that is the worst thing possible they could say. I would never talk about your mother like that."

"And you think they won't say that? You are in an alternate reality, I think. Welcome to this world, brother dearest."

"I don't care what they write. I care about you. I care about my mother. I want to protect you both from this."

"I haven't told Pablo. He will be upset when he finds out," she said, knowing that her secrecy about this would infuriate him more than the scandal.

"If he loves you, he will understand," Alex replied. "But you should have told him."

She shrugged, knowing he was right.

They discussed a strategy, and Alex drafted a press release that would preempt any attempts to spin this story in the wrong direction.

"I will have to tell Pablo. I should do it sooner than later before your press release," she said, knowing she should have told him months ago. If he loved her, he would understand. But Pablo was a complex man, and she wasn't sure how he'd take it.

"Would you like to do it now?" Alex asked.

"Yes, I need to do it now," she said, and stood to leave.

"You can use Daisy's office next door. It is small but private," he said and escorted her to a door in his office that opened to a closet-sized office next door to his.

"Daisy used this office?"

"Yes, I made it small to irritate her when she first started working with me. It did. You should have seen it before I enlarged it and added the door."

"Amazingly, she married you," Maria said.

"She didn't want to in the beginning. She turned me down repeatedly."

"I see why. I think more of her for rejecting you."

"She didn't know she loved me then. But I'm thankful each and every day that she changed her mind. Besides, she was pregnant with our beloved child," he replied before shutting the door and giving Maria her privacy. And just like two days earlier, she could not get a hold of Pablo. His cell went to his voicemail, and his office said he was in a meeting. So, like the day she had arrived, she wrote him a long email filled with apologies, explaining why she hadn't been transparent about who she was within the Stark family. It was a conversation she wished to have in person, but what could she do? She wanted to tell him before he read it somewhere. Her voicemail explained it vaguely and directed him to her email. Until she heard from him again, she would feel uneasy.

She didn't want to think of his reaction when he read her email, but she hoped it opened a deeper layer of trust between them. This should not be a problem, despite Pablo's volatile temper, which had never been directed at her, thank goodness.

Then why did she get the dark feeling that it would be a huge problem and potentially the first time they'd have a real fight?

Spencer walked into Alex's office seven minutes late because he liked to watch Alex lose his ever-present cool. And if anyone could irritate Alex, it was Spencer. Spencer had learned to let go of the little things in his life. Ruby had changed that for him forever. Alex still needed to learn that lesson.

"Mornin', boss, what's happening?" he asked as he dropped into one of the oversized, chocolate leather chairs in front of Alex's desk, like an impudent kid called to the principal's office.

Alex ripped a piece of paper off the tablet he had scribbled on, wadded it up, and threw it at Spencer, who caught the paper ball midair.

"Is she really that pissed off?" Spencer asked.

"I don't care if she is. You were too friendly last night, and I didn't like it."

"Alex, I like her, okay? It isn't like when we were in school. This is different. Considering what I've gone through in the last three years, it is amazing I can find another woman attractive after Ruby. Listen, I've beaten myself up enough with that guilt, and I wonder why Maria makes me feel this way, but that is the way it is," Spencer said, straightening his Hermes tie. The very act of wearing a tie still felt odd to a man used to jeans and cowboy boots. "Hell, I can't get her out of my mind. I didn't sleep last night, remembering how it felt to dance with her, hold her, and brush my lips against her cheek. I should have gone for her lips, but it didn't feel right. You know I haven't felt this way in a very long time. It is crazy, but I don't want to discount it or let her go."

"I should kick you all the way back to Texas," Alex said.

"Listen, I told you a month ago that Maria did something to me. Seeing her in Rome was such a pleasant surprise, but now talking with her, holding her, just intensified my feelings. Alex, I felt things I haven't felt in years. She is amazing. I see it. But don't worry, I will keep a handle on it, chillax," Spencer said.

Alex looked angry but said nothing. The usual granite jaw looked even more solid than was possible.

Spencer leaned toward the desk as if conspiratorially speaking to his cousin. "I'll be real with you. I don't think it is over yet. I think it is just beginning. I appreciate your understanding and sensitivity in the matter. I can't remember the last time I had a crush. I'm kind of out of my element, but it is coming back to me. I'll be respectful until she gives me some encouragement. Then the gloves are off, comprende?"

Alex folded his arms, his mouth forming a tight, angry smile. "Listen, you asshole, you are messing with my sister. Knock it off and remember where your brain is located. Consider that you might start thinking with it. I don't care about your past, your pain, or how this feels to you to find another woman attractive after all this time. She. Is. My. Sister. Aside from that, the press found out that Maria is my half-sister and now wants to run a story meant to bring about as much pain to the family as possible. My mother will be shattered. Her marriage, her love for my father, his love for her: everything will be questioned. My older sister is worried about our mother, and my younger sister, well, she has a fiancé that we didn't know about until about five minutes ago—plus the staff, everyone at her hotel will see her differently from this moment forward. So I could give a shit about your little crush. But listen to me, if you cause her one moment of pain, I'll kick you back to Texas. That will be the least of it. I'll probably do more, and you've been warned. Got it?"

"Whoa there, cuz," Spencer said. "Maybe we should have a little cocktail or a Xanax and think about this, talk it through. You know how the word scandal has always been near and dear to my heart. I love this shit."

"Is that how you spend your money now? On drugs and alcohol?" Alex asked, looking angry. "That sounds like someone I want to have near my sister."

"Come on, Alex. I'm teasing, so calm down. I should feel good that you are treating me like a normal person instead of that quiet, comforting tone you've used in the past. And just for your information, I don't do drugs or drink more than one or two cocktails on any social occasion. Here is something new. I don't stress the small things, and this is definitely a small thing. No one has died, so chillax. You know that I've walked through my own fire, so I appreciate opportunities and life for the luck that is given us. But something is happening here. I don't know what it is, but it involves Maria. I can't get her out of my mind. The need to protect her is extreme. I need to figure out how to get rid of her fiancé, so I can move forward and explore this."

"Maria is going to eat you up and spit you out in little pieces, and I'm going to enjoy watching her do it," Alex said with a cunning smile. "The gloves are off, my friend."

"I love how you don't give me any slack. You treat me like everyone else should but won't because they still feel sorry for me. I think I'd enjoy Maria being rough on me," Spencer said with a smile that showed his ample dimples. Toying with his cousin was great fun. "And if she wants to eat me up and spit me out in little pieces, well, I think I'd enjoy it."

"That's enough. You know I don't do pity, and I stopped feeling sorry for you long ago. But having you have thoughts about my sister is another level," Alex said.

"Get comfortable because I'm going to win her over, and you aren't going to stand in my way—just wait and see," Spencer said. Teasing Alex was a hobby of his, and Spencer was enjoying seeing Alex's ears turn red with rage.

Alex stood, ready to vault over the desk and hit his cousin, but Maria stepped into the office and sighed loudly.

"Let's get this over with," she said as she sauntered across the room and eventually sank into a chair near Spencer.

"Hey, Maria," Spencer said, lasciviously. "Looking beautiful as usual."

"Look what the cat dragged in, the sewer rat," she said, her lips pursing as her eyes narrowed. He loved her spunk.

"I deserve that for upsetting you last night. Again, I'm sorry. Once we get to Rome and I'm officially your boss in front of the staff, I know that you'll show me some respect. But when we are alone, you call me anything you want, darlin'."

Maria let out a sigh that sounded like more of a growl.

"You'll get used to me, my Maria. Everyone does," Spencer said. He was a little forward with her this morning, but he really was enjoying himself. It had been a long time.

"Don't count on it," Maria said. "And I'm not 'your Maria,' Mister Sewer Rat."

"Alex, could you please calm your sister down?" Spencer complained. He could see through this little act that she liked him. She was fighting her attraction, but she wasn't going to win.

"She can do anything she wants when it comes to you," Alex said with a smile. "I hope she treats you like an annoying… what was it? Oh yeah, sewer rat."

"Nothing like being ganged up on," Spencer said.

"That's what you get when you threaten to remodel my vibrant, beautiful hotel," Maria said. "It is gorgeous, and people love it. But how would you know? You were only in Roma for what, three days?"

"I was in *Roma* for five, but with your help, I want to make it even more vibrant and beautiful. I've got many ideas that will make it the top destination hotel in Italy. Now, why wouldn't you want that?" Spencer asked, turning toward Maria.

"I'm appalled to ask, but what do you want to do?"

"We will remodel the rooms and add bold colors to attract a slightly younger crowd than you currently have—the next generation. Wouldn't that make you happy?"

"If you wanted to make me happy, you'd go away, and I'd never see you again," she said, making Alex smile.

Spencer laughed, "Not possible. I'm in your life as long as you are the hotel manager and maybe even if you aren't. I love your energy." He loved the way she sparred with him. There wasn't anything he wasn't attracted to about her. Except for the fiancé—that guy needed to go away.

"Are you threatening to fire me or stalk me?"

"Neither. I want to work with you. Is that so bad?"

"Just like a sewer rat who has found his way inside your house, the space may not be large enough for both of us," Maria said and folded her arms.

CHAPTER SIX

Maria kept on the dark blue Armani suit for tea with Rebecca, but she added a chunky gold charm bracelet filled with memories. If she ran out of things to say, she could look down at the bracelet for inspiration. Nothing else in her wardrobe felt appropriate. After the long meeting with Spencer, where he took her through his ideas to turn her hotel into something like a concert venue, accented with neon and lots of black leather, she wasn't in the mood for any other color than something almost black. He had listened to her protests and suggestions, but who knew if he was paying attention? The whole meeting left her feeling on edge and angry, and her earlier tingle was replaced by fury.

Arriving ten minutes early to tea, she was surprised to find Rebecca already seated and waiting at one of the preferred tables: an antique red damask couch with a low marble-topped coffee table before it. Rebecca was perusing a small afternoon tea menu. She was dressed perfectly in a starched white blouse, camel cashmere pencil skirt, and a Burberry plaid silk scarf, artfully tied around her neck in a way Maria had never mastered. Her hair was up in a twist, but several tendrils were loose and framed her face perfectly. The outfit looked like individual pieces that went together flawlessly and as if a stylist had spent hours putting them together.

She had yet to notice Maria, who observed that Rebecca

looked nervous. She was fidgeting with her perfect scarf, pulling it this way and that, and repeatedly putting the menu down and picking it back up again.

Maria bypassed the gregarious and helpful hostess and went directly to the couch where Rebecca waited. When the other woman glanced up and saw Maria, she dropped the menu and stood. Then, after a moment of awkward decision, she hugged Maria, shocking the other woman.

Maria smelled Rebecca's Chanel No. Five and expensive hair products. She could also feel the other woman's nervous tremors. It prompted her to ask, "Are you okay? You are shaking."

Rebecca shook her head, "I'll be honest. I don't know what to say or do. This is so weird for me. I barely slept last night, and I've had a bunch of coffee. I'm a damn mess."

"Me too, why don't we just relax and chat? Start by telling me if you put this outfit together or if you have a stylist. Or maybe fashion runs in the family," Maria said, pointing at the scarf.

Rebecca laughed nervously and said, "Do you mind if I have some alcohol in my tea or maybe just a cocktail?"

Maria smiled and replied, "I would love some prosecco! What a good idea!"

⋅⊶⋅ ⋅◈⋅◈⋅ ⋅⊷⋅

Alex found them there two hours and two bottles of prosecco later laughing like schoolgirls. Around them, plates with tiny sandwiches and cakes sat pristinely untouched. Of course, if they had wanted to drink, they could have just gone to the bar. Maybe ladies who wanted to drink in a classy way pretended they were having tea while proceeding to get shit-faced.

Regardless, it didn't look good in the lobby of the family hotel. And it was setting a bad example for the staff. But damn, if he'd be the one to throw water on this party. These women needed to get along if he was going to survive as the CEO and de facto head of the family. As disturbed as he was to find not one but two semi-drunk sisters in his hotel lobby, it warmed his heart to see them getting along and chatting like old friends. Thankfully, his mother was hidden away in her room upstairs and had yet to make an appearance today.

"Is this a chick party, or can anyone join in?" he asked as he sat on the arm of the sofa closest to Maria.

"You can join if you pay," Rebecca said, which elicited a laugh from Maria. "And don't call us chicks, you jerk."

"I think we all know you and Maria would never have paid for it anyway, being that you are family and own a piece of this hotel," he said, ignoring his older sister's snide comment.

"Well, that is a given, but we would tip, and well, I might add. So, okay, why didn't you introduce me to Maria earlier?" Rebecca complained. "We are so totally alike. It is like looking at an Italian version of myself."

"I tried," Alex said.

"He tried not at all," Maria said, and both women laughed.

"Can you imagine how much fun we would have had ganging up on him as children?" Rebecca asked.

"It would appear you two are getting along and have found a mutual target to pick on," he observed. "Maybe I should go upstairs and snuggle with my hormonal wife. I could use the comfort of a good woman."

"As if that would be punishment. You can't keep your hands off Daisy, ergo her current knocked-up state, you perv," Rebecca said.

"Last time I looked, it was okay for husbands and wives to enjoy each other's company," Alex said.

"I wonder if she knew that being married to you came with being barefoot and pregnant?" Rebecca asked.

"The second one was completely her idea," he countered.

"You just sat by and watched it happen?" Rebecca asked.

"I was a very willing participant," Alex said.

"Why don't you act like my protective, older brother and hurt that evil Spencer for making lewd suggestions to me?" Maria asked.

"Yeah, he's been very much in her space. I told you what he did at the party. Now, Emily wants to know when we are going to Rome. He practically forced her to remind me repeatedly that we need to book a trip to Europe, so thanks a lot. My four-year-old, the world traveler, who must now see Rome—and soon. I should send you the bill for our first-class airfare," Rebecca said to Alex.

"I'm very thankful you two never met before this moment. I don't think I'd have survived it," Alex said. "He only kissed your cheek, Maria. It was like a brotherly gesture, really."

"You know what I call him?" Maria ignored her brother and asked Rebecca.

"Him?" Rebecca asked, scowling at her brother, "Or Spencer? Let me guess. It is something in Italian that means bastard?"

"Spencer. No, I keep it in English so he knows what I call him, because no way does he speak anything but English, so I call him the sewer rat."

"Harsh, but I kind of like it," Rebecca said.

"Ladies, Spencer is a good guy. He's just been acting all weird because he likes Maria. He has an inappropriate crush on her. That said, he's been through a lot, and if it wasn't for that, I'd be all over his shit. Cut him some slack. He's a goofball. Somewhere a beach is missing their resident surfer."

"Yeah, but… our geeky cousin we used to torture whenever we could get away with it?" Rebecca said. "I guess he is nice looking now, but I still remember him as the little kid who liked to stomp in mud puddles when we were kids. Nothing was safe around him. He liked to destroy everything. Remember when he was twelve and disassembled his father's car to give it a tune-up, a little surprise Father's Day gift, and then couldn't get it back together?"

"Yeah," Alex said. "That was bad. The dealership had to send a flatbed truck to haul it away with two cardboard boxes filled with what Spencer said were unnecessary spare parts. Remember when you mixed up all those items from the kitchen shelves, told him it was poison, and forced him to drink it?"

Rebecca took that moment to ignore Alex completely.

"Hey," Rebecca said to Maria. "You want to go to Nordstrom? We can walk there from here and then call Alex for a pickup."

"Yes, that would be great," Maria said. She had always wanted a sister to go shopping with, to share secrets and to do a host of other things.

"Please, don't call me," Alex interjected. "Call the hotel and they can send a car. Daisy needs me."

"For what?" Rebecca asked. "I think you've done all you can to her. She's as big as a house." Both she and Maria laughed at this.

Alex waved his arm between the two women and said, "I'm not sure how I feel about this little merging of the 'Hey, Let's Torture Alex Club.'"

"You wanted me to get to know the family," Maria said innocently.

"Yeah, you got what you asked for," Rebecca said, standing and then smiling with a wobble as she looked at Maria. "Don't let me buy cosmetics or lingerie. They are my weakness."

"How about shoes?" Maria asked.

"I forgot shoes!" Rebecca exclaimed and smiled. "I like yours, by the way."

"There is a little Ferragamo store by my hotel. I got these there in three colors," Maria said, pointing at her shoes.

"Will you take me there when I come to Rome?"

"Of course, and we will also visit Gucci and MaxMara."

"Moncler for my husband?"

"But of course, Moncler is good for men. I prefer MaxMara for myself, but if I lived here, in the rain, I'd buy Moncler," Maria reasoned.

"Do you like Ferragamo over Gucci?" Rebecca asked.

Before Maria could answer, Alex sighed, dropped a couple of hundred-dollar bills on the table as the tip, and said, "Have a pleasant time, ladies." Then he hurried off to find his wife.

Maria and Rebecca arrived back at the hotel three hours later, heavily laden with bags from Nordstrom.

They had a wonderful time buying makeup, lingerie, and shoes. They even stopped in the café and had a couple more glasses of prosecco.

"Wait until you visit my *Roma*. Then we will buy handbags."

"I love handbags," Rebecca said.

She and Rebecca smiled at each other, and Maria again marveled at how easy the day had been. It could have gone so much differently, but it went well. It couldn't have gone better.

"Do you have dinner plans?" Rebecca asked as their car pulled to a stop in front of the hotel.

"Room service, or I was going to harass Alex," Maria answered.

"Forget that. You're coming to my house," Rebecca said and gave the limo driver an address.

Ten minutes later, they pulled to a stop in front of a large brick home with large white pillars.

"Hey, Randolph, do me a favor and take all these packages and have them delivered to Maria Medici's suite, okay?"

"Sure thing, Mrs. Wilder," he replied before driving off.

"My husband Mitch is making some chicken thing with lots of cheese and wine. I guarantee you've had nothing like it in Italy, but it is tasty," Rebecca said as they walked up the front porch. "I think he makes it when he wants to get laid. Tell you what, it is looking good for him."

CHAPTER SEVEN

M aria flew back to Rome two days after her tea and
dinner with Rebecca. Even Spencer Whitlow
couldn't dampen her feelings at having had met
and spent time with her sister, niece, and brother-in-law.

She had a family. A *real* family. She'd been to their house and
received an invitation to stay with them the next time she was
in Portland. And if she were reading the situation correctly, it
would only keep getting better and better. Rebecca, Mitch, and
Emily were planning a trip to see her in a month. She couldn't
believe it. And she was going to invite them to her wedding to
Pablo. Rebecca was going to help her find a wedding dress when
she visited. Maria was finally getting what everyone else had and
took for granted: a family, a history, and a sense of belonging.
Her life was coming together in ways she'd only dreamed of
before now.

She took a taxi from the airport in Roma to her tiny apartment on the edge of Piazza Navona so that she could shower
and change before going over to Pablo's palazzo. She always
wanted to look her best when she saw him. Although she knew
everything would be all right, she was still disturbed that she
hadn't been able to talk to him after the world discovered who
she was related to. It just wasn't that large of a deal, but she was
so nervous that she could barely contain herself.

Each time she'd tried his number, it had gone to voicemail
almost immediately. Indeed, her now-exposed heritage should

not make a difference to him. He loved her. She should be more worried about the kiss Spencer had given her than this question about how she had grown up. Pablo had known she was in an orphanage, but he had never questioned her heritage.

After watering her plants, organizing her mail, taking a long shower, and spending longer than usual with her makeup, she contemplated an outfit for the evening. She had some things at Pablo's house, but she chose an outfit he'd never seen from the Burberry store at Nordstrom, and it reminded her of her sister. It looked good on her, and she couldn't wait to tell him about her fabulous trip to America. It had been a life-changing experience. She'd left Roma as one person and come home another. Finally, she belonged to a family, and she understood how that felt like you belonged as a member of an exclusive club that you had to be born into to belong. She hadn't really known it to have missed it; but now she never wanted to let it go.

She wore one of her new American lace slips in peach and cream under her Burberry dress as she got ready to see her fiancé after five long days away. He probably hadn't even noticed she was away with how busy he could be. He was a businessman first and foremost. She knew his main business was fabric. The Stark International Hotels in Europe were one of his largest clients, but she knew his family had a very long heritage in Roma that was felt to the deepest levels of government. His brother was climbing the ranks with the police, and Pablo had discussed his own political aspirations. Once they had been married for a couple of years, he intended to run for political office. She'd encourage and campaign for him, knowing what a powerful team they'd make. She was already designing his campaign and had slogans in her mind.

She took a cab into the lovely hills overlooking Roma, counting the moments until she was at Pablo's. She couldn't wait to tell him all her news.

Before Maria had a chance to slip her key into the ornate

wood door of Pablo's palazzo, the door was opened by his rather large butler, Bruno.

"*Buonasera*, Signorina Medici."

"*Buonasera*, Bruno," she replied as he opened the door wider for her to enter.

"Signor Tino is waiting for you in the library."

Maria made her way to the library and found Pablo standing by a roaring fire in the fireplace. He looked older than when she'd left him less than a week earlier. He didn't smile when he saw her, just raised his chin in defiance and stared her down with his dark eyes. It was not only unsettling, but it also scared her a little bit.

"Pablo!" she exclaimed and crossed the room to him with arms outstretched. He turned, just enough so that she bumped into his side as she kissed him. He kissed her back, but there was something different about the kiss. Something had changed.

"What is wrong?" she asked.

He pointed to his desk, her eyes following the direction of his hand. Stepping away from him, she crossed the distance to the desk and saw her reflection looking back at her. The headline on the largest newspaper in Roma was tall and blunt: "Hotel Manager Secret Lovechild of Hotel Baron."

"Explain yourself," he said.

Taken aback, she stared at him. She had seen him mistreat his employees, but he had never been that way with her. She supposed there was a first time for everything. It worried her. There were some jealous moments, but she thought they'd gotten over all that. "I tried to call you. I tried to prepare you, but I didn't know it was going to become public knowledge this week. I left you several messages, emails, and voicemails. Did you not get them?"

"This wasn't the kind of conversation to have over the phone. When did you know you were a bastard?"

She felt slapped but tried to recover as she explained, "I had suspicions after Alex started coming to the hotel. He looked like the man who visited me in the orphanage, my angel. He was always so kind and only wanted to see me. The one who had me call him 'G.' I always thought he was handsome. Only later did I figure it out that he was my father. Alex and I did a DNA test and discovered we were siblings, but I begged him to keep the information private, and he did until a few days ago."

"Until he decided to tell the world. Why didn't you tell me earlier? Before the engagement?"

"I didn't think about it because I didn't want anyone to know, so I told no one," Maria admitted. "Once I found out, I've tried to forget it. It doesn't change who I am. It doesn't change what we have. Nothing has changed."

"Everything has changed. I told you. I thought I was very clear. I will not tolerate scandal. I thought you were above reproach when I proposed to you," Pablo said as he stood and walked toward her. "People are counting on me to run for and win office. Powerful people who I've made promises to."

Maria was at a loss. This wasn't all that bad, was it?

"All it means is that I'm worth a lot of money. My brother Alex has been paying me into an account I haven't touched. And there is a trust fund that I can access in several years. I don't want any favors. My parents, the only parents I ever knew, were Giuseppe and Isabella Medici. This… this legacy isn't me. But now I have a sister I didn't know and who didn't know me. I've always wanted a sister. And I have Alex. I also have nieces who I already love. And I will have extra money to help with your political campaign."

Pablo cursed in Italian, then he said, "You think it is only about money? You are a naïve little girl."

"People won't care. Now you'll have my family backing you. It will be better."

"The people who matter will care about this."

"It isn't a problem. They won't think any differently. This

isn't going to be a problem." She was backpedaling. It was new to her, and she didn't like it.

"It already is. They already care." He proceeded to call her names that she had never been called, which immediately ripped her to her very core as if he'd used a knife instead of his words. She was once again the dirty orphan that no one wanted. Something less than human, undoubtedly unworthy of someone like Count Pablo Tino.

Tears burned in her eyes. What was going on? What had happened? "Pablo? I don't understand. Nothing has changed. I still love you; don't you love me?"

He added a final blow, calling her a whore in Italian, "That is what I think of you for your deception." He spat at her. "I'm only glad I found out before the wedding. I cannot believe I considered marrying you. You are nothing but a bastard child of a whore. Love you? I can't stand the sight of you."

"Pablo, how dare you say those things to me?" she asked. "I thought you loved me."

"I have no tolerance for lying whores," he said. "Love you? You can't be serious. How can I? I now know you are the daughter of a whore. Common trash. You aren't worthy of me. You don't get to have the honor of my family name."

"How dare you? I'm not a bastard. I'm not the daughter of a whore. I'm a businesswoman who had a complicated childhood. I've risen above it. I was going to tell you the truth—"

"But you didn't," he said, getting so close that she could feel the heat radiating off of him. Felt his spittle hit her face. "I fell for your beauty. You intoxicated me, but now I know who you are. I see you."

She was reminded of one jealousy incident that had given her pause when they were first dating. It had only happened once, but she had vowed never to forget it. They had gone to one of their favorite restaurants. The waiter was too friendly with her one night. Pablo, at first, was angry with him but then scolded her in the car on the ride home. Had she flirted? Had she used a voice that was too sexy? Was her dress too revealing? It had led to a fight and a week of not speaking. Then he had shown up at her apartment door with roses and a sincere apology. But that was a year ago, and this was now. How quickly he'd forgotten; how quickly she had remembered.

"Pablo, I didn't think it would matter so much to you. I didn't think it would change how you feel about me. I love you," she said pleadingly, but it was too late. She could see as well as hear his anger. She needed to leave while she could. Every instinct inside of her told her to run. He was about to blow up, and then it would get worse.

"It does not matter what you say. You are still the daughter of a whore."

She saw his hand raise in slow motion, not understanding the intention, then he backhanded her across the face. The blow shocked her much so that she didn't feel the pain, not right away anyway. It was such a powerful blow that she ended up on the floor, her legs crumpling beneath her as her hand immediately went to protect her face, although it was too late. She crouched near the desk legs, her arms raised, protecting her face, her hands feeling for lacerations or blood on her skin.

Had he really hit her? What had just happened?

He didn't love her, not like she had thought he did. Never had their love been like what her brother and sister-in-law had, but they did care for one another.

"You are nothing to me but an embarrassment," he said as she lay cowering on the floor.

Maria wondered if she should get up or stay where she had fallen. Her fear was for the notion that he might knock her down again. She would have to crawl away to someplace safe, but there was no place to go in the library. And what about her things? She had clothes and toiletries at his home. In an instant, they no longer mattered. The only thing that mattered was getting away from him. Could she make it to the hall? If she could get to the entrance, she could open the front door and run, run away from this house. Would he strike her again, or worse? She couldn't be a target for him, but the slap had caused her a moment of confusion.

He had knocked her with such force that her engagement ring had flown off her finger. It lay a few feet away. It had hit against one of the walls and bounced off the paneling.

He followed her eyes and said, "Don't even think about it. That was my mother's ring, and you have no right to even look at it, let alone wear it. I pray to my mother that she can forgive me for ever deciding that you were worthy of it."

"I wasn't going to touch it, but I was worried about where it had gone," she said as she scooted backward from him. She wanted to be anywhere but in this room. How was she going to get away from him?

He picked up the ring, then lorded over her once again. "I want to be very clear. We are through. I wish we were in a different country where I could kill you for the shame you've brought to my family."

He turned to leave, then changed his mind. As Maria cowered, he illustrated his point. Pulling back his foot, he then brought it forward until it connected with her stomach—not once or twice, but enough times that she was curled into a ball and sobbing, the pain on her cheek long forgotten.

"Now, you begin to understand what I think of you, whore," he said.

"I'm sorry," she managed.

"I hope I never have to see you again. But, if I do, it will be very bad for you. Do you understand? I could easily find a way to make you disappear. No one, not even this new family of yours, would find you if I didn't want them to. Do you understand?"

She nodded, understanding him quite clearly. If she got out of this alive, she would not be lucky a second time.

Pablo spat on her again. This time she felt the moisture as she lay curled into a ball, trying to protect herself. Finally, he left the room, and the first sob wracked her.

She lay there, sobbing for what felt like an hour, until Bruno appeared. He picked her up unceremoniously, tossed her over his shoulder, and she almost screamed out in pain. Had Pablo decided to make her disappear after all? She should have crawled out. Why hadn't she?

She should have tried. But she couldn't move. She possibly had some broken ribs. She hurt, but this humiliation was worse.

"Bruno, please, I'll go."

But he ignored her.

A moment later, Bruno tossed her into the backseat of a black Alfa Romeo with as much grace as someone might throw a bag of potatoes or dog food into their car. The clothing she'd left at Pablo's was dumped on top of her, as were her toiletries which spilled on her and her clothing. Her shoes were pitched in with force, striking her when they landed.

After a short ride, the car stopped by the front door of her apartment. Thankfully, she realized she wasn't going to be tossed into the Tiber or killed.

Bruno opened the back door, grabbed her, and dumped her on the doorstep like common trash, her clothing and what was left of her toiletries then fired at her like missiles. She rested with her pain on the cobblestone steps for a few moments, then she managed to crawl up to her fourth-floor apartment on all fours, where she collapsed and waited for the world to end.

CHAPTER EIGHT

T hey kept Spencer waiting. The staff of his own hotel in Rome didn't think enough of the owner to have a bellman waiting to take him to the corporate suite. Spencer would have a lot to say to Maria when he finally saw her. He didn't expect special treatment, but in this case, he should have gotten it. This lapse could not be tolerated.

It was as if they didn't even know he was going to arrive. Surely, Maria had prepared them to be on their best behavior. Yes, he'd been there earlier, last month to observe, and he had kept a low profile, but this time, he was there to take ownership and change things up. Maybe he should have given Maria more time. He knew she had only returned to Rome yesterday, and he wouldn't be meeting with her until tomorrow, but still, what was going on? Something felt off, and it was time for him to get to the bottom of it. And where was she?

He called the front desk while looking at the view from the corporate suite where he had been deposited not ten minutes earlier. The Colosseum lay just in the distance. He could almost feel all the historic pain and suffering emanating from the historic ruin.

"Yes, *Signore?*" A woman answered with a soft voice.

"I'd like to speak to Maria Medici."

"I'm sorry *Signore, Signorina* Medici did not come in today. Unfortunately, we believe she is home with illness. Would you like to leave a message for her?"

"No, but I want a car and a driver. Tell them the owner of the hotel requires their services. I'll be down in five minutes."

Spencer had her home address. He quickly changed into jeans and a t-shirt adding a suede jacket in soft chocolate.

The hotel limo, just like at all their hotels, was waiting for him out in front, ready to take him anywhere he wanted to go.

Spencer gave the driver the address and waited. Finally, there was a nod of understanding, and they were on their way.

Within five minutes, the driver stopped and opened the door for him. Spencer thought the proximity to the hotel meant Maria could probably walk, but he wondered how she managed it with her signature stilettos. The cobblestones would cripple a person if they tripped and fell. Heck, he'd tripped on them several times when he was last in Rome.

On the edge of Piazza Navona, the driver and Spencer stood in front of an ancient building that probably dated back two to three hundred years and was now renovated to individual apartments. Stark Corporation always provided an apartment for the hotel manager, and Spencer wondered who had chosen this location.

He could hear the sound of water from one of the three fountains contained within the Piazza. He wondered if Maria could listen to them from her apartment and guessed that she probably could.

There was garbage lying all around the front steps of her building. If he wasn't mistaken, some appeared to be high-end cosmetics, and they looked like they had been purposefully smashed. He made out a woman's red bra with a black lace edge and a broken stiletto. There was no doubt a story there. He'd have to ask Maria if she knew anything about the mess.

Finding the front door to the lobby propped open with a chunk of wood, he felt the heat of an unusually warm spring waft from the lobby of the building. Regarding the slip of paper again, he let out a breath and shrugged out of his jacket. Maria's apartment was on the fourth floor. He wasn't about to get in any elevator this old building might offer. He figured it could be days before anyone thought to look for him there if it failed. Perchance they should get her a nicer apartment.

He turned to the driver, handed him his jacket, and said, "I'll be back in a few. Don't go anywhere without me."

The driver nodded and got back into the limo to enjoy a bit of air conditioning.

Spencer didn't start breathing hard until he had passed the third-floor landing and was on his way to the fourth floor. He needed to keep up his exercise now that he was off the ranch. Maybe he'd start jogging or use the gym at the hotel. Either way, he shouldn't lose the momentum he'd started back in Texas three months ago as a way to handle his stress.

He should have brought Maria some groceries if she were sick, maybe some seltzer water since he doubted he could get ginger ale in Rome. He could have picked up some fresh fruit, maybe risotto, the only thing he could think of that was close to the comfort food of chicken and rice, but he didn't know what kind of sick she was, so he'd have to assess the situation and then decide what to do. Maybe the hotel could put a care package together for her.

He had a bad feeling about this situation, something he couldn't shake. Something that made him traverse the streets of Rome his first night in the city when he was both jet-lagged and sleep-deprived. Why hadn't she called? That was unlike her. She was on top of details like this.

At Maria's door, apartment 404, he knocked softly, but she didn't answer. He knocked harder and waited. In a matter of minutes, he knocked a third time.

The light changed behind the peephole, then a husky voice asked, "Spencer?"

Her voice sounded off, as he said, "Yes."

Slowly, Maria opened the door a crack, showing only part of

her face, and said, "Why are you here? What do you want, Spencer?"

"I heard you were sick."

"I'll be in tomorrow. I'm sorry about today, but I'm sick and need to get better. So, I'll see you tomorrow," she said and started to close the door again.

Damn, she was hurt, but there was more there. This wasn't flu or a cold. Something or someone was responsible for the look of fear he saw on her face.

"Maria, open this door," he ordered. Saying not another word, he waited. He sensed she was doing the same thing on the other side. Then, he heard her sigh.

"Fine, but it isn't that bad, so please don't react," she whispered and disengaged several locks, finally opening the door.

He'd be the judge. He'd seen a lot of bad. And it always seemed to happen to the women he loved.

Spencer had to step back at the sight of Maria. Less than a week earlier, he had kissed her flawless cheek, looked at her gorgeous face, and openly admired her beauty. He'd held her tight, but the thought of doing so to the woman before him gave him great pause. She had been battered.

Half of Maria's face was swollen and bruised. She had a black eye, and it looked like it hurt. She was devoid of makeup, her hair hadn't been combed, and she held her plush pink robe carefully closed in front, close to her body. She looked anywhere but at him. Who did this to my Maria?

"My God, what happened?" he asked, "Were you mugged?" He hoped that was her answer because if it were anything else, someone would pay. Hell, he was going to have to kill the responsible party.

Her face crumpled, and tears leaked from her eyes as she managed to shake her head.

Spencer didn't think. He just stepped forward and held out his arms. He wanted to pull her close but knew she was in pain and trying to hide it. When she did lean against him, words no longer were necessary. She keened in a way that let him know her pain was a lot deeper than her battered skin. Something very bad had happened to her. Spencer resolved that whoever had hurt her was a dead man walking.

He took two steps forward, just enough to shut the door behind him, then watched as she broke away from him and quickly went to work on the locks, slowed down by her trembling fingertips and the torrent of tears that leaked from her eyes.

She was terrified, and that made Spencer very angry. Maria Medici was the strongest woman he knew, and someone had tried to break her.

Spencer sat on the nearest flat surface he could find, her oversized couch. She joined him gingerly, sitting close enough for him to touch but not close enough for the invitation to be touched. He knew and respected the difference.

"Tell me," he said.

She looked away, and he said, "Maria, I need to know to keep you safe."

"My engagement is no more. Alex's announcement made Pablo... well, he was very upset. He didn't take kindly to the thought that I'd omitted details of my past. He wants to run for office and doesn't want any scandal. He said that I lied. I did. It was my fault. I should have told him earlier."

"Pablo did this to you?" Spencer said, already planning the man's slow and painful death.

"He had a bad reaction. I underestimated how bothered he would be by my past." Her words broke him in two. The Maria he knew wouldn't be this vulnerable, this frightened—she'd be plotting her revenge against the cowardly asshole. Pablo not only physically hurt her, but emotionally too, and that sometimes was harder to recover from.

"I wasn't there, but I know it wasn't your fault. No one has

73

the right to hurt you. A man doesn't hit his fiancée; a man doesn't hit a woman. What happened?"

"He slapped my face, and I fell. I was crying loudly, so he kicked me in the ribs to get me to understand how upset he was. I think a few of the ribs may be cracked. His butler drove me home, but I didn't feel like walking, so I crawled up the stairs to my apartment. My knees are hurt, but everything will be fine." It was painful to listen to her trying to convince him, trying to convince herself. Nothing was going to be fine until he killed Pablo.

"How long did it take you to pull yourself up the stairs?"

"Less than an hour. Everything is okay."

"Did he assault you in any other way?"

"No, he did not force himself on me," Maria said and added, "I'm thankful for that at least. I don't want him ever to touch me again."

Spencer stood and paced, his hand to his mouth stopping words that might be perceived as adding to her pain. He couldn't calmly discuss what Pablo Tino had done to her. He was having a hard time not reacting, not breaking something in anger. It would make him feel better to break something, but it wouldn't help Maria. It might scare her. The only thing that stopped him from running down the four flights of stairs to the limo and to Pablo's residence and murdering the other man was the knowledge that Maria was not only terrified but she was hurt and needed some medical attention. She didn't need to see him fly off the handle. There would be time to deal with Pablo Tino later. His priority was Maria.

Looking at her battered skin and the guarded way she held her body, he asked, "Have you been to the hospital?"

She looked at him as if he'd grown another head.

"If I go to the hospital, they will call the police. I cannot have a record of this. Pablo will kill me."

"Pablo almost did kill you. We need to make sure he is locked away from ever hurting anyone else."

"You don't understand. His brother is high up in the police force. Nothing will happen to Pablo, but something might happen to me. He told me they could make me disappear someplace my family would never find me. I think I would for sure disappear if I made trouble for Pablo. He told me he wished this was a country where women could disappear without repercussions."

Although Spencer wanted to hurt Pablo, he could tell there was something to her fear, and he didn't want to add to it. "Okay, we will talk more about Pablo later. Who is the hotel doctor on call?"

"Dr. Nonna."

"Let's call them and see what it would take to get a house call."

"We cannot disturb him so late at night," she protested, and he could tell the effort for her to breathe was hard. What if one of the ribs had broken and was now deflating her lung or stuck in it? What if her injuries could still mean life or death to her? He was terrified that she was hurt much more seriously than she appeared.

"We will pay him what he makes in a week of daylight calls," Spencer said as he pulled out his cellphone and waited for Maria to supply the information he needed. "I can't believe you have suffered from this since last night and didn't call someone. You should have called Alex. You could have called me."

Spencer continued to pace and sigh as they waited for the doctor, who arrived fifteen minutes later.

The doctor, a small-statured man with dark hair and a granite jaw, kept shaking his head. He also spoke very little English, so communication wasn't the easiest with Spencer's limited grasp of Italian.

"No Xray, but I think it is injured," the man said, pointing to Maria's abdomen, and shook his head.

Spencer pointed to his ribs and looked to the doctor, who merely nodded and said, "*Si.*"

"*Uno, duo, tre, quattro, cinque?*" he asked, pointing to his ribs. "How many?"

"*Quattro,*" the doctor said, holding up four fingers and nodding.

Spencer grabbed a tongue depressor the doctor had used on Maria. First, he cracked it, looking for the doctor's reaction, and then broke it.

The doctor grabbed another depressor out of his bag and just bent it.

"Cracked, not broken," Spencer said.

Maria sighed and said, "See? Not so bad."

"It is bad enough," he said and pointed to Maria's face.

"*Irritata…* eh… sore," the doctor said.

"It hurts," Spencer said and watched as the doctor talked to Maria, giving her instructions as she nodded.

"Would you please translate?" Spencer asked, knowing he wouldn't get the whole story.

"He wants me to use ice on my face, my knees, and my chest where the ribs hurt. It will take six weeks for the ribs to heal, and I'm to be very careful with myself for those six weeks."

The doctor handed her two pill bottles, accepted five hundred euros in bills from Spencer, and quietly started to leave.

Spencer stopped him at the door. He handed the man another hundred euro note and said, "Please tell the driver in the limo downstairs that I don't need him for the rest of the evening."

Maria translated to the bewildered doctor and added, "*prego,*" to the end of her message.

The doctor nodded, suddenly understanding that it was his

time to leave, glanced at Maria, and nodded again. Then he quietly slipped out, leaving Maria and Spencer alone.

"Are you hungry?" he asked. "Have you eaten anything today?"

She shut her eyes and shook her head as tears leaked down her cheeks. Her fear, hurt, even embarrassment to be in this position was palpable. She had trusted someone who had turned on her. The ramifications of that misjudgment were almost too much to comprehend, but she needed him, and he needed to help her or kill Pablo. It was one or the other.

"Okay, let me see what I can do," he said as he stepped into her kitchen as Maria sat on the couch and silently wept. It broke his heart. After seeing Ruby go through all she went through, he couldn't believe someone else he cared about was suffering. He made Maria a cup of tea, found some amaretti biscuits from a red tin for her to dunk in the tea, and prepared a tray. The more to keep his hands busy.

How could anyone hurt her like that? How could *anyone* hit someone, let alone someone they loved? He needed more details. He wanted to know everything from the moment she saw Pablo to when she got back home. He knew it would only make him angrier, but he didn't care. He needed to know.

Spencer returned to the living room area, where Maria was looking at him as if she had forgotten he was in her apartment.

"Try to drink this and eat the cookies so you can take the pills."

"I don't want to feel groggy," she said with pleading in her eyes. "I fear he will come here to check on me or send the police. Whatever happens, we cannot trust the police."

"Maria, you need to rest, and I'm not going anywhere, so you don't need to worry about anyone hurting you." He set the tray on the coffee table to grab her hand, gently sitting on the couch, hoping she understood he was here to help her as long as she needed.

He thought she'd protest, but instead, she began to cry again, silent tears leaking down her cheeks.

Spencer lifted the tray to set it in his lap, then gently lifted the cup off the saucer and handed it to her. She took it, looking at him over the lip of the delicate cup, and then sipped at the warm tea. He'd found a basic English tea in her cupboard and didn't worry about the caffeine. She was running on fumes, and he anticipated he'd have to grab the cup out of her hands at some point when she fell asleep sitting up.

"Why are you scared he will return?" he asked as he held up a cookie for her to take in her hand.

She nodded and said, "He is a very powerful man, and I've offended him. He will not forgive me for my betrayal. He will want to make sure that I got the point. Or he will stop being angry and want to make sure that I've forgiven him but still know my place."

"Listen to me. You are safe, but he isn't."

"I don't know if that is the right reaction. I don't know if we are safe," she said, the fear creeping into her voice. "I think you underestimate how powerful he is in this city."

Spencer got up and pushed a heavy table in front of the door without a word. He doubted that Pablo would bother them, but anything he could do to reassure Maria, he would do.

Her eyes met his, and she quietly nodded and then whispered, "Thank you. Don't open the door to anyone."

"I can't now anyway. You need your rest. Would you like a bath? I'll stand guard."

She nodded and started to stand.

"Why don't you rest here and let me draw you a bath? When it is ready, I'll come back for you."

She nodded and murmured, "Thank you. Hot, please."

"Finish your cookies and then take the pills, ok?" She agreed as he left the room.

Her clawfoot tub was ancient but elegant, and it worked. He

was reminded he was in Italy, with the elaborate tile on the walls and the ceiling, a geometric puzzle in black and white that would give an ordinary person a migraine. The floor was white marble with veins of black and dark gray. In the United States, it would cost six figures to get a bathroom like this, but in Italy, it was standard.

The only color in the space was a stack of neatly folded fluffy pink towels that matched the robe Maria wore as she rested in the other room. She was a girly girl down deep.

Spencer ran water that was a little warmer than he might have wanted for himself. He waited until it was three inches from the edge, then he shut off the water and went back for Maria.

After helping her stand, he gently walked with her to the bathroom and hesitated.

"Would you like my help into the tub?" he asked.

Maria reached for the knot on her bathrobe and slowly loosened it. Then she nodded and said, "I'm going to need your help. I can barely bend my knees."

"Anything you need, I'm here."

Spencer tried to put his feelings for the woman to the back of his mind, but the truth was, the last time he'd felt this way about a woman, he'd lost several years of his life.

Ruby. For three years, he'd ridden a rollercoaster with her that broke his heart each day until he stepped away. It had only been a few months ago but felt like years. He missed the closeness of a woman. It had been a long time since Ruby's accident. As Ruby recovered from her injuries and he realized she would never get significantly better than her brain injury allowed, he had put aside his feelings. But now, with Maria, it was hard to keep a rein on his attraction, but to do anything about it would make him a brute equal to Pablo. She needed a friend, a protector. He took his job seriously.

And here he was again, embroiled in another mess. His

thoughts, his emotions were shattering. The only difference between Ruby and Maria was that Maria had been fine until someone decided to make her a human punching bag and undermine her world. It hadn't been a random accident. Maria was perfection. And someone hadn't seen her elegance and tried to break her. He would hurt the party responsible for hurting this precious, beautiful woman.

Maria tried to push the robe from her shoulders but couldn't lift her arms without pain. Spencer stepped forward and eased the fabric away from first one shoulder and then the other, hanging the discarded robe on a hook on the back of the bathroom door.

Normally, he'd be distracted by the lace and satin bra and panty set she wore in blush pink, but not today. Instead, his eyes went directly to the bruises marring her perfect olive skin. It was worse than he'd imagined. He wanted to hurt that animal who had done this to her.

Maria either had little or no modesty, or she had been beaten down to a point it no longer mattered. Possibly, she had always been this way, as Europeans are not modest, but Spencer didn't think so. Maria stripped out of her lingerie and placed it in a wicker basket in the corner of the bath. Then, nude but not showing that it bothered her, she reached out her hands and had Spencer help her into the waiting tub. He watched her struggle and wondered if he shouldn't have just picked her up and gently place her in the tub. He would next time.

Later, during quieter moments, Spencer would try to picture Maria's lush body, but all he saw were the bruises. Instead of the pleasure he'd hoped to feel at the memory, all he felt was rage—white, hot anger.

Maria sunk into the tub with a groan and seemed to realize her mistake immediately. Having anticipated her need, he handed her a soft cloth in the pale pink and a bar of coconut-scented soap.

"Thank you, Spencer," she said meekly, and it broke his heart.

A warm bath had always calmed the anger that had lived within Ruby since the accident. He often wondered if her anger was just frustration at the broken shell of the body in which she would be forever trapped. He put these thoughts into the special compartment in his mind and turned all his attention to Maria. All he wanted was for this sweet Italian woman to feel better and not be in pain.

When she had thanked him, something inside of him broke. This was a proud woman. The last thing she wanted was to need his help, to be naked during something that was the equivalent of a medical procedure. The animal she'd been engaged to had done more than beat her physically. He'd broken a bit of the lively spirit that Spencer had so enjoyed.

Maria slowly, carefully, ran the cloth over her face, neck, and arms. He could see her shudder in pain when she ran the material over her large bruises and her tender ribs.

"Why don't I do your back for you?" Spencer suggested. "I'll be very careful."

She nodded and leaned forward awkwardly. He took the cloth, rubbed it against the coconut bar, and gently ran the fabric over her back, avoiding the bruises that existed there as well. It was becoming easier to document the areas not bruised or battered than making a note of all the injuries.

When that was done, she leaned back and shut her eyes, the full magnitude of her ordeal starting to sink in. Without help, she couldn't even bathe. Spencer could read her thoughts as if she said them aloud.

"Would you like your hair washed?" he asked.

Remembering that he was there, she slowly nodded and said, "You don't have to. I know it won't be an easy thing."

"I don't mind," he said. He was used to it. Up until six months ago, he washed Ruby's hair twice a week. It was one of his favorite times with her. He realized he missed those times, which were the last vestiges of intimacy he had with the first love of his life. Thankfully, she was happy in her new living situation. He only regretted that he had hesitated for so long to have her live away from him. He'd been selfish, believing she would suddenly get better and come back to him.

"Thank you. Pablo threw some of my toiletries at me, and one of my lotions ended up in my hair. I got the glass out, but the lotion stuck to my hair."

Spencer focused once again on Maria and asked incredulously, "Didn't that cut your scalp?"

"Only a little. It stopped bleeding quickly, but the different bottles hurt when they hit. I was just glad they missed my face. It's better today."

He'd see for himself when he was touching her scalp.

"Were those some of your things in the street by the front door?"

"Yes, but don't worry. I don't want them anymore. I can afford to buy new."

"I think that is a good idea. Same with the clothing."

"I'll drain some of this water to get fresh for my hair. I don't like sitting in bathwater that isn't clean," she said as she reached for the drain and cried out in muffled pain.

"Let me," he said, plunging his arm into the warm, soapy water and finding the drain. He could see her feet, her elegantly manicured toes that had the perfect shade of red polish, but he remembered that none of it mattered. Pablo hadn't cared to notice. Pablo hadn't cared about her at all. Well, when Spencer was done with Pablo, Pablo would know what he'd done was wrong.

"Do you have a bowl I can fill for rinsing your hair?"

"Just under the sink is a pitcher I use," she said and pointed with an elegant finger that was tipped in that perfect red.

He tried to keep everything matter of fact, and normal, as if he found a battered woman every day and helped her. But inside, he raged.

Filling the pitcher, he then leaned over Maria in the tub and watched as she bowed her head. He carefully poured the warm water over it.

"Could you please use the shampoo in the black bottle," she asked and pointed to the counter. Spencer retrieved the bottle, placed a small amount of the floral yet spicy orange-scented liquid in his hand and began to massage it into Maria's scalp, careful of any lumps, bumps, or shards of glass that may remain. Eventually, he saw the cut and tried to avoid bumping the scab.

He was careful to get the job done but also take it slowly and try to relax her with a scalp massage, just like he had always given Ruby. Maria responded by sighing appreciatively.

Spencer was well aware of the healing power of touch.

When he'd finished conditioning and rinsing her hair, he grabbed a brush off the counter and slowly brushed her long mahogany locks into a tame, silken mass, avoiding the cut he'd found earlier.

Grabbing two, soft, cotton-candy-pink towels from the stack next to the tub, he wrapped one around her head and helped her stand and then dry. When he'd finished, he wrapped the second towel around her battered, sore body.

"My skin is dry," she complained as she walked slowly to the counter, sat gingerly on a small stool, and then rubbed cream from a small jar into the normal side of her face and gently touched the swollen side that Pablo had attacked.

Slowly, she replaced that jar and reached for a larger one, white with black lettering.

"Would you like me to rub some of that into your back?" Spencer asked, trying to sound like the caring person he hoped she thought he was instead of the lusty beast who'd kissed her cheek and wanted more under the stars at the anniversary party.

He knew she didn't need that Spencer at the moment, and he wanted to show her there were more layers to him.

"Please," she asked with a small voice. He picked up the Byredo Bal d'Afrique body cream, took a sniff, and approved. He'd smelled the exotic mix of violet and jasmine before, when she was wearing it at the party just under some heady perfume. He wanted her to feel good, to return to some normalcy after the brutality. He hoped the lotion would help.

Gently as he could, he rubbed the lotion into her soft skin, remembering that he was privileged to have this opportunity.

"What would you like to do with your hair?" he asked as he slowly rubbed lotion down her spine, avoiding the bruises he saw that had formed on the lower part of her back — where she must have landed when she was tossed out of the car in front of her building.

"I'm sorry, I won't ask you to do anything else for me—"

"I don't mind at all. Would you like me to blow dry it?"

"You'd do that?" she asked.

"Of course," he said, trying to lighten the tone a bit. "I'll even add all the products I know girls like to have in their hair. I'm a full-service man." He added a wink and smile, which prompted Maria to roll her eyes..

She pointed out several products and gave him instructions on how to apply them to her hair.

Fifteen minutes later, he was brushing the dry waves of her hair and marveling at how soft it was. In his dreams, he'd wondered how it would feel to touch, but the reality was so much better.

"Are you tired?" he asked, knowing the answer. She'd had so much adrenaline surging through her body since the assault. She was probably going to drop at any moment as she had finally started to relax.

She nodded and then admitted, "But I don't know if I can sleep. I'm still scared. I know he will try to see me again."

"I'm here, and nothing will happen to you on my watch."

She met his eyes at that moment, and he could see the skepticism in them.

"I'll be on the couch. Just a few feet away from you and the front door," he reasoned.

"No, that is too far away," she said as she stood and took his hand. She then pulled him toward the bedroom to her double bed. Not quite understanding, he followed her into the bedroom.

"What would you like to sleep in?" he asked as she went to a low dresser and pulled open a drawer. She returned with an oversized nightshirt that depicted the Colosseum against a pink background.

"Here, let me help you," he said, looking for and finding the opening for the neck and her arms.

A moment later, the towel was on the floor, and she was looking adorable in the oversized t-shirt.

"I have to say it," he said, "You look cute in the t-shirt. Now, why don't I leave the bedroom so you can get some rest? I'll be on the couch in the other room."

She shook her head again, her eyes pleading. "No, Spencer, that is too far away."

"It's okay. I can sleep on the floor in front of the door."

"Not the floor, sleep on the other half of my bed, closest to the door," she said. "Please." The fear in her eyes cut him to the core.

He was trying to be good, but he wasn't an idiot. Lying next to her would be sublime.

"Sure, Maria—I want you to rest and feel safe," he said, kicking off his shoes and waiting until she got into the bed. He stretched out on top of the sheets next to her, a human barrier between her and the rest of the apartment.

He thought she'd be asleep the moment her head hit the pillow, but that was not the case. Instead, as the reality of the past day and a half took hold, he could hear her soft whimpers in the dark.

Carefully, he leaned toward her, and she immediately snuggled into the crook of his neck with the uninjured side of her face, seeking the presence of him.

She was small, fragile in his arms. The things that kept her awake and in fear filled Spencer with fury. Pablo Tino had no idea what he'd awakened within Spencer the moment he'd laid a hand on Maria.

CHAPTER NINE

Maria snuggled against Spencer. She felt safe for the first time in hours. Since Pablo had hurt her the day before, she hadn't eaten or slept. She didn't know what to do with herself. Fear had taken over, and that was something she was not accustomed to. Fight or flight; ever since she was a little girl, she would fight, but in this case, she'd just wanted to escape someone she never thought would raise a hand to her. Finally, Maria gave her heart to and trusted someone enough to marry them, and then he turned on her—lesson learned; she would never do that again.

When Spencer had shown up on her doorstep like a knight in shining armor, Maria couldn't believe it. She feared for his safety, too, though she soon realized Spencer was a man who could take care of himself. Pablo was unpredictable, but Spencer was a strong man and would keep her safe for now. She had to trust him, yet all she'd learned in the last few days was that no one could be trusted. She was betting everything that Spencer was different.

Whether or not he wanted to be her protector, he'd been drafted into the job. He'd made her feel human again, helping her to eat, washing her hair, and now being someone she could snuggle against who wouldn't raise an angry hand to her. But after this, would Spencer look at her as he had before? She wouldn't kid herself into thinking that she would ever have a chance with Spencer after this. He was her boss, and that was all he'd ever be, and that was for the best.

And to think just two days earlier, she'd been engaged. She shouldn't be thinking about dating anyone. Hadn't she learned her lesson? Trust no one. It had been her motto growing up through adulthood—but Spencer had made her feel something different.

Pablo had never been so into her. It had been evident from their first night. He wasn't a flirt. On the contrary, her ex was all business. Although Maria had no proof, she suspected Pablo had women on the side. He liked to be in control, and although he'd never been so with her, she knew he needed to exercise his power, as did his brother and their family. And that made Maria worry; she was sure she hadn't heard the last from him yet…

Men were all the same. Hell, Spencer probably treated women like that in every town he visited. Maria used to see through that kind of charm, why her ex's gruff exterior seemed real—you get what you see and nothing more. No one could be this kind, caring, and thoughtful—not in her world. Well, after this day and night, she wouldn't have to worry. Spencer wouldn't treat her like anything but a coworker.

Maria relived Pablo's violence in her dream. She felt the pain when he kicked her the first time, the second time, and the final blow that lit her insides on fire and had cracked her ribs. What if he hadn't stopped? Would he have killed her and hidden her body? Would anyone know what had happened to her, or would she have simply disappeared, her body hidden in the dirt in a shallow grave? Or would they have thrown her in the river?

And how long would it have taken someone to notice that she was gone? Who would have noticed? Would they have called Alex eventually? How long would it have taken him to figure it out? Would he ever have thought to look at Pablo? How hard would he have looked? Would the family have just been happy to have a problem gone?

She was as Victoria Stark undoubtedly described her—a bastard child that nobody wanted. In hindsight, Pablo probably thought of her as a safe armpiece for his aspirations in the political world. A foster child in the system was untraceable. And Maria wasn't outwardly messy ("You'll be a good wife, my love… you won't cause your husband any problems"), thinking of Pablo's words when they got engaged made her skin crawl. She'd switched from an asset to a liability in seconds. She should be thankful they hadn't married or had children.

Jerking awake, she pushed against the solid body that she was reclining against only to discover that it was Spencer. She clung to him, needing his protection and savoring his warmth.

"Maria, you're safe. I'm here," he said as he stroked her hair and tried to calm her down. "No one will ever hurt you again." The conviction in his voice gave her comfort.

He'd been asleep as well, and she'd awakened him. What hadn't she done to Spencer Whitlow since he'd arrived? What would she have done without him?

"*Scuzi*, sorry—I shouldn't. I'm so sorry."

"Hey, hey, it's fine. You're fine. I'm here," he said, continuing to touch her hair. "I think you were dreaming or reliving what that animal had done."

"I was," she said and snuggled closer to Spencer.

"Can I get you anything? Water? Another blanket? Do you want to talk?"

"Would it be too much to ask if you just keep holding me?" she asked, hating that she sounded like a weak woman.

"That is something I can definitely do," he said. "Hate to tell you this, but I kind of enjoy being close to you, although I hate the circumstances."

He had to be kidding, humoring her. She could smell his cologne, the clean cotton of the t-shirt he wore as they spoke to each other in the dark.

"Spencer?"

"Yes?" he asked, his voice soft and thick in the dark.

"I'm sorry about all this."

"I'm sorry that he was violent to you. I'm sorry that I wasn't there to bash his head in for hurting you. I hope it wasn't always like that between you two."

"No, he never hurt me. That was the first time he touched me."

"And the last time. But I have to ask, was he ever verbally abusive?"

She hesitated, then said, "Yes, there were a few times he was jealous and angry at me for talking to another man, a waiter, a taxi driver, or a guest at the hotel. At first, he thought they were too flirtatious with me, then he began to question me, that it was me who was too flirtatious. It happened maybe three or four times. He was always, always so apologetic afterward. He wouldn't speak to me for a day or two, then arrive at my door with flowers or jewelry and apologize until I forgave him. Italian men can be like that."

She paused while Spencer rubbed her shoulder, then continued, "The thing was, when he was so mad, I was scared of him, scared he might physically hurt me, but he never did, not until this time. Then he hurt me, and I didn't know if he'd ever stop. I've never been more scared in my life. I'm not going back to him, ever."

"It would kill me to think of him touching you ever again," Spencer said, tightening his hold ever so slightly on Maria.

"You've done so much, but there is one thing you could do for me if you wouldn't mind, but I do not like to ask."

His fingers played in her hair, gently rubbing circles in her scalp.

"I'd do anything for you," he said, his words saying more, conveying everything.

"Pablo, he kissed me when I arrived at his house. I just... I don't want him to be the last person who kissed me. And since you didn't seem to mind trying to kiss me at the party, I was wondering if you could kiss me now? Would it be okay for you? Or am I too ugly now? Maybe you don't feel the same way now, and that's okay."

"You are one of the most beautiful women I've ever seen," he said. "Nothing has changed except that I want to kill your ex-fiancé."

Spencer's body turned toward her, slowly, carefully, and she sensed more than felt that his face was very close to hers. A moment later, his soft lips kissed her temple, her eyelid, her cheek, and finally her lips with the delicate touch of someone trying to bring comfort but aware that pain was very close to the surface.

He kissed her not just once but three times. Then he said, "I don't want to hurt you. And I promise there will come a time when I kiss you that not only will you be a willing participant, but it also won't just end with kisses."

"After all you've seen tonight, your feelings for me haven't changed?" she asked. "I didn't think you were serious in Portland. There must be other women."

"There was someone else. She's ill and will never be the person I fell in love with, nor will she ever love me again. But yes, I still love her, I always will—but that love is different now. It took several years, but I finally figured it out."

Maria laid her head on his chest and let his words sink in. He hadn't been dissuaded. He'd faced something he was only just now starting to talk about. He didn't think that she was a mess and that he should run away. He was there. But until she knew about the other woman in his life, she needed to be careful.

The next morning the sun was bright and solid in the sky when Maria opened her eyes to discover she was alone in her bed. Sounds from her kitchen didn't go unnoticed. Spencer was there no doubt making breakfast. She couldn't tell him that she usually had an espresso and not much else.

As she was thinking about him, and all he'd done for her the night before, he appeared in the doorway to her bedroom with an espresso in his hand, as if he had read her mind.

"Good morning," he said, looking strangely domestic and comfortable in her apartment.

"Good morning," she answered and sat up, leaning against the headboard of her bed. She hurt, but it was less sharp and duller. A little of the sting had gone out of her face and knees thanks to the medication the doctor had given her. The ribs ached badly, but not like they had the day before.

"Would you like a double espresso?" he asked as he moved into the room and sat on the edge of the bed. He'd even thought enough to add a large sugar cube to the edge of the saucer.

She took the coffee, tossed in the sugar cube, and began to sip it when a sudden noise from the hallway outside her apartment had her spilling the drink down the front of her pink t-shirt, creating a dark stain reminiscent of dried blood.

"Maria, open the damn door," an angry male voice shouted in Italian. The voice was accompanied by loud banging that had a violent quality.

Spencer looked questioningly at her, but she could tell he knew who was there.

"That's Pablo," she murmured and all but dropped the small espresso cup on the edge of the nightstand.

"Does he speak English?" Spencer asked.

"Fluently," she whispered, pulling the covers to her like a child seeking protection. "Please don't open the door. Don't let him in. I don't want to see him again. I don't want him to see me, see what he has done to me."

"Of course not. Don't worry. I won't open the door."

Spencer walked to the front door, still barricaded by the heavy table. Pablo's angry fists battered the other side of the door, making Spencer take several steps back and away from the door.

"Pablo Tino, this is Spencer Whitlow. I own the Villa Roma, and I am Maria's boss. This apartment is hotel property, and you need to leave. I saw what you did to Maria. Soon, everyone on our board will know what a vendor did to one of our hotel managers. And just in case you want another run at her, I've hidden her far away from here. I'm encouraging her to report you to the police for assault. Now, go away and never bother her again, or you will have the full power of the Stark Corporation and her family coming after you."

"Who the fuck do you think you are?" Pablo bellowed from the other side of the door. Maria cringed and placed her hands over her ears, but it made no difference. Pablo's anger was deafening.

"To repeat, I'm Spencer Whitlow. I own ten of the Stark International Hotels, including Villa Roma. I don't take kindly to you hurting one of my people. Men who beat up women are the lowest form of human existence. You will pay for every one of her bruises."

"How dare you! She… is… my fiancée. What happens between us is none of your business."

"According to her, you ended the relationship with your boot. It's over, you coward. You mess with someone who works for me, and I make it my business. We are one big family at Stark, and I think you know she is my cousin's sister, which makes her family to me. And from what she told me when I put her on a flight yesterday, you are no longer engaged, so get that idea out of your head. Besides, you have your emerald engagement ring back that says the engagement is over better than I can."

"We had a little fight, a little misunderstanding that got out of hand, that is all. But of course we are still engaged."

Maria shook her head. Was Pablo delusional? Spencer did the same, looking similarly incredulous.

"You are delusional if you think I'd let her marry you—or Alex Stark, her brother, would let her marry you—after what you did to her. You aren't engaged, and here is a little more news for you. I can also tell you that you are fired from our hotels. Our company no longer has a need for you to supply any of our hotels in Europe or anywhere else for that matter. All contracts are void as of this moment. I'll send written notice within the hour."

"You can't—"

"I can," Spencer replied with a smile. Noticing that he finally had this asshole's attention, he continued, "Now, you need to understand, this apartment belongs to the Stark Corporation. You need to vacate the area and never bother Ms. Medici again, or I will call the police right now on her behalf and the behalf of my company."

"You don't begin to know what war you are starting," Pablo said.

"No, sir. You don't begin to understand what you've done. The war started the moment you raised a hand to her. I've seen what you did, and soon everyone will know. It is unforgivable."

Even though Maria was just a room away, Spencer vowed then and there she'd be gone as soon as he could get her dressed and to the airport. She needed to heal with family while he cleaned up the mess here.

"No one speaks the way you are speaking to me and lives to talk about it."

"Are you threatening me? Well, let me be clear. Come near Maria again, and I'll kill you myself," Spencer said before going back to the bedroom where Maria cringed. "But go ahead, threaten me again, and I'll take measures to protect myself, so what I do to you will be in self-defense. I have been the Texas State Shooting Champion for the last fifteen years. Trust me, that means something."

They could hear Pablo screaming obscenities, but Spencer ignored them as he made his way back to the bedroom where Maria waited.

"Spencer, what have you done? Do you know how dangerous he is?" Maria whispered as she looked at him in a way that conveyed how worried she was.

"He doesn't know how dangerous I can be, but he is about to find out," Spencer said and held out his arms for Maria, who clung to him as if he were the last life preserver on a sinking ship. Spencer held her to him and murmured every reassurance he could think of, but Pablo was a much bigger threat than he'd imagined.

The call from Alex came a half-hour later, which was noon local time but the middle of the night back in Portland.

Pablo had been busy. Now, it was time to retaliate.

"Hey," Spencer said, having coaxed Maria back to her bed.

"Why is one of our suppliers, Maria's fiancé, going ape shit crazy and calling me in the middle of the night? He was talking about suing us and said you, whom he refers to as that 'Texas Bull,' threatened to kill him."

"You will want to kill him too when I tell you what he did to your sister," Spencer replied and then told Alex everything, from finding Maria to Pablo's tirade outside her apartment.

"Holy fuck. Is she okay?"

"No," Spencer said. "Doctor confirmed cracked ribs, but he didn't speak English, so I have to take Maria's word for it."

"If I ever see him myself, I'll kill him," Alex said.

"Too late, I already called it. I get to kill him. You can provide an alibi and help me clean it up."

"Agreed. Why aren't the police involved?" Alex asked after Spencer finished.

"I've been asking Maria since yesterday. She finally gave me an answer that made me pause. Pablo's younger brother is on the police force. He is the one who didn't get the title of count, but he has political ambitions like his brother, so he is making his way, proving himself. From what she has said, it doesn't appear that he is worried about who he might have to step on to get to the top. He is General Inspectorate of Public Security, which is Italian for 'Pablo can get away with anything he wants.' He and Pablo could make Italy a very uncomfortable place for anyone they didn't like."

"Shit. This is all we need, some psycho with a Mussolini complex and a focus on Maria," Alex murmured. "I don't think that he is someone to disregard."

"No, I am much more concerned than I was yesterday. He seems to have a failure to connect to reality. Or else we are completely underestimating him. He thinks they are still engaged despite my contradictions."

"Is she safe?"

"An hour ago, I'd have said yes, but I don't think so. Not anymore. The guy was beyond pissed. He came back today, probably to reconcile by getting Maria to submit to whatever he demanded, but he ran into me instead. Not only was I in her apartment, but I fired him from his hotel contract and alluded to the fact that I'd hidden Maria far away from him."

"Yeah, this is bad," Alex said. "I'm concerned."

"I think he'll be back. I want to move her to my executive suite at the hotel and then send her somewhere safe, preferably out of Italy. Possibly to you in Portland."

"Let me think on this for a minute or two. I'm not sure the executive suite is safe enough. There are a lot of places she could go, but I agree. I'm beginning to think that Europe isn't safe. I don't think it is far enough away from Pablo. I don't like the way this feels."

"Me neither. She could hide out on my ranch, but I think she'd hate it," Spencer said.

"Is Ruby still at her care facility?" Alex asked.

"Yes, nothing has changed in the last six months. Ruby isn't going to leave the care she is receiving. She is thriving in the group home and has made friends. She is happy."

"That's what I thought when we visited her a couple of

months ago. I know I've said it before, but I'm sorry. I know how much you loved her in the beginning. I know how much you wanted Ruby to recover. It is such a waste. You've gone above and beyond. I am just so sorry things didn't work out better, but thanks for being there for my sister."

"Thank you. Ruby would have done it for me. But she's happy now, and that is all I can ask for. That was a strange time in my life, I've never felt so powerless, but there is something I can do in Maria's case. Pablo will never get another chance at her."

"Good, thank you. But what about you?" Alex asked. "I think you are squarely in his crosshairs."

"I need to take care of this without any distractions," Spencer said. "If he comes after me, so be it. I'll take care of him. But one way or another, I have to neutralize the situation. Just be there if I need you with an alibi or bail money. Please find me a good international attorney. If I get into trouble, send me someone good. Get me off with time served." Spencer was kind of joking, but not really.

"Spoken like a Texas Bull. Count on the family's full support, my support. And in the meantime, let me think on it for a bit."

"Don't take too long."

"I'll call you back in fifteen minutes."

Spencer hung up and turned to find Maria watching him. "We think your apartment isn't safe."

"I'm glad you've come to that conclusion, and for the record, I think you're right," Maria said. "He was so mad. I thought he would kill me the other night. I don't know if breaking off the engagement is enough."

Spencer nodded and asked, "How fast could you pack a few bags?"

"Give me ten minutes, but I will need your help," she said.

As Spencer watched, Maria pointed to three suitcases in the closet. Spencer laid them out on the floor. With his help, she carefully packed several of her suits, casual clothing, and things that surprised him—photo albums and sentimental trinkets she did not appear to want to leave behind.

Eventually, he helped her dress and then made a call to the hotel, where he talked to the head of security. Handlers were dispatched to the lobby of Maria's building to keep Pablo from entering. The men talked for a few minutes, then Spencer hung up and said to Maria, "Change of plans."

More calls were made. Alex called back and offered assistance from half a world away. Plans were made, airline tickets were hastily purchased. Cars were found. It was not lost on him that Maria's lack of fighting them on this was further proof of her fear and, to him, that they were doing the right thing. They needed to get out of Rome; the sooner, the better.

By the time an unremarkable, small silver Alfa Romeo SUV pulled up in front of Maria's apartment, they were ready. Her bags quickly joined Spencer's in the back of the car, and they were on their way to the airport in Florence, about a three-hour drive but away from Pablo and the connections he might have locally. It was purposefully away from the airport in Rome, where Pablo might or might not be monitoring the comings and goings of Maria and her companion.

Five hours later, they were on board a Lufthansa flight to Chicago with a layover in Munich. Once in Chicago, they boarded a flight to Portland, Oregon. They arrived at the Portland International Airport four hours later, tired and still a little scared from their hasty departure.

The entire flight, Maria kept to herself. Spencer tried to engage her in conversation, but she didn't want to be noticed and tried to hide within herself, looking out the window almost the whole flight with the biggest, darkest sunglasses he'd ever seen. She never turned when the attendants stopped with food and drinks, so Spencer accepted the items for her. Halfway through the flight, he noticed she was shivering and covered her with a blanket, tucking it in to show how much he cared, yet she said nothing. At one point, she reached for his hand and held tightly to it for the rest of the flight.

Spencer considered getting her a wheelchair to make it easier maneuvering through the busy airport. When he mentioned it, his strong Maria would have nothing of it—which made him proud, as it was a little of her old self coming back, and he was happy to see that she was finding her edge again.

Alex waited for them in baggage claim with Mitch, Rebecca's husband and head of security for Stark International Hotels, on his right side. Another equally large man named Frank, flanked Alex's other side. Alex took one look at his sister's face and visibly flinched.

He held out his arms to her, and she gently went into them, her tears beginning before she could speak. "I'm so sorry," he murmured, gently rubbing her back. "No one does this to you and gets away with it."

Over her shoulder, Alex said, "Thank you for taking care of my sister."

"I'm not done yet," Spencer said, giving his cousin a knowing look.

"I don't doubt it," Alex responded, returning a look to scare primal fear into anyone that would dare cross any member of their family.

Pablo had no idea what he was in for. Between Spencer and Alex, he didn't stand a chance.

CHAPTER TEN

Despite the fact the corporate suite at the Stark International Hotel Portland had two large bedrooms, Spencer and Maria shared one bed. They didn't even discuss it. By silent, mutual agreement, they settled into the first bedroom they found that first night, hanging their clothes in the same closet, using the same shower… just not at the same time, which Spencer spent a lot of time second-guessing.

They lay under the covers of the king-sized bed together and held each other. Maria wore another oversized t-shirt, this time of the Pantheon, and laid her head on Spencer's shoulder. He carefully wrapped an arm around her, thinking of all the twists and turns their lives had taken in the last couple of days. He didn't know if she was warming to the idea of having him in her life, but he thought this continued closeness was a good sign. She had just lost a fiancé and was battered and bruised, so he needed to tread carefully. He needed to make sure he didn't overwhelm her.

He didn't know what he would do if she chose to walk away from him. He wanted his strong woman back—wanted to be by her side—and it was right then and there Spencer realized he had strangely strong feelings for Maria.. He'd felt it the moment he saw her at the anniversary party, but now he knew for certain. The need to protect her had taken his feelings to a completely different level. Something told him, this was going to be serious.

The differences between Ruby and Maria were vast. Ruby was never interested in wealth or status, and she was secure in a simple life from the first day they met. Maria was brunette, and Ruby a redhead with blue eyes. She was the woman he'd thought he'd spend his life with until fate intervened. So what was this unstoppable attraction to Maria? It was physical for sure, but more. He could vividly see a future with her… a family. Did it frighten him? No, not in the least. Did he worry that she was the first woman he'd been attracted to besides Ruby in six years? Yes. It had happened quickly, but there was no one else like Maria. He knew that for sure.

When Spencer had called the hotel in Rome to order a car to pick them up outside of Maria's apartment, he'd been told that not only was Pablo cruising the hotel lobby, but the police were asking for Spencer at the hotel. They had shown an interest in the waiting company limo. Were they watching it? Possibly. That information was good enough for Spencer to change up his plans. Now he wondered what awaited him back in Rome when he returned in several days.

He had been very excited about the idea of the renovation. He had wanted to work side by side with Maria. Now, he was very excited about the idea of evening the score with Pablo. He and Alex had yet to discuss it, but by unspoken agreement, he knew Alex would bless his plan to enact revenge on Pablo for what he'd done to Maria. He just wondered if he needed a couple of wingmen, so his ass didn't get kicked. He could easily be in over his head, and that could land him in a Roman jail or shot, his body buried in a shallow grave in the Italian country-side. Needless to say, he had to be careful.

Having been exhausted the night before and then arriving in the middle of the night, Spencer and Maria slept in until mid-morning the next day. Spencer awoke first but didn't want to wake Maria, hoping that the longer she slept, the better she might feel, and the quicker she might heal. The bruises were already changing color from that dark blackish-blue to a more purply color.

Gently untangling from her, he walked into the main living area, hoping to brew some much-needed coffee. On the way to wipe away the cobwebs of sleep, he found his cell and saw that he had a message from Alex that showed his usual familiar warmth for the man sleeping with his sister: "Call Me."

Spencer gently shut the door between the living area and the bedroom where Maria still slept. Then he called Alex.

"How is she?" Alex asked.

"Hello, cuz. She is still asleep. We were exhausted. And if I'm being honest, I'm still tired, so I can only imagine how she is feeling."

"Daisy got Maria an appointment with Daisy's doctor for two this afternoon. It isn't that we don't trust the fine doctor you found to make a house call in Rome, who didn't speak English and could be paid in cash, but we want a second opinion before she makes any next steps."

Spencer, too, had hoped to get Maria to another doctor once they got stateside. "You've got no argument from me, I agree." Then said, "I don't want to wake her, but I will at 12:30. That should give her enough time to get ready."

"Will she fight this second doctor's appointment?"

"You do know Maria, don't you? Hopefully, she will fight us on it because that means she is getting better."

"I love my baby sister, but damn, if she isn't stubborn and moody at times."

"Gee, I wonder where she gets it?" Spencer asked, only to find himself talking to a dial tone.

At precisely 12:30, Spencer slipped into bed next to Maria and gently started kissing the uninjured skin on her face until she gradually woke up.

"Spencer?" she asked, "What time is it?"

"It is a little after noon, and your brother and sister-in-law have made you an appointment with their doctor to check on your progress."

Maria swore in Italian but opened her eyes and gave Spencer a small smile.

"Good morning, my sweet Maria."

"Good morning, my Spencer," she replied and reached for him. He gave in and slowly, gently enfolded her in his arms.

By 2:15, they were in the examining room of a doctor who had office space at Good Samaritan Hospital, a five-minute drive from the hotel. Spencer had helped her into a gown, and she waited, looking sad and small on the examination table.

By 3:00, the doctor was showing Spencer and Maria an image of four neat cracks along her ribs that almost precisely matched the impression if someone had kicked her hard with the tip of a shoe.

She was given about the same advice as the Italian doctor had given her, only this time Spencer could understand it.

"Ice, rest, be careful. If you do all these things in six weeks, they will be as good as new." He then examined her medication, taking the tops off the bottles, sniffing, examining the pills, and nodding. Then he said, "They gave you the good stuff. Be careful you don't use too much of it, and when you finish the pills, don't get a refill. If you still have pain, take Advil or Aleve."

That night they had an early dinner with Alex and Daisy, who asked for a detailed account of everything that had happened since Maria left Portland five days earlier. Neither Alex nor Daisy said much, but for the tight lips and what wasn't said, the food that wasn't eaten, Maria knew they were upset.

As they made their way back to the suite, Spencer felt Maria take his hand. He clasped her small hand tightly in his own. She was getting more comfortable with him, which pleased him.

That night, they slipped into the same king-sized bed they'd slept in the night before, but this time when Maria slipped into his arms, she kissed him lightly on the lips. Not to be outdone, he kissed her back but let the kiss linger and grow.

Much later, Spencer said, "I know we should stop. I don't want to hurt you, but I want to make love with you, and I know that isn't possible. You're hurt, and I'd feel like an ass. Hell, I already do."

"I can't wait to be well. I've decided that I want us to be together," she murmured as she reached down to touch him intimately.

"You have?"

"Yes," she answered without hesitation.

"Well, tonight, you need your rest, and I need a cold shower," he said, kissing her as his hands gently roamed over skin that he knew hadn't been involved in the cruel acts of her ex-fiancé.

"You make it hard to stop," she admitted.

"Touché, but it does crazy things to me to know that you don't want me to stop."

"I'm starting to crave you, Spencer. That is very dangerous for a woman. When she meets a man, she just knows. Yes, I will make love with him, or no, he will never touch me. We will make love someday, and it scares me that I know that so soon." She then looked at him, searching his face, "I should not want any man after what has happened. But I want you. Why is that?"

"Don't be scared of it. I promise to be careful with you, Maria. We were meant to be, you'll see." The sincerity in what he said seemed to give her comfort.

The following day, Maria and Spencer had a late breakfast in Alex and Daisy's apartment. Maria's bruises were starting to have greenish-yellow edges, and she contemplated makeup around her black eye for the first time, but when she gently touched the area, the pain was still so intense she had second thoughts. At least her knees were starting to look less scratched and just a little discolored.

Maria didn't know how to feel about her sister-in-law's scrutiny at breakfast. She wasn't used to having people care so much about her. First, Spencer had bent over backward, then Alex had looked uncharacteristically upset. Maria had seen it the day before and was surprised to see it carry over to a second day. If Daisy kept the frowns up, she would get wrinkles.

"It doesn't hurt so bad, not like three days ago," she said, trying to reassure Daisy.

"Maria, when I think about it, it turns my stomach. I can't believe someone who told you they loved you treated you like this," Daisy said and reached down to give her pregnant stomach a reassuring rub. "I'd kill Alex if he ever touched me in anger."

"And I never would, my darling," he said, reaching across the table to take her hand.

A knock on the door brought Rebecca and Mitch to the table. This was Rebecca's first look at Maria, and when she did, she took a step back, as horrified as Daisy had been.

Rebecca put her hand to her mouth, grasped Maria's hand, and shook her head in horror.

"Damn it, Mitch. I'm sorry, but this is so much worse than what you told me. I just can't believe that we were having fun just a few days ago, and then this happened. Maria, I'm so sorry."

"I warned you," Daisy said, looking at Rebecca.

"Rebecca, honey," Mitch said, trying to pull her to him.

Alex cleared his throat and said, "I'm just sorry the information about Pablo's character and connections didn't come out earlier. It might have prevented Maria from ever meeting up with Pablo in the first place or choosing to engage in a personal relationship. At least she didn't marry him or have children with him."

"Gee, that was so lucky," Rebecca said, shaking her head. "I think I want to kill him."

"The line starts behind me," Spencer said. "I think she got close enough. Aside from what he did to Maria, he had a finger in our business. It shows me that we need to vet our vendors a little more carefully, and then Maria would not have met him in the first place." The correction was noted by Alex with a slight nod.

"We don't know if he would have done anything further or will do anything further, but he has done enough," Alex said. "We need to make sure he is handled, and it doesn't need to be delicate."

"What are you planning to do about it now that we are here in Portland?" Spencer asked.

"I've been thinking about this. I want Maria to file a complaint with the local authorities and take it from there. I don't want you to be a vigilante, although I would enjoy seeing Pablo get what he deserves. I'm concerned it would backfire. We could end up on the wrong side of this. It goes without saying; we've fired him, and that is a significant blow to his business and standing in the industry. It is an embarrassment."

Before Spencer could say a thing, Maria decided she needed to say something.

"Alex, think about it. Nothing will happen from filing a complaint, but Pablo will know that I'm here in America. I don't want him to know where I am," Maria said as she sipped her coffee and felt the familiar feeling of dread that had so occupied her thoughts for the last three days.

"She's right," Daisy said. "She can't call the authorities. It will expose her location and make her vulnerable again. She needs to disappear."

"I don't want him to know where she is," Spencer said. "I want to return to Italy and start the renovations we've discussed. Business as usual just without Maria as if she has moved on to bigger and better things. Maybe we needed her expertise elsewhere. Then, when Pablo least expects it, I'll take care of him."

"I think you should leave Pablo alone," Alex said. "I don't know if we have enough power to bail you out of an Italian prison."

"I don't want you hurt, and I want to have a say in what you do. I want to know how you are remodeling my hotel," Maria interjected. "You can't just do it without me. I intend on returning to *Roma* at some point. Besides, Pablo has security. I fear he would do worse to you than he did to me. From what Alex tells me, I need you for your talent to remodel my hotel."

"That is the first time you've sounded like the Maria I first came to know," Spencer said, gently placing his hand on top of hers and giving it a gentle squeeze as he winked at her. Everyone at the table noticed and exchanged knowing glances.

"I have an idea, I just don't know if it is ideal, but it will take care of our immediate issue of making sure Maria has disappeared," Alex said as he took a bite of his bacon. "That way, Spencer can see if Pablo lets it go or tries to talk to her again. We hide her for a month or two. Then if everything is settled, she can return to Rome."

Daisy shook her head as she rubbed her belly.

"Daisy has voiced her concerns to me," Alex said. "She thinks the location is too far off and that this idea is too extreme. Despite what she thinks, I've been listening and considering what she said."

"As if you'd expect any less from me than an honest opinion," Daisy said with a slow smile to her husband.

"And I listened because I love you, and you are the smartest woman I know," he replied. "And the mother of my children."

Daisy rolled her eyes and smiled.

"And if Daisy wasn't already pregnant, I'd tell you to spare us all and get a room," Rebecca said. "Please get back to the matter at hand."

Ignoring his sister, Alex said, "What I'm going to suggest, the place I'd recommend for Maria, well, it is off the beaten path, which is why Daisy doesn't like it."

"I think I already do. Tell us about it," Spencer said.

"The Caldera Lodge at Crater Lake," Alex announced. "Our manager left two weeks ago, and we need a replacement from May first until October fifteenth when we close for the season. Maria wouldn't need to be there for the entire season, just in the beginning to ensure everything is running smoothly, a month or two at most."

"It is in the middle of nowhere. It will bore her to death," Daisy said. "It is the exact opposite of Rome. No vibrant city, no shopping, no restaurants, just a big ass lake in the middle of nowhere."

"It is so out of the ordinary. It will be perfect," Spencer said. "Pablo would never think she would go there."

"Where is this Lodge? This middle of nowhere lake?" Maria asked. She already felt a little out of sorts away from Roma, but now to be sent to a place she'd never heard of had her concerned. And the details they were sharing made it worse.

"It is in the middle of nowhere," Daisy said. "Wilderness. Forest. And don't forget the altitude. It makes me feel sick."

"Peaceful, isolated, and very beautiful," Alex said. "It's right next to Crater Lake, one of the most beautiful places in the world. Daisy and I went up there last summer, and it was wonderful." Maria's brother missed Daisy's eye roll and scrunched up face in obvious disagreement.

"It's a great place to hide in plain sight," Spencer added. "And within a month or, heck, if you decide to stick it out until October, hopefully, this will have died down. Pablo will have been dealt with, and the hotel renovation will be well underway. I can come back and collect Maria in October and take her to

Rome or even my ranch if she'd like for a few more months of downtime."

"Collect me? No. I decide what I do. And as for my hotel, what about my input?" Maria asked. They must understand her need to be involved! It was all she has left. All of her was her work and the Villa Roma. "It is my hotel that you are ripping apart. I want a say in it, especially if I'm a partner in Stark Corporation."

"Or she could come back here full time if she prefers," Alex said, ignoring her and Spencer. "The world of Stark is her oyster."

"You both are talking about her as if she isn't here. Knock it off and listen to her," Daisy said and shook her head. "Remember, aside from having your own ideas, you must convince others that they are good. And even I'm not convinced."

"Yes, sorry, darling," Alex said to Daisy. Then he turned his attention to Maria.

"I need a competent body to manage The Caldera."

"Alex," Daisy warned with a sharp tone that wasn't typical of the pleasant woman. It worked, garnering Alex's attention immediately.

"Yes, my darling?" he asked, looking at Daisy.

"You aren't listening to what Maria needs. Spencer will go forward with the renovation, but what about Maria's input? It has been hers for several years, and she has run it well. You told me yourself it was one of your most profitable hotels because of how Maria manages it. Remember? You gushed when I first went to Rome with you. You couldn't stop talking about what a wonderful manager she is. So, stand behind your words and trust her. She deserves a voice. Shame on you and you, Spencer, for not valuing her thoughts and opinions. I expected more of you both."

"Go, Daisy!" Rebecca said, toasting her with a cup of coffee.

"I'm sorry, Daisy, we got ahead of ourselves. Spencer, you

will need to connect with Maria each day to receive her blessings and thoughts, but I'm sure you were planning on this. I can mediate if you have a difference of opinion. Maria has excellent taste, and her finger is on the pulse of the tourist scene in Rome. Does that sound reasonable?" Alex asked.

"Very, but only if Maria agrees," Spencer said. "I will be checking in with Maria each day. I planned on it anyway."

"But how do I know it will be alright?" Maria asked. "My staff will need an explanation as to my disappearance. What if you forget me?"

Spencer smiled and shook his head. "Um, I don't think you have to worry. I'm not going to forget you. As for your staff, I'm going to tell them your talents were needed elsewhere, and since we are planning on a remodel, it seemed like a good time to send you to another location. Maybe it is a sabbatical, but you will be back. Besides, if they have a heartbeat, they have probably read that you are a Stark and not just a Stark employee."

"But I didn't tell them goodbye." She was so bothered by this upheaval and angry at her ex for all that has happened. He'd cut her to the core, but she needed the security of her hotel, and she hoped Spencer was true to his word. He had been her rock to this point.

"They will get over it. Besides, you were needed elsewhere immediately," Alex said. "And you will be safe, which is our main concern."

"But *Roma* is my home," Maria said, thinking it was the closest thing to normal that she had. "I don't want them to think I was a coward and ran away in the night."

"I know this isn't easy," Spencer said.

Maria looked down at her breakfast as her lip twitched. Then she said, "This is hard. I've never been scared of anything. Even when I was in the orphanage, I knew I'd survive. I've never run away from anything. He hurt me, but he didn't break me. I can't be driven out of my hometown. I want to show him that. If *Roma* isn't large enough for the both of us, he needs to leave."

"And you will show him eventually, but for now, I can't think of you in Rome. I was there. I heard the anger in his voice, my Maria. More to the point, I saw what he did to you," Spencer said. "I don't think he is done yet. I don't want you within a thousand miles of him. Not until I know you are safe. I can't risk anything happening to you. You mean too much to me."

A look passed between them, one that was more powerful than any words they'd said to each other in the last two days.

Alex sighed, breaking up their intimate moment and put it succinctly, "The bottom line is that we need to keep you out of Italy until the matter is resolved. This isn't forever, but it is for a little while. Please, I need you to leave your hometown with the knowledge that you will return to it someday. Can you please trust us?"

"Oh Maria, trust him, for crapsake. He's wanted to be the protective older brother for a long time," Rebecca said.

Maria looked around the table of worried faces and finally admitted defeat. "Okay, I will follow your advice and go to the vilderness."

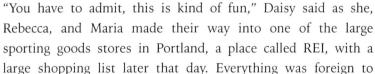

"You have to admit, this is kind of fun," Daisy said as she, Rebecca, and Maria made their way into one of the large sporting goods stores in Portland, a place called REI, with a large shopping list later that day. Everything was foreign to Maria, but she didn't argue with her sister and sister-in-law, who seemed to know what they were doing.

"I'd like to see her in a bunch of Patagonia and Columbia Sportswear Jackets," Daisy said to Rebecca. "We can think of them as her substitute for Armani suits."

"What about my Armani? I brought four of my Armanis with me," Maria said.

"I'm thinking jewel tones with her coloring," Rebecca chimed in, ignoring Maria.

"I like that idea. Just not black, but a few, so she has a bit of variety."

"I agree. Maybe ruby or emerald," Rebecca said. "Polar Tech."

"Will I need everything on that list?" Maria said, indicating the large list that both Daisy and Rebecca scrutinized and added to with little or no input from her. She let this go on because, for once, she could admit they knew better.

"Yes," they answered in stereo.

That morning after breakfast, they had insisted that she needed to be outfitted and begun their immense list. They had taken over like jackals on a fresh carcass. They bought Maria what she had called *vilderness* gear, laughing each time Maria said it. It had provided a good distraction when her mind wanted to focus on so many other, less pleasant, things.

Maria knew Oregon had lots of outdoor enthusiasts, but she had been surprised by all the various merchandise. Because there was a lot of skiing and outdoor activity in her own beloved country, a lot of these items were familiar, but not being an enthusiast, she hadn't spent any time in a store like this. Picking up an odd-looking device, she'd shown it to Daisy. The other woman replied, "Yaktrax. I cannot believe I forgot them! We will take them, just in case." In case of what? Maria thought better than to ask.

"How could we have forgotten Yaktrax?" Rebecca asked, joining them and dumping an armload into their already full cart.

At Maria's further bewilderment, Rebecca explained, "In case of snow, they grip the ground. You put them on your shoes."

"Oh," she said and then asked, "Wait, there will be snow?"

"That area can get a surprise snow this time of year, but probably not," Daisy responded, "But we want you prepared, just in case."

Maria tried on brownish-gray hiking boots and wondered what she had gotten herself into. They were just so ugly. Her feet liked them, but her fashion sense was offended.

"Those are good," Daisy said. "I saw those on a documentary Alex wanted to watch. Hikers at Everest Base Camp wear those on the days they aren't climbing."

"Yeah, look at the brand. Loro Piana from Italy. Ironic, huh? They are top of the line," Rebecca said.

"Does everyone dress like this at The Caldera Lodge?" Maria asked.

"Yes, it is wilderness terrain around The Lodge, lots of rocks and ledges and stuff," Daisy said, "Trust me, you'll need this. You'll start to love those boots. Hmm… maybe we should get two pairs. I like the blue. I bet they match the lake."

"Are you serious?" Maria asked. "Could they be any uglier?"

"It is a way to avoid breaking your ankle," Rebecca said. "Although I think they dress up for dinner at The Lodge. You can wear your other Italian shoes there. Daisy, you and Alex were there last summer. Do you remember? Was there a dress code for dinner?"

"Yes, we dressed up for dinner, but I wouldn't have worn heels outside of the lodge. Not even on the steps, which are wood planks and uneven. The dress code is more of a suggestion. With all the hikers, you can't toss people out for wearing jeans in the dining room. Clean, new jeans are the dress apparel of the lake crowd."

Maria thought she must have audibly gasped because her sister and sister-in-law stopped what they were doing and looked at her. She said, "I like to dress for dinner. I'd never wear jeans. I don't even have a pair of jeans." Both women looked shocked and then laughed at her.

There was a wide variety of "just in case" items Daisy and Rebecca put in the shopping cart that eventually got charged to Alex's black Centurion American Express card. Although spring and summer would be warm, Daisy and Rebecca insisted that it got very cold at night at Crater Lake, and they wouldn't let Maria go into the *"vilderness"* unprepared.

They even insisted that she get two pairs of jeans she vowed never to wear.

"Don't knock it until you try it," Rebecca said.

"Jeans are amazing," Daisy said, but Maria only groaned.

They added something that looked like candy bars but was labeled Cliff Bars to the basket with the added comment, "Just in case."

"In case of what?" Maria asked.

"If you get stranded in your car. You keep a few bars in your glove box," Rebecca said. "That altitude is nothing to mess with."

"Rebecca is right. It is high up. You'll feel it, especially in your lungs," Daisy warned.

"What what will I feel?" Maria asked.

"The altitude. It will take a bit of time for your blood to adjust to it," Rebecca said. "Surely, you've felt it when you were in the Italian Alps skiing."

"I don't ski. Are you kidding? I don't like the cold. What is this about my blood? First, you talk about my lungs, now my blood? Tell me, what happens to my blood?" Maria asked, feeling a bit panicked.

"It gets thicker because there is less oxygen," Rebecca said. "You produce more red blood cells. We all do it when we go to a higher altitude, but your body will eventually adjust. You might feel nauseous for a few days."

"What?" Maria asked, horrified.

"After a week, you won't notice it at all. I promise. Oh my," Daisy said, giving her tummy a rub.

"Are you okay?" Maria asked.

"Yes, I still have a few weeks, but the baby likes to kick a lot. It feels weird but wonderful at the same time. I can't believe we are having a second daughter. I'm so happy. Alex is over the moon. I swear, I thought he'd be disappointed it isn't a boy, but he is ecstatic."

"A daughter is perfect for Alex," Rebecca said and added with a sly grin, "He will be a good father to daughters. He deserves daughters."

"It is so hard to think of all that pregnancy does to your body," Maria said.

"You'll see when you are pregnant," Rebecca said. "It's terrifying but wonderful at the same time."

"Oh, I don't know. Having a baby seems a long way off, if ever," Maria said, "Especially after Pablo. I don't know if I'll have children."

"Would you like to?"

"Yes," Maria said shyly. And she did; she had always wanted a family primarily to replace the one she didn't have growing up.

"What she is trying to say is that we've all seen how much of a crush Spencer has on you. He is a puppy dog," Daisy said. "Heck, he might be in love with you."

"He's very protective," Rebecca said.

She was thankful once again for all he'd done. But loving someone again so soon seemed too dangerous, though possible... if it was Spencer. But Maria realized she needed time, so maybe being at the lodge would be good for both of them to decide what they wanted. It would prove to each of them if fate really had a hand in all of this. She didn't even know what it was like to make love with him. He might be terrible. Who was she kidding? He—they—would be fantastic.

"Your babies would be cute, with Spencer's dimples and your beauty and fabulous green eyes," Daisy said.

"Babies?" Maria asked, slightly amused at the idea these ladies had already picked out the father of her children.

"They would be damn cute children. I've known him my whole life. I've never seen him so... so smitten. Well, it has been a long time. He's all into you," Rebecca said. "I know your ex-fiancé just abused you, and my question might be way too early, but do you have any feelings for sweet Spencer? Maybe it is just too soon to ask."

"He is a good guy," Daisy said.

After a long pause, Maria said, "I don't know how I feel. Everything is strange, but I like it when he touches me and kisses me. It is good. I'm missing not being with him. But, Rebecca, why did you say that it has been a long time for him? Who was before me? He's talked about some woman in his life that he loved, but there was something that happened. He's never gotten too specific."

"I'm sorry, it isn't my place, and the moment I said it, I knew I shouldn't," Rebecca said.

"Too late," Maria said, "Is there someone who I need to worry about?"

"Damn it, no," Rebecca said. "I shouldn't have opened my mouth."

"Tell me," Maria ordered. "I need to know."

"I'm telling you so that you understand Spencer. Maybe you'll understand why he is so sad sometimes, so protective. You see, there was someone who we thought would be in his life forever. Ruby. Ruby Taylor. She was this beautiful redhead." Rebecca stopped, then corrected herself, "I'm sorry, she is a beautiful redhead. She is still alive.

"They met about six years ago. Everything was wonderful in the beginning. They planned to get married and have kids. We all thought they were perfect for each other. They were just two peas in a pod. I think, hell, I know Spencer thought she was his soulmate, but then about three years ago, she had a car accident.

She was on her way to see Spencer, which made it worse, but it was heartbreaking. I remember when I first heard about it. It was just horrific. I couldn't make sense of it, you know?

"You see, she got out of the car when she was hit initially. When she got out to look at the damage, she was hit by another car. Her body flew, like, seventy feet. She landed in a plowed field, which probably prevented her from being killed outright. I'm not sure if that wouldn't have been better to end the suffering that was to come." She stopped again, gathering her thoughts.

"It's so hard to talk about, so sad. Anyway, she ended up with a bunch of broken bones and a severe brain injury. When we first heard about it, there was talk that she wouldn't live, but she did, and it became apparent that she would never be the same. Spencer had her living with him until about six months ago. She would sometimes get angry and violent. Spencer was the only one who could reason with her. But then she stopped recognizing him and was violent all the time. Things just got progressively worse to where she needed full-time care."

"That is why Spencer hasn't been involved in the business," Daisy added, "He's been taking care of Ruby. He dedicated his life to her. It was sad because a part of him died when she had her accident."

Rebecca continued. "Things got bad about six or seven months ago. Spencer realized that he could no longer take care of her, so he put her in a care facility."

Daisy added, "Alex visited Spencer three months ago, and they went to see Ruby. He said she was the best-dressed woman at the care facility and seemed very happy to be around others. However, she still didn't know Spencer and didn't know Alex either. Spencer and Alex had a heart-to-heart after the visit, and that is when Spencer decided to step away from everything in Texas and start back in the business. We were all so worried about him."

"He tried so hard. They hadn't married yet, but Spencer showed up for her, for better or worse. She is still beautiful, but she will never be the person she was. He pays for her care and makes sure she gets the best of everything. He insists. You don't know for how long we have hoped and prayed that he would find peace and happiness again," Rebecca said.

"And with Adam's tragedy, I think the Stark and Whitlow families deserve a happily ever after," Daisy said. Turning to Maria, she continued, "If you are part of that, fabulous. If not, at least you've helped Spencer to live again."

"Spencer is a good man," Maria said. "I had no idea he had been through such a tragedy."

"Just be kind to him. He's been through a lot," Rebecca said.

"And Ruby?" Maria asked.

"She is happy," Rebecca said. "Spencer says now that she's around others with similar afflictions, she seems more at peace, at home. Sadly, she won't ever recover. The brain injury just gets progressively worse."

"I like him now better than I did when we started this discussion. He put his life on hold for the woman he loved. I often wonder if anyone would care that much for me," Maria said.

"I can think of several people. Spencer is one, and that is a good start. Give it a little time to let the dust settle," Daisy said.

"I don't think he is going away anytime soon," Rebecca said with a twinkle in her eye.

In her heart of hearts, Maria hoped he wasn't going away anytime soon either.

CHAPTER ELEVEN

Spencer returned to the corporate suite with Maria early in the evening so they could spend some of their remaining time together before she went off to the *"vilderness."* These family dinners with Alex, Daisy, Mitch, and Rebecca were becoming a little too familiar. If they lived nearer to each other, they would all be so much closer than they already were, and it reminded Spencer of their childhood, leaving him both sentimental and a little sad. Noticeably absent was his Aunt Victoria, who was still loath to accept Maria as part of the family. She'd taken the corporate jet and gone to Texas to see Spencer's parents. The juxtaposition was not lost on Spencer. He didn't know how to make the other woman come around, and right now, he didn't think it would be possible. Maybe his parents could make some headway. After they heard the news, they were more than supportive of Maria. Spencer always wondered why they'd never had more kids. Growing up, he would've liked having a brother or a sister, or both, but it just never worked out for them, he guessed. Regardless, there was no question in his mind they'd come to love Maria. He was sure.

As always, he thought of how short life was and that you had to make the most of each day. He was falling for Maria hook, line, and sinker, and he couldn't deny it.

Spencer looked out at the skyline and spoke from his heart, "This is our last night together for at least a month. I'm going to miss you. I don't know what I'm going to do without having you in my world each day."

He wasn't sure that Maria could hear him, but when he turned, she was leaning against the door frame, smiling that Mona Lisa smile that she had perfected. She'd heard him. "Please call me. Please don't forget me in the middle of nowhere."

"That would be impossible."

She smiled and turned away as she muttered, "*Molto bene.*"

He was learning Italian, and he knew enough to understand that his comment made her happy.

A moment later, one of the bathroom doors shut, and he could hear the shower running. He missed the last couple of days when she had needed his help. With the large, walk-in showers in the two baths in the corporate suite, his assistance wasn't necessary. She could easily walk in and out without him. She was getting better. He should be happy that she was healing. The swelling had gone down on her face, and the bruises were very light now—heck, she could probably cover up with makeup if she chose.

But he missed being needed so intimately. At least she still had him help her get dressed, but with each day, she was recovering and getting stronger. She needed to. She would be on her own at The Caldera Lodge. He didn't want some eager young summer student with a constant hard-on helping her in and out of her clothes. Her bra still gave her a bit of trouble, but now she'd started hooking it at her waist and moving it up her body. She was nothing if not independent.

Had he hoped she might invite him to share her shower? Yes, but no invitation had been forthcoming.

He'd seen her naked. He'd held her in the dark. Last night, his hands had taken their time and touched every part of her he'd dreamed of, but she hadn't invited him into her shower or her body, and he was confused. Was she purposefully distancing from him?

Putting an end to his misery, he stepped into the other bath in the suite and took a cold shower. It had been a long day, strategizing with Alex for Rome and several other hotels when all he wanted was to relax, snuggle up next to Maria, and go to bed with her in his arms. He didn't know how he'd make it without her over the next month. Not only had he gotten used to her, but he also needed her. Tomorrow and every day after would be hell until she was back in his arms. Then they would talk, and if he didn't do it right, she'd run away from him as if he were a cobra chasing her through the brush.

Women like Maria didn't want to feel trapped by a man. He knew that. She would always want a certain level of independence. He just hoped that he could be the man in her life.

But he had to give her her space now. She'll be at The Lodge, and he'll be in Rome. Spencer only hoped that distance would indeed make the heart grow fonder.

Twenty minutes later, Maria breezed through the suite wearing a pink silk nightgown with black lace trim and a matching robe in pink silk with black lace around the cuffs and hem. When she saw him, she smiled broadly, almost teasingly. She knew the effect she had on him. Hell, he acted like a pubescent schoolboy any time she got near him. Her effect was immediate, a visceral reaction he could no more control than stop. He was a confused idiot with an erection.

Spencer wondered how in the hell he was supposed to get any sleep tonight, knowing he was sharing a bed with her. He was glad to see she was feeling a bit better, but he wished he could be around her when she was fully recovered.

"You look beautiful," he said.

"I bought this today at Nordstrom while shopping with Rebecca," she said. "Do you like it? She picked it out for me."

He didn't know whether to thank or curse his cousin.

"Yes, I like it," he said. "But then I'd like you in anything or nothing at all."

She smiled at the compliment.

"Did you buy it for The Lodge?" he asked, hating The Lodge. "I hope not."

"No, I bought it for you," she said, looking up at him with the full force of her emerald eyes.

She had been sitting on the edge of the bed as he watched her, gathering odds and ends she wanted to take with her to The Caldera Lodge with several new pieces of luggage and those older pieces she had brought from Rome that she would leave behind in Daisy and Alex's care.

She stopped moving after she told him about the nightgown. It left him speechless.

"Don't you like it?"

"I love it," he managed. She looked too good for the likes of him.

"I'm glad because I bought it for tonight," she said.

"Tonight?" he asked, the air gone from his lungs.

"Our last night together for a few weeks," she said, looking down, looking sad. "Hopefully, you won't forget me."

"Of course, I will not forget you. Are you kidding? I will be counting the hours until I see you."

She shrugged and smiled.

"You know, I could go with you to The Caldera Lodge for a few nights," he said, hearing the pathetic edge in his voice. "Help you get settled."

If he went with her to Crater Lake, he'd never leave. He knew it.

"I know you must get back to *Roma*. The hotel has been without management for too long. The staff needs one of us. They need to have guidance," she said. "But I need to know you will be careful. I'm scared to have you go back. I don't know how you will protect yourself. I'm worried. Not only did you defend me, but you also fired Pablo's company."

"Don't worry about me. I'll be careful. I want to come back to you. This won't be our last night together," Spencer said as Maria slowly walked around and turned off the other lights in the suite, and finally made her way to the bed.

Standing in front of him, she said, "Thank you for taking care of me."

"I've enjoyed every moment. I want to take care of you every day. I want us to take care of each other."

"Maybe we will have to do that. Take care of each other. I will miss you," she said and leaned over to kiss him on the cheek.

He sighed, he didn't know what to say, and it wasn't like he could pull her to him and show her how much he'd miss her. She was injured. He could still see shadows of the bruises on her body.

She pushed him back on the bed. Until that moment, he didn't know how close he was to it. One minute he was standing, the next, he was on his back, sitting up on his elbows and watching the woman he loved, wondering what might happen next. It appeared Maria had plans and had already choreographed their last night together. He didn't need to be in charge. He could play along.

He sat up on the edge of the bed, holding his hands out to her.

As the thoughts formed in his mind about what she might do, Maria grabbed his hands in her own and then sat on his lap so that her body was facing his. Her face was just inches from his as she brought her feet off the floor and encircled him with her legs.

"Well, hello," he said, and leaned his face into her chest.

"I wish I didn't hurt," she said.

"Me too," he said, looking up and meeting her emerald eyes. "Am I hurting you now?"

"No, I like having you right where you are, well, until I need more," she said and rubbed her breasts against his face as her hands landed in his damp hair.

He needed to be careful. This would not be anything but gentle. With her injured ribs, he didn't want to add to her discomfort. He placed a hand on each of her butt cheeks, pulling her to him, his face more level with her breasts.

Bending down, she kissed him. Unlike his kisses, which had been meant to comfort and reassure, her kiss was meant to convey passion, and it did. He kissed her and wondered if she was feeling what he was feeling—the need to be close, the longing to have her body against his, and the longing to be inside of her.

Reaching up, he ran his hands into her hair, which was still up from the shower. He started pulling out pins as he went. The masses of dark mahogany strands fell into pools in his palms until they overflowed and cascaded around her shoulders. Some of the tendrils were still damp from where they had gotten wet in the shower.

Pulling back from him, she struggled to push away her robe. He helped her and then watched as it fell to a soft pink puddle at his feet.

"I don't want to hurt you, but I've never wanted you more," he said. "What do you want? Do you want me to make love to you? I'll be careful. I'll do my best not to hurt you."

"You won't hurt me," she murmured as she kissed him again. "We just need to be a little careful."

He knew without a doubt that he loved this woman, but by the same token, a week earlier, she had been in love with someone else. He stopped himself from telling her how much she meant to him. He had a feeling she already knew. And if she didn't realize what they had yet, he didn't want to scare her.

Removing one of the pink satin straps of her nightgown, she then reached for the other strap and let it fall with the front of her gown, exposing her full breasts. This time, Spencer didn't look away. How he had missed this gloriousness earlier, he didn't know. It was like he was seeing them for the first time.

Spencer gently lowered his head and took one delicate pink nipple into his mouth and then the other. He did this with gentle finesse, reading each little moan and purr from her lips, listening for any sign that he was hurting her instead of bringing her pleasure.

Eventually, Maria threw her head back and moaned as she ran her hands through Spencer's damp hair and sought to bring him closer to her.

He kissed his way down her body, being extra careful of her bruises.

They were starting something, and he had no idea how to end it so that neither of them would get hurt, emotionally or physically. In this moment, his only thought was to show her how he felt, to erase some of the pain she had gone through.

"Maria," he managed.

"I need this, Spencer. I need you," she murmured as she kissed him. "Please. We will be careful."

Spencer hadn't made love sitting up in a long time, and the fact Maria was sitting on him was a bit of a game-changer. Any kind of sex was a bit of a game-changer. He hadn't made love in over three years, not since Ruby's accident.

⁘ ─────── ⋅◉⋅◉⋅ ─────── ⁘

When it came to sex, Maria knew what she liked, but this was different. She was injured and had to be sensitive to positioning. She couldn't have Spencer's weight on her, but she could have her weight on him. So they might have to get creative and would have to improvise. It would be different but good.

"Help me to take this off," she said, indicating the night-gown. He did as he was told. The cool fabric slipped over her head and off her body. She reached down and untied the belt on his robe, then pushed the fabric away from his bare chest.

"Maria, I want you. I've wanted you since that first day we met, but are you sure about this?"

He was going to need a lot of reassurance, but she didn't want to think about being anything but a woman responding to a man's loving touch on her skin. Being with Spencer now was a healing moment for them both. After what Daisy and Rebecca told her today, she knew they each needed this for different reasons. Hers was to rid herself of her ex's memories, baptizing herself into a world without him. Maria wanted her body to feel Spencer and his loving care. And by chance, he needed to have a healthy woman respond to him in a way he hadn't been responded to for a very long time.

"Don't you want to make love with me?"

"Ah, yes, I just am trying to put your needs ahead of my own, which doesn't come naturally for me. I've wanted you since the moment I saw you in your hotel. I'm trying to be the kind of gentleman who puts his woman's needs first."

"Good, you can please me first," she said and pushed him back on the bed as she straddled him.

"Um, I don't know how to say this, but I don't have any condoms. I didn't think this kind of activity was even in the cards. I didn't want to make any assumptions."

"Don't worry. I'm on the pill, and I take it every day."

"Okay, if you're sure," Spencer said, sounding slightly overwhelmed.

"I'm sure," she said. She didn't want to tell him that Pablo had been obsessed with condoms and was certain she'd try to get pregnant to entrap him and eventually get his money. It was easier to double up with the birth control and not worry about his fears ever coming true.

She let her lips say what her brain had a hard time articulating. Before long, Spencer's pajama bottoms had joined her nightgown, and she was easing herself onto Spencer's erection as his hands tried to touch her without hurting her. Once she had fully taken him inside her, his blue eyes searched hers as he said, "I've died and gone to heaven. Do anything you want to me."

Then she began to move, taking him in and out of her body.

Reaching between them, Spencer stroked her intimately and slowly to match the rhythm to their bodies, making her forget everything around them but him. And when Maria could take it no more, she succumbed to her most primal of emotions and screamed in a release.

Once she could open her eyes, she saw Spencer watching her, his eyes clouding over, and then he was coming inside of her, screaming in his own release.

The waves of pleasure continued and built again, bringing on another orgasm for her that continued with Spencer's.

Much later, after they'd had another round of what they would later call "careful lovemaking," she fell asleep stretched out on top of Spencer. If he minded her weight or the added burden, he didn't say. The next morning, he smiled the crooked grin she'd gotten used to when he was being mischievous.

"I thought of something. Please indulge me, but if it hurts, we'll go back to the standard from last night. I mean, it was great," he said as he extracted himself from under her, leaving her to feel bereft for the loss of his warmth and solid feel of him.

The bed was tall, with four posters. Spencer stood at the edge of the bed and faced her, his body glowing in the early morning light, his erection casting a long, diagonal shadow on the bed.

"I think I like where this is going," Maria muttered as she pushed away from the sheets and let Spencer slide her over the smooth sheets by grasping her ankles and pulling her toward him and his waiting, early morning erection.

This is what he wanted, she realized, to be in control. That was what she wanted too, but she'd never tell him. It was his turn, and she let him lead.

Before long, her body was at the edge of the bed, her feet on Spencer's shoulders as he slowly moved inside of her, stroking her to complete loss of control.

When he reached between them to rub her clit, she threw her arms over her head and lost herself to the man she knew she was falling head over heels in love with.

CHAPTER TWELVE

"**I**f you need me, just call," Spencer said as he and Maria stood next to a Land Rover from the hotel's fleet, his arm gently around her waist. The words seemed inadequate after all they had shared in the last week, even in the previous few hours.

"I will be fine. How will I know that you are being careful?" she asked. "I don't want Pablo to hurt you. I don't like thinking of you going back there. Promise me that you won't take any stupid chances."

"You will have to trust me, and please, please drive carefully," Spencer said, his arms now loosely circling her body. "And the next time we meet, you'll be recovered." What he wasn't saying didn't need to be said. They'd made love last night and this morning, carefully. It had still been good, but when she was fully recovered, it was going to be fantastic, and they both knew it. The countdown to their reunion had started.

With their assorted family members looking on, Maria kissed Spencer goodbye with a passion that made the witnesses look away. It had been a long time since anyone had made his heart beat this wildly in his chest. He would do anything he could to protect her, and unfortunately, that meant sending her away.

"Please be careful," Spencer said, and Maria hugged him tighter, almost to the point of hurting herself. Maria didn't need to look to know that Alex was giving Spencer a predatory look over her shoulder as Daisy winked, which said it all. So much for keeping their private life private. Maria wondered what Alex would say to Spencer after she left, and then she decided she did not care. Spencer had proven himself in every area. Alex could see that for himself. And she didn't care what anyone thought. This felt like love. The way she always thought love would feel.

Then she remembered Rebecca's words. He had once had a love, and he had lost her even though she was still alive. Eventually, she and Spencer would need to discuss it, but it could wait. Maria could not be jealous of an injured woman. She thought more of Spencer for what Rebecca told her he'd done. Yet another reason to fall in love with this man.

It was interesting. They both had much to overcome when it came to past relationships.

Up until a week ago, Maria thought her life was finally on the right track—that marriage and a family were in her future. But that had changed, and now she was back to where she'd started, only this time she had the Starks. However, that was not like having a family of your very own. Having children was important to her. She wanted to give them everything she'd never had in the orphanage or with her adopted parents. They were good people, but it never truly felt like home to her. Fortunately, her work at Villa Roma felt like home. And in the last few days, being with Spencer had felt like something close to it. Possibly, home was wherever he was, and she could be.

But after all he'd been through, Maria couldn't help but wonder if Spencer was ready for more? He acted like he was ready, but she needed to spend time thinking through everything she'd learned. Spencer, according to her sisters, lost his way after Ruby's accident. It sounded as though her chances of recovery were just not there. Maria held no false illusions;

however, if a miracle happened and Ruby recovered, Maria would want Spencer to be happy, even if that meant losing him to another woman because that other woman had come first.

Over the next few hours, Maria followed the Land Rover's GPS directions with precision as she made the five-hour drive to The Caldera Lodge. The truck, which belonged to Stark International and was on permanent loan to her, was the largest automobile she'd ever driven. After a harrowing drive just to get out of the city limits of Portland, she decided it wasn't as easy to maneuver as the little Mini she owned in Roma. But on the open road, she couldn't help but notice that drivers in Portland and all of Oregon were polite and drove slowly, unlike her beloved Italians, who threw caution to the wind when it came to driving on the Autostrada. She had to be mindful of her speed and not drive her usual 150 kilometers per hour, or 90 miles per hour. For the first couple of hours she drove down an interstate, which was so easy that it gave her mind time to wander, especially at the reduced speed.

She'd been engaged to Pablo a week earlier—her life, her future, her everything had been planned out, but now she was exploring something new and fragile with Spencer. The question that went through her mind was, where would the flirtation with Spencer have gone if Pablo had stayed in the picture? Last night, although remaining reserved, Spencer had been a better lover than Pablo had been, even on his best night. Spencer seemed to know her better than Pablo ever had. She felt adored, loved, and satisfied in a way she had always wanted from Pablo but had never gotten.

But what if it all went wrong? Spencer was her boss. They had friends and relatives in common—it would all be messy. And she had made love with him last night and this morning. It wasn't like she'd never see him again. She'd see him at every family gathering from here on out for the rest of her days. But if their time together had been a mistake, it had been epic.

She got off Interstate 5 at the Hwy 58 interchange and headed into the mountains. As she drove through deep forests, the terrain slowly changed as she drove over the mountain pass. The soil turned red, and the forest thinned only to be replaced with large volcanic rock formations. Stopping at a rest area to get out of the car and stretch, she saw a huge lake and several snow-capped mountains in the distance. Looking down at her red dress and matching shoes, she was momentarily glad that Daisy and Rebecca had taken her shopping. She was a fish out of the water and wondered if she should change.

The Rover was filled with luggage holding an assortment of hats, gloves, shirts, shorts, pants, thick, ugly socks, and two different pairs of hiking boots. She even had a couple of pairs of trousers that became shorts with a zip of the zipper. There was a day pack and a regular pack for longer outings—as if she would use either. The only item she remotely liked was her new red Titanium jacket, and a light pink jacket Daisy had picked out, made of a soft fabric called Polar Tech. Italy probably had similar fabrics, but she hadn't ever darkened the stores where they might be kept. When she'd explored the outdoors with her adopted father, they kept to nicely manicured trails and walkways. There was no need for wilderness gear.

An hour after her rest stop, she passed a sign letting her know that she was now in the Crater Lake National Park. The Caldera Lodge was situated on land leased from the National Park Service. Stopping at the khaki-colored little house that was the entrance booth by the ranger station, she rolled down her window and faced a nice-looking man in his early forties, whose face lit up when he saw her.

"Good afternoon, Ms. Medici," he said, appraising her in a way she was used to being appraised.

"How did you know it was me?" she asked as she removed her Gucci sunglasses.

"They called ahead, specifically Alex. He told me you'd be in a Land Rover. And pardon me, but with your accent and clothing, you don't look like a typical hiker. I didn't even need to look at the car you're in," he said with a wink.

"Oh, no, I don't hike. I'm here to manage the lodge, The Caldera Lodge, but you probably already know all that," she replied, wondering for the hundredth time what she'd gotten herself into.

"Nice shiner. Alex said you'd been in a car accident."

Oh, so that was how he was explaining it to people. The swelling had gone down; heck, she didn't think anyone would necessarily notice unless they were looking. Alex had told this man, so now he knew.

"Thank you. It hurts much less each day. Where is the lodge from here? Am I getting close?" she asked.

"Eight miles down the road. You can't miss it. If you need anything, the name's Finn. Peter Finn." He handed her an official badge and told her to hang it from the car's rearview mirror.

"Thank you, Mr… er… Finn," she said after affixing the pass.

"Call me Peter. I get up to the lodge every week or so. I'll check on you next time I'm there and see how you're getting along. I know Alex wants to make sure that you settle into the lodge and have no questions."

"He's very protective," she said flatly.

"I've gotten to know him over the last few years. I like him and his new bride. What a gorgeous family."

"Yes," she said, but it sounded more like *chess*.

"Anyway, I'm sure you want to get to The Lodge and get settled. Welcome to Crater Lake. Please call on me if you have any questions."

"Thank you, Officer Finn."

She smiled fleetingly and waved as she pulled away. Great, the last thing she needed was this man checking on her. She already missed Spencer terribly, and she had seen him a few hours earlier. Heck, they'd been making love a few hours earlier.

Meeting men like Ranger Finn only seemed to illustrate the loneliness she'd be facing. She didn't know how she would sleep without having Spencer hold her. She was still tired from all the stress she'd endured, but still, she was already missing him. When they were together, she hadn't had the time to dwell on Pablo and all that happened in his library. Spencer had taken away her fear.

Tears flooded her vision. Pulling to the side of the road, she allowed herself to cry, to feel and release some of the pain she had carefully hidden. She cried for the life she thought she would have. She cried for her naivete. She cried for Pablo's false love. She had believed him, and for that, she was mad at herself. What if she'd married him? Would he have eventually made her disappear?

After a few minutes, she regained control, wiped away her tears, and checked her makeup. Assured that everything was in place, she pulled back onto the road. She'd cried more in the last week than she had in her entire life. It hit her in waves. One moment she'd be fine, the next, something would remind her of what had happened, how vulnerable she'd been, and she would lose it. She had to find a way to control herself. It was easy when Spencer was by her side, but now he was flying back to Italy, and she had the extra burden of being worried about him. What if Pablo or his brother came after Spencer? How would Alex get him out of jail or harm's way? People thought they were almost immortal, but each body was fragile. She knew how easily someone could get hurt, how frail the human body was… Spencer thought he was invincible. He was wrong. And what if Pablo came after him with a knife or a gun? She couldn't think about the endlessly bad possibilities and resulting outcomes.

Her new employees at the lodge wouldn't understand, nor care, nor would they respect her weakness if she kept up with the crying and worrying about something that was happening half a world away. She had to get a grip. Taking a deep breath, she drove on.

She caught a glimpse of brilliant sapphire water appearing from behind a cut in the beautiful deep green foliage. It was her first glimpse of the famous lake. She could only see a small portion of the entire landscape, but what she could see took her breath away. Crater Lake was amazing. And at that moment, she thought of her adoptive father. He would have been speechless at the view. She had no one to share it with, so she needed to enjoy it for herself.

Realizing she had to concentrate on driving, she forced herself to keep her eyes glued to the road. A few minutes later, the enormous wooden lodge came into view. The Caldera Lodge was her home for the next couple of months. It was nothing like she'd ever seen before. It wasn't rustic. It was elegant. It was as much of a part of the landscape as the trees and the water beyond. She could imagine what her father, Garrison Stark, had seen in the place when he had bought it. Alex had done the right thing by keeping it in the family, although it was a far cry from the Stark family's usual business interests.

She parked in the paved lot, grabbed her briefcase and hand-bag, and made her way to the massive front porch. The view stopped her. From her vantage point, she could see the entire lake in all its splendor. The size reminded her of Lake Como in her homeland, but everything else was different. Bellagio, on the edge of Lake Como, was a trendy tourist town catering to movie stars and royalty. Crater Lake was pure and unspoiled. Yesterday, she'd spent some time researching the area online. The fact that it was a mile from the top of the crater to the water's edge prevented it from being spoiled by large crowds of people. At Lake Como, everyone wanted to jump in and swim or drive around the lake in drunken splendor. Crater Lake didn't allow private boats. Good. She was glad it had stayed pristine.

The air smelled clean, fresh, and slightly woodsy from all the pine trees. It was a scent she had never smelled before but would forever associate with The Caldera Lodge. The air felt warm, one of the last days of spring that boded well for a warm summer.

She took it all in for several moments, hearing people talking and the occasional car, but overall, it was the quietest place she'd ever been. Figuring there wasn't a Vespa within a hundred miles, she smiled and inhaled the fresh scent of sun and evergreen. Despite the fresh air, her lungs felt tight in the 7,200-foot elevation. Rebecca and Daisy had told her about the phenomenon, and she knew it would pass as her body acclimated, but now, her body felt like she'd run a marathon. Even walking from her car to the front of the lodge would be a tough workout.

As she started up the steps to the front door of the lodge, her narrow heels caught in the grooves of the wood, making the walk up the wide, uneven wooden planks difficult. Opening the massive door, she stepped inside the enormous space and immediately felt insignificant in the cool air. A large stone fireplace that was twice her height had several trees worth of wood cut and stacked, waiting for someone to toss in a match or torch.

Large, oversized leather furniture with craftsman-style tables and low, muted, stained-glass lamps gave the impression of a library in the middle of the forest. Native American-inspired designs adorned large area rugs that suggested walking paths through the lobby. In contrast, exposed box beams that were the largest she'd ever seen in dark, shiny wood provided an interior framework for the ceiling.

Light poured in from the windows on the other side of the lobby, displaying a one-hundred-and-eighty-degree view of the lake. She stopped and stared in wonder. The lake was so dominant and gorgeous in front of her. It was hard to find words to describe it. She had traveled a lot in Europe, especially in Italy, and this view gave Bellagio a run for its money with Lake

Como. The water was so blue; it was hard to believe it was real.

No wonder people milled around lazily looking at the exposed wood architecture, staring at the impressive view, or just waiting for a table to open in the restaurant. This vastness reminded a person of their place in the world and reinforced each person's vulnerability.

People were reading on the back deck, lounging in Adirondack chairs while they enjoyed a cocktail. You could see them gaze at the lake and shake their heads in disbelief. Yes, this was real, not a picture.

Everywhere, the pace of life was slow and easy. She realized she was suffering culture shock of the difference between where she had been only a week earlier and where she was now. This was about as far from bustling Piazza Navona as one could get, but it was so much more impressive. To think that this land had been untouched and potentially undiscovered during the time period when gladiators were fighting in the Colosseum was almost more than she could take.

She walked to the front desk, a massive piece of wood from which the staff, dressed in forest green polo shirts and khaki shorts, casually chatted with guests. Aware of the stares she was receiving, she realized what brought on the curiosity. She was a city girl, looking entirely out of her element and everyone knew she didn't belong with just one glance. Besides, she had what Peter called "quite a shiner" on her eye. Wishing she'd taken Daisy's advice and worn one of her new wilderness outfits, she tried to smile at one of the young women who continued to stare at her from behind the desk.

"Hello," she said to a pretty blonde, hoping her accent didn't give her away.

"Ms. Medici? You have finally arrived!" the girl asked, big blue eyes taking on a doe-like innocence.

So much for blending in. "Yes, I'm Maria Medici. I have

arrived." Smiling, she extended her hand and waited for the girl to take it.

"Wow, all the way from Italy. That's so cool. I'm Ashley, and this is, like, Jennifer." She seemed to bubble with excitement as she introduced the almost identical blonde girl next to her. They weren't sisters, but they could be with the almost identical makeup, hair, and tans. They had to be college students. She only hoped they were old enough to drink.

"We are, like, so excited to meet you."

With a sinking feeling, Maria accepted that the professionalism and formality she was used to back home in Roma might not exist at The Caldera Lodge. She would observe the behavior for a while before making any drastic changes. Like it or not, this was now her home. She'd spent too many years being lonely at Villa Roma. Having a friend at work would make all the difference. She was terrified of what Spencer might do to her hotel, but the idea of having him as an ally was not lost on her. They would have had such fun together in Italy. She had quietly put together a list of places to take him, both sightseeing and some of her favorite hole-in-the-wall restaurants.

Trying to stay focused on her current management assignment, Maria wondered if all the female employees of the lodge were blonde, blue-eyed women with unnatural tans. Had Alex had a hand in the hiring of these women? He liked smart people above all others. She wondered how intelligent these women were.

"Thank you," she replied to the warm greeting. "You have a beautiful… lodge. I'm looking forward to working here. I hope you can teach me about the nuances of running such a space. I'm only familiar with hotels in the city. The *vilderness* is all new to me."

"She's so cute. Did you hear the way she said 'wilderness?'" Jennifer asked Ashley as if her new boss was not standing in front of her. "It was more like *vile-deer-ness*."

"She reminds me of that actress in that old, old movie... *House* something," Ashley replied and then contemplated the idea.

"*Houseboat*," Maria interjected, feeling every one of her twenty-eight years as she remembered the Sophia Loren movie. These vapid girls were going to drive her insane.

"Yeah, that's the one. Have you, like, seen it?" Ashley asked.

"Once," Maria replied, changing the subject. She'd seen it at least ten times and liked it less each time she saw it. "So, how long have you each been with the lodge?"

"About two months." Ashley offered. "We started in April, and we were here for the May opening. Like, it was crazy."

"We're both students from the University of Oregon. Ash thought this would be a fun summer job, and she was right. It has been like an epic blast. Like, so much fun!" Jennifer said with a beaming smile.

"When do you go back?" Maria asked, wondering how these two girls could think that working in the middle of nowhere was a blast.

"First week of October," they answered in unison.

Almost four months away. October could not come fast enough. She wanted to say how much that knowledge pleased her, but she wanted to get off on the right foot. It was new for her, being in such easy company.

Next, she was shown to her quarters—a small one-bedroom apartment with a kitchenette and small sitting room. Without a staff bellman, Maria and one of the blondes from behind the desk (she wasn't sure which) carried her luggage to the small space.

She would need a few outfits for the evening, as Daisy had predicted, to maintain a presence in the dining room, but she wouldn't be wearing her stilettos any time soon. Glad she had taken Daisy's advice, she ripped tags off her new gear and fed laces into her ugly new hiking boots. Twenty-four hours earlier, she would not have thought she would wear the offensive items. Now she couldn't wait to see if they offered some comfort against the uneven hardwood floors.

Thinking of her beautiful shoes on the dirt trails that she saw headed down toward the lake's edge, she shuddered. Along with her job title, she'd been given a uniform of green polo shirts and khaki shorts. Seven shirts and shorts were neatly folded on the end of her bed. She unfolded one of the t-shirts and looked at the label, L.L. Bean.

"What is an L.L. Bean?" she wondered aloud. Yet another American label she'd never heard of before. She'd have to ask Daisy or Rebecca. Who knew all these brands existed?

Thinking the color of the cotton top would be complementary to her eyes, she slipped out of her tight red sheath dress and matching jacket, kicked off her heels, and put on the comfortable yet shapeless outfit. Luckily, she had a fake alligator patent belt that would work and give her some shape. Just because she was in the middle of nowhere didn't mean she could completely forget her fashion sense.

Glancing in the mirror of the old-fashioned-looking-yet-modernized bathroom, she checked her reflection. She had been in Spencer's arms less than twelve hours ago. Why couldn't he be with her? Oh yes, she'd turned him down and told him to get to her hotel in *Roma*.

She let down her hair and pulled it back into a casual ponytail. Her large, gold, chandelier earrings were the next to go, replaced by simple gold hoops. Looking more casual took years off her age, turning her into a contemporary of the blondes at the front desk despite the black eye that had started to fade.

Checking her cellphone, she frowned—no service. She should have known from the literature she'd read, but for some reason, she'd hoped it wouldn't be true. Alex and Spencer seemed to think she'd have cell and internet access.

She glanced at her text messages. She kept expecting to hear from Spencer. He might be somewhere over the Atlantic flying to Roma. They had made a pact. They were supposed to talk each day. How would they do that if she didn't have cell service? How would he keep her aware of what was happening in Italy? She wondered how email would work. She wondered how she could be away from Spencer for so long.

She went to the window and opened the thick, dark drapes. Her room was on the second floor above the lobby. She had a great, unobstructed view of the lake out of every one of her four windows. The hotel manager shouldn't have one of the best views, but she refused to feel guilty. She had enough on her mind. The dark azure water in the pristine lake was perfect, although reminiscent of someone's very blue eyes, whom she missed dearly.

A single boat, holding a dozen little stick people, cut across the water, making waves in the otherwise pristine surface as it headed toward Wizard Island. She knew the boat visited a dozen points around the lake during a two-hour tour. People could get on and off the boat at their leisure. You could have a picnic at Wizard Island or go fishing for Kokanee, a fish she'd never heard of before. All she knew was that the restaurant served it, and she intended to try it when and if she ever got her appetite back. Since leaving Roma, food held no appeal. Aside from needing to quiet her growling stomach, she rarely ate unless Spencer fed something to her.

She spent the rest of the day exploring the lodge. Her two front desk charges, Jennifer and Ashley, seemed in awe of her, each of them eager to answer any question she had about the lodge. With one hundred and two guest rooms, they were booked months in advance for every night of the summer season, which had begun after Memorial Day weekend two weeks earlier.

Each room was decorated comfortably but didn't have televisions, phones, air conditioning, mini-fridges, mini-bars, Wi-Fi, or wired internet. Although this was clearly mapped out in the brochure and on the website, about one guest a day still complained.

At least they would return to civilization within a few days. She might be without internet and cell service all summer.

Her office was a small space right behind the front desk. She had a basic desk with an older computer with email, but she was told the service could be intermittent and was currently down. No real surprise there.

An hour before the restaurant closed, she took a small table by a window in the bar and asked the waitress to bring her the most popular appetizer dish along with a glass of the local wine, an Oregon Pinot Noir. A few minutes later, a large platter arrived, and she was told it was called "nachos." Special nachos with chunks of marinated bison instead of beef. Experimentally, she tried a few bites and was immediately hungry for the fresh, wonderful antipasto of her homeland. She wondered how far she was from a supplier of *meloni* and good prosciutto. Too far, she decided. After a few more bites of the nachos, she decided they were as awful as they looked but found the pinot to be quite pleasing.

Again, she checked her cell for service. None. The ladies from the front desk had sent an email on her behalf to the Stark corporate office to let them know that she had arrived in case any of them were curious.

By the time she was unlacing her expensive Italian hiking boots (which she had a new appreciation for) and getting ready for bed, she was exhausted. Part jet lag, part stress, she knew she would fall asleep as soon as her head hit the pillow. Unfortunately, despite her exhaustion, she lay awake thinking about Spencer and how accustomed she'd become to having him next to her… or below her as he had been last night.

Homesick for Italy as well, she missed her hotel and her tiny apartment with its proximity to the sounds of Piazza Navona.

She missed the friendly people who didn't think she was different, but part of Italy. She missed the smells of delicious food and polluting Vespas. But most of all, she missed the company of Spencer.

Last night, she'd been holding onto Spencer, and the future didn't look so bleak because she had him in her arms with his arms protectively around her. But now, only a day later, she felt homesick and lost without the familiarity of Italy but mainly without the familiarity of him. And she couldn't even tell him how much she missed him because she had no cell service. Tears silently rolled down her cheeks, sinking into the too-soft pillow in the too-soft bed that would be hers for at least the next month.

CHAPTER THIRTEEN

"Is everyone ready to go into the *vilderness* and see *Vizard* Island?" Maria asked eight children under the age of ten, gazing up at her with wide-eyed admiration. Shy smiles mixed with an occasional giggle made her ask, "Are you all laughing at the way I talk?"

"You sound funny," a six-year-old girl with pigtails replied.

Maria leaned down to the little girl and smiled. "That's because I'm from Italy. We don't have any place like Crater Lake in my country, but you can eat pizza every day if you want." This brought on a few oohs and ahs.

It had been two weeks since her arrival at The Caldera Lodge. She was still finding her way, very frustrated by the intermittent internet and lack of details from Spencer when he called. He'd taken to writing her letters, letters that she would later describe as love letters, and mailing them with photos and swatches of fabrics and ideas. With him in Italy, and she in Oregon, it took his letters a week to make it to her, and by the time she offered her input, most of the decisions had been made. She did not feel this was at all a coincidence. She admired him a bit. If the shoe was on the other foot, it was exactly what she would have done to make sure her chosen agenda was followed.

She wanted to be able to talk to him anytime she wanted, and she did pick up the phone, or he called her every couple of days, but it wasn't the same as being in his physical presence, and she missed him. The time zones were also a bit of a problem. She wondered if he regretted the feelings that he had so passionately proclaimed for her. Some of their phone calls were a bit abrupt. Did he still feel the same way about her? When had she felt so insecure and needy before? Was this insecurity the result of how much Pablo had disappointed her? Why did she want Spencer to proclaim his love? What was wrong with her…

At least it sounded like things had cooled down in Roma with Pablo.

According to Spencer, Pablo had, for the most part, left him alone. The police had shown up at the hotel a week after Spencer got back. They were investigating a missing person's case, concerned about a report made by Pablo who was playing the part of the concerned fiancé. Alex had to call the police and tell them to drop the inquiry, but he wouldn't tell them where Maria was except to say that he was her brother, that she had broken off the engagement to Pablo, who wasn't taking it well, and that she was safely out of the country.

Her ribs hurt less each day, but they were still sore, and if she moved too fast or did too much, they reminded her to take it easy. Everything since the rooftop anniversary party had felt like a dream. She didn't know what to believe. One thing was for sure; she would never return to Pablo. Spencer had ruined her for anyone else, not that she needed any convincing when it came to her ex.

Her young charges followed her like a pied piper out the back door of the lodge and onto the observation deck, where she began the Fact Chat of her now famous "Wilderness Walks." It had started with Maria needing to get away from the lodge to think about what had led up to the dramatic changes in her life. As she walked the trails, she found peace. Her curiosity got the better of her, and she started studying everything she had discovered. Soon, the walks became less about distraction and more about exploration.

Her adopted father, Giuseppe, would be so proud of her. In the spring and summer, they used to walk around a different area of Italy, admiring the countryside. She only wished he could see all this area in Oregon. He would be awestruck by Crater Lake and the beautiful surrounding area. When she gave her Wilderness Walks, she felt like she talked directly to him. And to prove the point, she had done some rehearsals in Italian.

On one particularly warm afternoon when Maria had headed out for her mid-morning walk, a little girl of eight, who was a guest at the lodge, asked if she could join Maria. Maria so enjoyed showing the child all the treasures that Crater Lake National Park offered. The idea of the "Wilderness Walks" took form from that day. Now, she gave her ninety-minute walks five days a week. Guests were starting to call several weeks in advance to reserve a slot for their children.

The success was so surprising that Maria was thinking of training a couple of other staff members to make the walks an everyday event. There was interest from the nearby campgrounds to include children staying at different locations inside the park. There was enough interest that she could give two walks each day. As it was, she didn't like to turn anyone down and rarely did. But when the group size got to over ten children, she thought they lost the intimacy she liked.

After the tour concluded with each child getting a Caldera Lodge hat, she returned to the front desk.

"How is the afternoon going?" she asked Jennifer.

"Maria, it has been, like, crazy busy. We only have five rooms yet to check in. I, like, don't know what to do about the dining room. Everyone wants to eat at seven."

"Let's just make sure they all eat. There isn't another restaurant near here. Try to accommodate them, give them free appetizer vouchers if they are very unhappy about the time. Maybe we set up tables in the lobby if we don't have enough room in the dining room. Just make sure the chef can handle the volume. I don't want hungry guests. And I don't want an angry chef."

Over the last few weeks, Maria had slowly adjusted to the quieter, more relaxed way of the lodge, which included her casual staff. They called her by her first name and treated her more like a colleague than a boss. She thought it would bother her, this lack of respect and breach of formality, but on the contrary, she enjoyed it. Her staff felt more like friends, and they worked together well as a team. She found that despite the dark cloud that hung over her head with Pablo and her complex feelings for Spencer, she was laughing more than she had in years. Her new carefree surroundings were having a positive effect on her appetite, too. She was always hungry and forgot her carefully monitored diet to the point she worried about fitting into her designer clothing once it was time to return to her life in Roma.

Her injuries had all but mended. The bruises were gone, and the few shadows that remained were easily covered with makeup. However, Maria found herself wearing less and less makeup and liking this new natural look. She hadn't spritzed on perfume in weeks. When she inhaled each morning, she smelled clean air, a scent that couldn't be bottled and one she did not want to mask.

"Please make me a list of the overflow, and I'll handle it," she replied.

"Oh, and that gorgeous forest ranger guy called for you."

Her head snapped to attention. "Are you talking about Ranger Finn?"

"Yep, he really wanted to talk to you. I think he seems interested," Jennifer offered with a wide grin.

Maria pursed her lips into an indignant pout but only got a wink from the other woman in response.

"Did he say what he wanted?" she asked, with an indifferent shrug. They knew a little something about Alex. If he called, they were supposed to find her unless she was out giving a Wilderness Walk. Their curiosity was piqued as to why Alex called her so often, but they didn't ask her. Spencer called her directly on her office phone, but Alex liked to hear how the front desk answered calls coming into the lodge because he was a control freak, so he never called her directly. Rebecca and Daisy called every few days, and she enjoyed talking to them about things like fashion and gossip.

"Duh, obviously he wants you. He said he'd like to drop by later. He asked when you would be free tonight. For an old guy, he is, like, kind of hot."

Maria groaned. Peter Finn was becoming a bit of a pest. He dropped in every couple of days to see how she was adjusting. When he'd discovered the popularity of her Wilderness Walks, he'd beamed with pride and asked if he could attend one of them. She had turned him down. He was a nice man, but her romantic feelings were reserved for Spencer. To think of Peter Finn romantically only made her think of Spencer, and she'd come to realize that no other man on this earth compared to Spencer.

"What did you tell him?" Maria asked.

"I said any time after nine, and you could be found chatting with guests in the lobby and restaurant."

Maria knew she was very predictable. Each night, she circulated, trying to make sure everyone was having a good time. Usually, there were two or three guests who would dominate her attention, and she let herself be distracted. Sometimes she joined them in a cocktail or after-dinner coffee. Nighttime was, by far, the worst time for her. During the day, the mere setting of the middle of nowhere distracted her. But after sunset, everything changed. The hours between sunset and whenever she could fall asleep were the worst.

She missed Spencer a lot more than she should. He'd become her definition of the perfect man. But what if that wasn't who he was? Pablo certainly had changed, though Rebecca and Daisy confirmed Spencer was the real deal.

Maria couldn't help but want to know more about his first love, Ruby. If the woman recovered, would Spencer decide to go back to her? Of course, he would. From what Rebecca said, recovery was unlikely, but it didn't keep Maria from playing out different scenarios in her mind.

How could she have fallen in love in a matter of days? Maria knew in her heart he wasn't just a rebound. But how could her feelings have gotten so strong so fast? She had to be sure. She had to be careful.

"Maria?" one of the girls asked, pulling her out of her thoughts.

"Yes, Jennifer?"

"Like, that Alex guy is on the phone for you. Do you want to talk to him?"

"Always. I need to tell you both. I should have told you earlier. He owns this lodge, and he is my brother," Maria said frostily. What she wanted to say was that he paid their pathetic wages, but she was trying very hard to be that kinder, gentler, more Americanized Maria.

"He's, like, your brother? Why didn't you tell us?" Jennifer asked, "But he isn't Italian."

"He is my brother, and the timing is right to tell you now, so I'm telling you."

"Isn't he, like, the head guy at Stark International Hotels?"

Ignoring the girl, Maria stepped into her small office, purposefully left the door ajar, and took the call. "Hello, Alex, is everything okay?"

"You're an aunt again! Daisy had the baby about an hour ago."

"Is everyone okay? The baby? Daisy?"

"Everyone is great. I was in San Francisco when her water broke. I barely made it back in time. When I got to the room, she was ready to push. Things started to happen then. I caught the baby. I was the first person to touch her. Isn't that cool? I'm the first human to touch my baby girl."

"Wow, exciting!" Maria exclaimed, and she meant it. "How much does she weigh?"

"Seven pounds, five ounces," Alex said, the pride evident in his voice.

"And, who does she look like?"

"I'll email you photos. I think she looks a little like Lexy, but Daisy says she looks like you and Rebecca."

Maria felt a warmth in her heart that had never been there before. "Is there anything I can do to help Daisy or you?" She was happy she'd sent a cute pink outfit for the baby and a stuffed animal for Lexy the week before.

"The doctor is sending them home tomorrow, easy birth— well, it's never easy, but as births go, it was smoother than the first one. Thank you for asking, but her mother is coming to stay with us for a couple of days, and that never ends well, so think positive thoughts."

"You don't like her mother?" Maria asked, having never heard this before.

"No, she loves me. I think she is fine. She and Daisy are like oil and water. It is never good when they are in the same room for more than ten minutes. It is like a couple of angry wildcats going at it."

"Make nice. Be the peacekeeper. Look what you've done for Daisy and me. I do believe I love her like a sister."

"You both get along much better than you did when you first met," he observed.

"See, anyone can change," she said. "Maybe Daisy and her mother will find peace."

"Yeah, no," Alex said with a chuckle. "But I do have some other news. This is great. Speaking of surprises. Our cousin

Adam has a little baby boy, and I think a new future wife who I met today."

"Wait, I'm confused. I thought Adam lost his wife and baby and was heartbroken. I wrote him a letter before the funeral—"

"Adam met someone last summer when he was renovating The Bay Shore. She was staying with her friend, Kat Russell. I'm friends with the woman's husband, William. Anyway, Adam met Laura, who paints amazing watercolor landscapes. They had what was supposed to be a summer fling, but they fell in love. She got pregnant, and he just found out about the baby because he's been in Dubai for the last few months."

"She just told him?" Maria asked.

"Yeah, it was a surprise, but she had her reasons. Adam had his head up his ass about his grief, said he never wanted another baby, but that was then, and now, everything is different."

"Is Adam happy?" she asked.

"Blissfully. He told me he was going to ask Laura to marry him. He showed me the diamond, a big one, like he should get her after the hell he put her through. He might be doing it as we speak. And the baby, his name is Sam. He's a charmer. He looks exactly like Adam. They look like an instant family. It is crazy, but it is so right. It is such a blessing. I'm so happy for him Hell, I'm happy for me, for Daisy, for our family."

"I'm happy for everyone, but especially Adam," Maria said, thinking of how she had heard about the tragic news of Adam's first wife and child when they'd been killed by a drunk driver almost two years earlier. He had found love again, and for that, she was beyond thankful.

"I am too. If anyone deserves to be happy, it is Adam. The only fly in the ointment is that he refuses to go back to Dubai. He wants to stay in San Francisco or anywhere that Laura is going to be. I can't say that I blame him. We are talking about him for Portland. It wouldn't change things between you and me, but it would give Adam a chance to settle in and run things for a while. He is very capable. I was just offered the position first by the older generation because I'm the oldest son of this generation. And now I have a bride who'd like to travel a bit. I want to indulge her before the girls are ready for school."

"What happens to Dubai? Would you go there?" she asked, missing his proximity already.

"Well, I wanted to ask you. Do you have any interest in Dubai? If you and Spencer would be open to it, I think it might be great for you two, or Daisy and I will go in a few months. I think she'd love it for a couple of years, but I wanted to check in with you. There is also New York, which I know Spencer wants after Italy, but everything is negotiable."

"Spencer is going to New York after Italy?" she asked. This news was a surprise.

"That was the plan, but everything is subject to change. If you and Spencer want Dubai, I'll go to New York."

"I wonder if Spencer was ever going to tell me about this," she said, feeling uncomfortable.

"We only started seriously talking about it last week. It was a very casual conversation. Adam is a little territorial about New York, but he is better away from there, so I tried to persuade him away. He is doing great in Dubai. New York needs a charismatic leader. But after what happened today with Adam and Laura, everything is different."

"Spencer would be great in New York," she said, trying not to let her sarcasm flood into her tone.

"Ideally, I'd want you with him. You two would make a great team."

"That isn't proven yet," Maria said, ignoring the fact it was technically Spencer's hotel. "I don't know what Spencer has done to my hotel in *Roma*. I might have to spend the next six months changing it back to make it profitable. And it isn't like he has discussed his plans with me. I don't even know if I'm going to see him again."

"What? Of course, you will see him again," Alex said. "Say the word, and I'll ask him to go to The Caldera Lodge to free you today. And he has been showing us his ideas all along, and I haven't heard you protest up until now, so I'm sure everything will be fine."

"Well, with the internet and email issues we have in the middle of nowhere, I approved some of his ideas or vetoed them after he had them installed."

"I'm sorry, internet and cell service have always been questionable at The Caldera Lodge, which is why we don't offer it to guests, but all his choices looked fine."

"How convenient," Maria said with the appropriate amount of sarcasm.

"You know that Rome is Spencer's hotel. Do you think he'd mess it up?"

"I'll have to see it to know," Maria said dismissively, knowing Alex had a point, but still she wanted to be there.

"Should I send Spencer? Would that make you feel better? I can have him there the day after tomorrow."

"Do nothing of the kind. I'm uncertain of how things were left. I want him to come here on his own without the big Hotel Baron ordering him."

In a softer tone, he said, "It will all work out, I promise. I get a feeling for things—Daisy and I, Adam and Laura, Rebecca and Mitch, and finally Spencer and Maria. I've warmed up to the idea of you with Spencer. I think it is a good thing."

"What, you now read the tarot?"

"Maria, please, trust your big brother. Spencer has it bad for you. I see it, and I know it."

"We will see. As my brother, I need you to be thinking about my interests because I'm not sure there is anything to discuss with Spencer. I want to be successful in my own right. I don't know if Spencer is a part of that."

"You are successful. You are one of the best we have in the

company," Alex said. "I want you to do more. We need to show-case your talents."

The silence extended on the line.

"I've got to get back to work," she said and offered a final, "I'm glad Daisy and the baby Lily are alright."

"Me too, thank you. Maria, it is going to be okay. Think about what I said. We will figure it all out," he said and feigned having to get back to his wife and child. She would have done the same thing in his shoes. Something had been uncovered that wasn't good. And now, Maria had to deal with it. Alex and Spencer were making plans, and it seemed as though Spencer hadn't thought to include her.

CHAPTER FOURTEEN

S pencer walked through the lobby of Villa Roma and felt more than heard the hush that fell over the guests and staff.

The concierge was a serious pain in the ass. Marco intercepted Spencer just before he could duck into the private employees-only hallway. "Have you heard from *Signorina* Medici? I would like to know she is alright."

"I talk to her every few days. She is fine. In fact, she is thriving. She is just busy whipping another hotel into shape. She will be back, and she misses all of you." Marco gave him a look like he didn't believe him. He couldn't blame Marco.

Spencer was missing Maria too. Her quick departure hadn't settled well, and now they looked at him with disdain, blaming him for what was not discussed. They were worried about her, and more than once, one of them would get up the nerve to ask about her. They were shocked about her being a Stark, and they wanted to know how that affected her.

Rumors were running rampant. She might be a Stark but was she sick? Had something happened? Was she injured? He was the last one they knew that had contact with her, and now she was missing. They knew something had happened with her engagement, that it was off. But what had happened? Had she had an affair with Spencer, and Pablo found out? Suddenly, Spencer was running the hotel. They were suspicious. And as much as it bothered him not to have their loyalty, he respected the devotion they showed to Maria.

She should be there. They should have been doing this remodel together. He had wanted her input. The lack of internet at The Caldera Lodge had made a mockery of his choices. As it was, Maria was not going to like some of the decisions he'd had to make, keeping on the tight timeline. She was going to make him remodel some aspects of the redesign, and he couldn't blame her. This hotel was her baby, and he was messing with it. And the hotel and its staff missed Maria, the force behind the hotel's success.

He went into his office, really Maria's office, where her perfume still lingered, and picked up his cell. He didn't trust the hotel to make any of his calls to her. He didn't know if the numbers could be traced, but he didn't want to put her in danger, paranoid as he was about Pablo's reach.

He dialed the number for her office and waited.

"The Caldera Lodge," Maria answered.

"Hello, gorgeous, how goes it?"

"I like it, but I miss good mozzarella and prosecco. I miss the food and the people. Are you enjoying everything there?"

"How could I without you here? There are places that I want to go to, but I want you to show them to me. Without you, there is no reason."

"Like what?" she asked. "You need to see everything while you are in *Roma*."

"I've been to the Trevi Fountain, the Colosseum, and Vatican City, but they weren't anything without you. I've been to every restaurant you suggested. They are okay, but the food is bland because you aren't there."

"The food is not bland. You sound like a lovesick puppy," she laughed with amusement.

"I am. I miss you," Spencer said. "I'm enough of a man that I can admit it. I want you here. I want to see you and be with you."

"Maybe we will meet up in New York," she said.

"New York? No, I want to have you show me *Roma*. I want to be with you in *Roma*. See? I'm calling it *Roma*, like a native Italian."

"Alex told me about New York," she said, and he could hear the anger in her voice.

"I'm not thinking of anything but you. New York was a conversation. I want you to understand this. Being with you is a certainty."

He wanted to have her show him around the most romantic city he'd ever been to, but she was at some damn lodge, thousands of miles away. As it was, he was a weekend tourist seeing a lot but enjoying nothing. Weekends away to Naples and Florence were simply out of the question unless he wanted to torture himself.

He craved her. It was like having a bite of your favorite dessert and then having it taken away from you. Their time together had been too brief—just long enough for him to fall in love. Alex wasn't helping, telling her part of the story. New York? As if he'd go there without her. He was tired of being without her.

"How does the hotel look?" she asked, ignoring his earlier words.

"I'm mulling over a couple of ideas. As soon as I think they are valid, I'm sharing them with you."

"I hope I will see it soon," she said.

"You will," he said as he sat down and saw the designers enter his office with several tile samples. They didn't respect him, and he couldn't blame them. His Italian was still rudimentary. "I've got to go handle something, but I'll call you back. I have an idea to share with you," he said and then tried his best to channel what Maria might like for the hotel despite the fact he owned it.

His life was a mess. Aside from their distance, he was keeping a big secret that was burning a hole in his gut every time he thought of it.

He hadn't told Maria the truth about Ruby. He'd mentioned her casually, but he gave the impression that Ruby wasn't around. She was part of his life, and he had possibly misled Maria. The timing had never been right for him to correct assumptions. She'd been hurt, injured, and threatened. And for the first time in his life, he thought of Ruby as stable or at least unchanging. She was in a special home where they understood her injury and took good care of her. She was protected and safe. He could not say the same of Maria. He still worried about what Pablo might do to her if he found her. The angry ex had been too quiet, and it bothered Spencer.

Spencer couldn't help but wonder what Maria would think of Ruby. If Ruby hadn't had her brain injury, he would be with her now. They would no doubt be married and maybe have a child or two. But it wasn't meant to be. They had three glorious years. That was all they were going to get in this life.

How could he explain it to Maria? What was there to say? It's not like Maria was his second choice. She had just appeared after Ruby. And if Ruby were well, Spencer would not have entertained being with Maria. He would have noticed her beauty, though he would have kept to his vows. Cheating in a committed relationship was not an option. As they liked to say in Texas, Spencer was loyal as the day was long.

Would Maria want to meet Ruby? Would she understand that he had to keep visiting the other woman? That she had once been the love of his life but was still important to him?

His old, familiar frustration that he'd come to think of as a dogged enemy raised its head and reminded him not to forget his past and who he'd pledged loyalty to before he'd met Maria.

Ruby was the injured one. Did that mean Spencer had to give up on his life and die right along with her? She wouldn't want him to. She would want him to live his best life. Hadn't she said that to him often enough? Hell, they'd said it to each other. "If something happens to me...."

What a morbid conversation to have, and they'd had it, more than once. Maybe all couples talked about mortality at some point.

Six months earlier, Spencer had admitted to himself that she needed more care than he could offer at his home, and it had broken his heart. It was just another kick in a sea of pain that surrounded Ruby. He hadn't kissed her lips in over three years. He hadn't held her or made love to her since the accident. He had thought she might remember him on some level and want some sort of affection from him. A hug, the occasional kiss, but no. She didn't like to be touched by anyone, especially him, except she would let him wash and style her hair, which always broke his heart.

He'd existed in her shadow, always near but never touching her except to help her dress or to wash her hair. He had hired extra help, but Ruby hadn't liked the strangers in her space. It was a revolving door of caregivers, but only Spencer was the constant.

One of the designers tapped his pencil, and Spencer refocused on what the man was saying. Spencer had a bit of trouble following the rapid-fire dialogue of the designers at the table.

Several tile samples were placed before him, and he immediately chose the one that was the most sedated of the samples.

One of the designers threw up his arms and started swearing. Spencer had no idea what the problem was, but he knew without a doubt that he was the cause.

CHAPTER FIFTEEN

S pencer picked up his cell and redialed Maria after the
designers had cursed him in Italian. She answered on the
second ring.

"Twice in one day? This is becoming a habit that I think I
might like."

"Good. I have an idea that I'd like to run by you," he said.

"Oh, my goodness, you are asking my opinion. And it would
be?" she asked. She almost sounded lighthearted. They had
come a long way since she dismissed his ideas outright. Then he
realized she was probably being sarcastic. On some level, it
warmed his heart. She was sparring with him again.

"I want you to meet me at the Eugene airport tomorrow
afternoon."

"You're coming here? Tomorrow?" she asked, and Spencer
could hear the excitement in her voice.

"Yes, I don't think I can handle another week without
seeing you. So, I came up with a good excuse. I have a couple
of hotels to show you, so pack a bag and meet me at the
Eugene airport tomorrow afternoon. We need to visit The W
Hotel in Bellevue just outside of Seattle, and then we will jet
down to San Jose to visit another hotel called The Valencia.
They each have elements I want you to see to consider for
Villa Roma. You'll be gone about three days and two nights,
but we will just be tourists, so you can dress comfortably,
preferably clothing that can be removed quickly by me. I wish

I had more time, but this will give us a bit of time together, and you can see what I envision for Villa Roma. What do you say?"

"I'm so excited!" she said, a lightness in her voice that he hadn't heard before.

⋅⊙⋅⊙⋅

Packing had never felt so fun. The following day, Maria bid goodbye to the surprised Ashley and Jennifer, spent too much time on an outfit selection and made the three-hour drive to Eugene.

Spencer called her from the family airplane she knew so well, and she drove right to the private hanger.

Parking in a reserved space, she bounded out of the Range Rover, wearing her new jeans and a soft cotton peasant blouse she'd bought in Klamath Falls, and into Spencer's waiting arms.

There was no time wasted on awkwardness or ceremony—she kissed him, and he kissed her back, his arms holding her lightly, still careful of her recent injury as he lifted her off the ground. It had barely been five and a half weeks since her injury, but she felt recovered. Being lifted was a sign of strength, but unlike the power Pablo displayed, this didn't scare her. Spencer was strong, and she liked it.

"Well, hello," he said, as they broke free from their kiss. He gave her a long look from head to foot, then smiled, his dimples making him look sexier if that was possible. "You look, well, fabulous. Crater Lake agrees with you. How do you feel?"

"I think that I'm very healed," she said, rubbing against him. "You won't break me when you touch me."

"I don't intend on ever breaking you. I like you just the way you are," he said and kissed her again. "Still, I'll be careful."

Quickly, they boarded the Stark family jet and started the forty-five-minute flight to Seattle. Maria never left Spencer's lap.

And later, she couldn't recall any conversation, just the feel of his lips on hers as they kissed their way through the flight.

A limo waited for them on the tarmac.

"It is about a half-hour drive to Bellevue," Spencer said as they got in the car.

"I wish it were longer," Maria said, patting the seat next to her.

"I think I'm a little scared of you, and not for the first time," he said and kissed her heartily. "Let's hope there isn't traffic and the room is ready for us."

They made excellent time.

Eclectic was one word to describe the techno feel of the lobby of The W Hotel in Bellevue. The silver stand-alone check-in stations were bathed in ultraviolet light, or something similar. They could see the glow the moment they stepped off the escalator, taking them from the street to the hallowed entry of the modern hotel.

"If you do this to my lobby, I will kill you in the night as you sleep," Maria whispered with a smile.

"Never, baby," Spencer said as they walked by the bright neon-colored pictures displayed on the walls, and bars that sported names like "Civility" and "Unrest." Possibly, it was a homage to Henry David Thoreau. Still, the meaning would be lost on the younger generation.

"The feature I want to show you is in our room, and I'm not just talking about the bed."

They walked down a hallway to an elevator bay where a recorded voice told them coquettishly, *"They were in the right place."* Maria felt out of place. Her senses were assaulted by the colors, and although Villa Roma was bright, it was classy. The same could not be said of this hotel. This interior felt too edgy. Maria felt old in her late twenties, just walking through the lobby.

They took the elevator to the seventh floor, and Maria

walked hand-in-hand with Spencer to a door at the end of the hall.

Turning to her, he asked, "Ready?"

"For the room or you?" she asked with a small smile.

Spencer dropped the keycard and had to bend to pick it up.

"The room first, then me," he said nervously, opening the door and letting her go first.

She made a sound akin to eating something bitter and shook her head as Spencer followed her inside.

"Wow," Spencer said as he looked around at the stunningly bad décor that assaulted his eyes. "Even I find it a bit… um…"

"Awful," Maria said, looking at the deliberate magenta smears on the gray carpet and the silver lamé leather headboard. But what took her breath away was the shower in the middle of the room. She'd heard of the attraction of the voyeur shower, but this was the first time she'd seen one in person.

"I need to find who the designer was so that we never hire them," Spencer said.

"It looks like someone was murdered on the carpet, and the body was dragged away," she observed. "This would look more at home in Italy."

"Um," Spencer began. "I have something to tell you."

"What?" Maria asked, checking out the most hideous wallpaper she'd ever seen in the room that contained the toilet. Black, cream, and mauve flowers were on every flat surface, including the ceiling. Taking in the small room and the rest of the hotel room with the prominent shower, she asked, "People like this hideous décor?"

"Yes, very much, and one floor of Villa Roma now has these kinds of showers to attract younger tourists. Let's not knock it until we've tried it."

"How do you say in English? What the fuck? Are you crazy?" Maria asked as she shook her head. She didn't know what to think. How could he? She supposed she was lucky that he hadn't converted the entire hotel to this voyeur shower concept, but one floor? Was he nuts? She wouldn't get angry until she saw it.

"It looks better than this. You have to trust me."

"I will try to remain, how you say... open-minded."

"You might not like it, but you'll respect the revenue it brings us."

"I think I need a cocktail," she said.

After a dinner at a faux Italian restaurant that claimed authentic Italian food, they arrived back in the room, and as Maria watched, Spencer started shedding clothing.

"I'm still upset," she said as he removed the peasant blouse without incident.

"Take it out on me," he said.

"Why do I think you'd like that?" she asked as he unhooked her bra, tossed it aside, and began kissing a trail down her body, paying special attention to her breasts and their rosy tips.

"I'm counting on it. Let's try out the shower," Spencer said as he looked up from her breasts with innocent blue eyes, still managing to have her nipple in his mouth. The image made her laugh.

Maria didn't care about the damn shower. She wanted to be with Spencer. Now that she was feeling better, the ribs no longer hurt. She wanted to make love with Spencer with abandon—in the way she had dreamed many nights when she was trying to sleep alone at The Caldera Lodge.

"Fine," she said as she leaned against the glass doors and let Spencer push down her jeans and then last of her clothing, in this case, a pair of red silk panties that matched her bra.

He threw his remaining clothes off as if they were on fire. And as she ran her eyes over his body, one word came to mind: hot. His body was hot.

She'd felt the firmness of his muscles under taut skin in Portland as she'd taken him, but she hadn't let herself adore his perfect male form. She'd been selfish, just wanting to take him and feel satisfaction. Now, she wanted to take her time. She didn't want to miss a thing.

He was all solid male and silky skin under her fingertips. A nice dusting of blond hair covered his chest. She knew how good it felt rubbing against her skin, especially her breasts. As he picked her up in his arms, she sighed as he stepped into the shower. This was going to be good.

Under the soft lights they'd left on, she noticed that her olive skin matched his tanned, toned skin almost perfectly. He held her as if she weighed nothing as she wrapped her legs around his waist and felt the tight muscles of his body with each step he took. If she moved only slightly, he'd be fully rooted within her. It took an iron will for her to hold back until he couldn't wait any longer, but she wanted him to give in first.

Holding her with just one arm, he turned on and adjusted the water. She stole a glance at his face, only to see him looking down at her with that damned sideways grin.

"How hot do you want it?" he asked, and she wasn't sure if he meant the water or himself. She decided not to take any chances.

"As hot as you can stand," she managed as he bent to kiss her. He kissed her until her lips felt swollen, and his tongue mimicked what he was about to do with his body.

Pushing her against the cool glass, he held her suspended as the air around them turned to steam.

"Take me," she ordered, forgetting her earlier resolve.

"Yes, ma'am," he said in his best Texas drawl.

Maria's heart threatened to explode in her chest as Spencer entered her in a hard thrust that made her gasp.

Had he always been this large? She felt impaled, in the best possible way, pinned against the cool glass, his body holding her up. Then he started to move, and her eyes rolled northward. Nothing had ever felt this good. She opened her eyes to see

Spencer watching her as he slowed down his rhythm, filling her and retreating. She cried out with each stroke, feeling it all the way to her heart.

She loved this man, and by the way he was looking at her, the feeling was mutual.

Just as the thought entered her mind, the orgasm took over, making her scream Spencer's name. Before long, he was joining her, his breath coming out in short gasps that matched hers as he gently murmured, "My Maria, damn it, you feel so good."

Later, Maria lay naked on the bed, panting, the sheets damp around them from the shower and their own sweat from the unhinged lovemaking. That damn shower was quite the aphrodisiac. Spencer lay next to her, gripping her hand, his breath labored.

"That was fucking amazing," he said, and not trusting her voice, Maria nodded. Then, she managed, "Okay. But only one floor."

"One floor," Spencer said, turning to kiss her cheek as his arm snaked around her waist and pulled her close. Then he kissed her slowly and thoroughly. "Have I told you lately that I'm falling for you?"

"No, not since dinner," she said, her hand running through his damp hair, "But I never get tired of hearing it. Say it again."

He pulled her close and started his sensual assault all over again as he said, "I think this might be love."

"I think you might be right," she said as she gave over to his touch.

They checked out of The W after having breakfast on black patent leather cubes in a room called The Living Room Bar.

"I think I prefer the Starbucks," she said as they stepped into the waiting limo.

"I know I do," Spencer said and shook his head.

"You've told me nothing of Pablo," Maria said out of the blue as they drove to the airport.

"He has asked about you, but he hasn't approached me yet," Spencer said.

"Promise me that you will be careful and not take any chances," she said.

He kissed her and said, "I have a lot to lose, more than I had the first time I spoke to him. You have my word. I'll be careful."

Four hours, including a two-hour plane flight to San Jose, later they were in a limo on their way to The Hotel Valencia on Santana Row.

"What did you want to show me here?" Maria asked as they drove past shops and restaurants on streets lined with palm trees and tourists in shorts and tank tops. After The Caldera Lodge, it felt busy and noisy. Didn't these people want to hear their own thoughts? Was she ruined for large crowds for the rest of her life? Possibly. Maria wished she and Spencer could steal away to someplace quiet, where they could be alone and to explore their new relationship. At the thought, she snuggled closer to him.

"The Hotel Valencia has some design elements that I think will appeal to you, but I'll let you decide."

"That is generous of you," Maria said thoughtfully but slightly sarcastically as they walked through the lobby to the elevator.

"This, I like," she said, gesturing to the open space.

"Well, I'm glad because your lobby in Rome looks more like this now that I've been redoing things. You can now see into the interior garden like this open space."

"I've often thought of doing that. I like the metalwork," she commented.

"We now have lots of wrought iron in the form of walls that separate the garden from the rest of the lobby. I've even added these kinds of cobblestones."

"What about the beautiful marble floors?" she asked in horror.

"They were dated and cracked in places, so they are gone, but the cobblestones look great."

"I think I need to see for myself."

"I would expect no less, my Maria, my beautiful. I can't wait to show it all to you."

Spencer used his keycard to open the room at The Valencia. It was unusually dark until Spencer opened the equivalent of large barn doors and then louvered French doors, which opened to a balcony overlooking a city square.

"What do you think of the French doors?"

"I like them," Maria said, crossing to touch the louvers and said, "They look very Italian."

"They look authentic in our hotel."

"Where are you putting them?" she asked.

"The third floor has the showers. Think of that little amenity as a substitute for no view. Then floors four through ten have these doors opening to the Roman sky and views. What do you think?" he asked, opening his arms in invitation.

"I think it is a good idea," she said and fell into his waiting open arms.

"To make you happy makes me happy," he said and kissed her.

"Then before dinner, make me happy," she said as she reached down to cup him through his jeans.

That night at dinner, he asked her a question for which she'd dreaded answering.

"Can I ask you something?"

"You can ask me anything," she said, hoping that this might open the communication to discussing Ruby, but sensing this wouldn't be easy, whatever he was going to ask.

"Alex never really shared how you all figured out that you were related. I've been very curious. I don't want to ask anything that makes you uncomfortable, but I'd like to know.

And just so we are clear, nothing you say will change how I feel about you."

Maria took a deep sip of her wine, hoped it would give her courage, and nodded. Then, she began.

"From the time I was very young, I knew I was different than the other children at the orphanage. I had my very own guardian angel, who asked that I call him 'G.' I didn't understand it until I was much older. This mystery visitor was a man that looked like Alex. It was our father, Garrison Stark. He was so handsome, and he would only come to visit me, none of the other children. Maybe once a year, sometimes twice. Each time he arrived, he would hold me on his lap, hug me, and tell me that I was beautiful like my mother. He always smelled good and was in a suit and tie. The nuns, they would fawn over him. Now I know it was because he donated a large amount of money to them. And for me, he would always bring me a new outfit and a toy that would get confiscated for the communal toy box as soon as he left, but I didn't care. He'd come to see me, and that made me feel special. The other children would let me know they didn't appreciate the special attention I received. More than once, I was beaten up after his visits, but I didn't care. I wanted to be with him all the time. I think he was my first love.

"I almost didn't want to be adopted because I didn't think he'd know where to find me, and I was right. After I was adopted, I never saw him again, but from what we've been able to piece together, he continued to help me. He acted as a secret benefactor as I got older. School debts would be instantly paid in full and extra money would get deposited into my bank account without explanation when I was at university. I questioned it at first, only to be told by the bank that there had been no mistake.

"When I got my degree from the university after my parents died, there was a too-good-to-be-true offer of employment with the Stark International Hotels. Knowing what I know now, I wish my father had shown up and introduced himself to me.

That would have been priceless." How she wished he'd just shown up on her doorstep and explained everything to her. She wished she could see him one more time and hug him like she had when she was the dirty orphan child. He never seemed to notice how dirty she was, never hesitating to hug her close to him.

"Did you ever hear the story of how he met your mother?" Spencer asked as he grasped her hand across the table.

"The nuns told me that she was a waitress in a restaurant, was unmarried, and died in childbirth. Of course, they wanted me to think she had died because she had sinned. They were nuns," she said dismissively. "I wish I could have asked my father, but now I can't. I should be grateful; he had wanted to help his youngest child, but he didn't want to acknowledge me. I have Alex and now Rebecca. Those relationships are more precious to me than anything, probably my greatest gift." She added, "The nuns would be shocked, but they knew he was my father all along and didn't tell me. That is hard to forgive."

"My Uncle Garrison wasn't an easy man," Spencer replied. "He was hard on Alex, which is why Alex rebelled after Wharton. I never thought he'd go into the family business. I thought he'd either sell cannabis out of a van or become a Wall Street tycoon and buy Stark Corporation to prove to his father that he could."

"But Alex stepped up after our father died."

"No one expected that," Spencer said. "Uncle Garrison's death was so unexpected. I mean, he and Aunt Vic were traveling in Greece. They were having a wonderful time. I couldn't believe it when I heard he died."

"He died with secrets. He didn't tell anyone about me," Maria said and realized her glass was empty.

Spencer poured her another glass and said, "Well, I'm glad we found you. You've added a very wonderful branch to this family tree. We are the lucky ones. You take up our brains and attractiveness quotient by tenfold."

"I don't think your Aunt Vic would agree."

Spencer kissed her hand and said, "I hate cilantro, but everyone else seems to love it. It doesn't make me a bad person. It just means that I don't like an herb that I think tastes like soap. I've tried to like it, but something always holds me back."

"It tastes like soap," Maria said, enjoying the fun tone that had made this serious conversation more palatable.

"Exactly," he said. "Good thing is, I love the taste of my Maria."

"Well, thank goodness for that," she said and looked down shyly as she remembered how he had run his tongue over every inch of her flesh, tickling her before he tasted her.

"I haven't answered your question," she said.

"But you will. You're getting to it," he said.

She couldn't help it; she smiled. Spencer was patient, and she loved him for not pushing her.

"After our father died, when Alex took over and started showing up at the hotel, looking like a carbon copy of my angel, I started talking to him. I was just a lowly front desk registration clerk, but I told him about my guardian angel. It was Alex who noticed the color of our eyes. He was shocked at first. I remember he went back to the United States only to return a week later because he couldn't stop thinking about it. He remembered that his parents had a rough patch when he was about ten. They had separated, and Alex was sure they'd divorce, but after about six months, they got back together. He said they were stronger and more in love. His father had spent most of those six months away from his family in Italy, renting a small apartment and having a serious midlife crisis.

"He asked me to submit to a DNA test. Within a few days, what we suspected was confirmed. Alex went to the estate attorney, and that was when he discovered the trust I wasn't supposed to find out about until I was thirty. Alex hired an investigator, and she confirmed my mother's identity, Sophia Rossi, and that she had died in childbirth. Garrison Stark paid for her grave and headstone in a graveyard just outside Roma."

"Have you been to see it?" Spencer asked.

"I visit on my birthday, every year since I found out the truth. The day she died was the day I was born."

"I hope you don't blame yourself for that," Spencer said, stroking his thumb over the back of her hand as he looked into her eyes.

"I did for a while, but then I came to understand that I can't change what happened, so I've learned to live with it."

"I don't know if this helps, but I think Alex, Daisy, and Rebecca are very happy to have you in the family," Spencer offered.

"My siblings have pulled me into the family fold. I'm thankful, but I'm pretty sure Victoria Stark will never warm up to me. I am the physical evidence of her husband's infidelity."

That night, she and Spencer made love, but unlike the day before, there wasn't a frenzy to reach the most intense orgasms of their lives. Spencer had never been more gentle, more caring, more adoring. He held her close, maintained eye contact, and for the first time, she didn't feel like they were scratching each other's itch. On the contrary, they were sharing something that was far more intimate. They truly were making love.

That morning she had to say goodbye to Spencer again, and the drive back to The Caldera Lodge was hard. This time, she'd had to blink back tears. She had wanted to talk to him about Ruby, but after discussing her father and upbringing, she didn't want one more moment of heavy conversation. As it was, she was feeling especially vulnerable.

Spencer was planning to see her when the rest of the family visited The Caldera Lodge in several weeks. The last three days felt like a wonderful mini honeymoon. They had walked along

Santana Row, eaten meals together, drank wine, and then made love and slept together, entwined, at night. If this was a taste of what life would be like with Spencer, she wanted it to feel like this every day. Was it too much to dream about; too much to ask? Had it ever been this easy, this fun with anyone else, including Pablo? No

There were only two little items that stood in her way: Ruby and New York. Before they took one more step forward, she needed answers to both.

Chapter Sixteen

rriving back at The Caldera Lodge, Maria settled back to the slower pace, taking her position very seriously. Her time at The Caldera Lodge was coming to an end. In a matter of weeks, she would be back in Roma with Spencer. She wanted to make sure she left a positive mark on The Caldera Lodge.

Certain patterns were starting to develop that she noticed and did her best to control. Her biggest concern was children who wandered away from their parents and got lost. Each week, it seemed, she had to help find a missing child who'd decided to have an adventure. If she was lucky enough to have children of her own one day, she'd never let them out of her sight. She was currently contemplating different tracking devices for children to wear for the duration of their trips to Crater Lake and, more importantly, The Caldera Lodge. Maybe what she really wanted was a tracker for Spencer so she'd know what he was doing. She missed him like she had never missed anyone.

That evening, she wore a simple black sheath dress in a crepe silk fabric with a matching black cashmere sweater and a strand of simple pearls, which had been a Christmas present to mark her first year as a manager with Stark International Hotels. She walked through the lobby taking in the nightly scene. When she had first arrived at The Caldera Lodge, she would look at each table and make sure Pablo wasn't lying in wait. It was a stupid paranoia, but one she was finding hard to let go of considering her fear. It had been several weeks, and he hadn't tried to find her. Other than the missing person's report, which Alex had addressed, there hadn't been anything else. Maybe she was finally rid of him. She hoped beyond hope that it was over. Her time with Pablo had developed soft fuzzy edges—the good memories hiding, only the bad memories playing like movies in her mind. That last night, the night he could've killed her, had removed those good memories with Pablo. Now she feared him like children feared the monster under the bed. She would forever be looking for him in the dark corners.

Tonight, she was happy to have Spencer, her family, Alex and Daisy, Rebecca and little Emily, not to mention her little nieces Lexy and Lily in her new life. Her life had turned for the better, and she liked it.

She wanted a crystal ball or maybe Alex's fictional tarot cards to see if she and Spencer had a relationship that would endure. It had been several days since she'd spoken with him, and that was several days too long. She was physically and geographically isolated, and she felt lonely. The rest of the world, beyond this wilderness—Italy, Portland, her hotel… It all felt very far away.

Fires had been lit in the two gigantic fireplaces at opposite ends of the massive lobby to ward off what she had come to expect as a very cool evening chill. She noticed a family of four playing a spirited game of Monopoly at one of the game tables. Maria noted that someone on staff had brought them popcorn and beverages. She only hoped they'd been offered before having to flag someone down.

Another family, whose children had been on her Wilderness Walk, were putting together a puzzle of Crater Lake that had been assembled and reassembled many times at that same table by different guests. She got hugs and excited chatter from the children, who abandoned the puzzle when she walked by as if she were a celebrity. Such attention always flattered her. She joined them for a few minutes and even helped them out with the puzzle.

Happy-looking couples relaxed with cocktails and chatted in low, comfortable chairs. A few people sat by themselves, reading books, blissfully unaware of anyone around them. Maria envied their serenity. The lobby was like a big living room for the travelers, uniting them into one large family.

She'd never seen anything like it in any other hotel. As she made the analogy in her mind, she realized when she returned to an urban hotel that she would miss this family feel, a strange intimacy somehow caught for this moment in time. This was the kind of thing she had wanted for her childhood, but it had never been close to this kind of family feel. Her adoptive mother and father had never played a board game or put together a puzzle with her. Possibly, they had outgrown board games and puzzles because they were older. Her adoptive mother had taught her how to cook, her adoptive father taught her a love of nature, but they respected her privacy, and when they were all together, they were a bit formal with her. It was as if she was a stranger in their home. It was better than the orphanage or foster care, but it wasn't what she had wanted it to be.

She was also sad for not having these kinds of fun memories with her adoptive parents. By the time she came into their lives, they didn't have the time or energy for a child. Aside from the explorations with her father, she didn't experience a lot of family togetherness. She wondered for the millionth time why they adopted her. More than once, she wondered if they had just been bored one day and showed up at her orphanage. Possibly, if they had gone another direction, they might have ended up with a puppy from the local animal shelter instead of a little girl.

Once, she had heard them fighting, her mother second-guessing the idea of bringing a child into their comfortable lives. Her father fought back, defending his love for Maria. She'd never forgotten the casual way that her adoptive mother had considered Maria's fate with only the barest of parameters that easily could have resulted in her removal from the only home she'd ever known.

From that day forward, Maria became the super daughter, the best guest who cooked and cleaned. She gave more than she took. She cooked most of the meals and cleaned the house. She did whatever she could to earn her keep so that they would love her. Her father saw what Maria was doing and eventually had a conversation with her when they were out exploring nature.

"My girl, you never need to worry. You are our daughter. Your mother, well, she had problems with everyone—the butcher, the farmer who sells her vegetables, and even her sister, Sophia. Don't fall into that trap. You are mine, and I'm never going to let you go. I need you more than you know. Even if your mother packed your bags and sent you back to the orphanage, I'd drive right back there and get you. You are my daughter. I wish we could have shown you a more loving household. I know it isn't easy. But know this, you always have my unconditional love."

It was later that Maria discovered her mother's medication for bipolar disease. When she would skip her medication her disease would come back in a way that not only affected her mother but affected Maria and her father as well. And in the end, she didn't feel like she knew her mother at all.

Maria's parents died when she was away at college at the age of twenty. An auto accident in the South of France where they were vacationing killed them together—so coincidental to how her real father died. She missed them, especially her father, but she had them in her life for less than ten years. Loss was something she'd gotten used to from an early age. And this was no different, except she no longer had a place to go when she was on school vacation. The holidays were incredibly lonely.

If Maria was fortunate to have children one day, she would play board games with them, put together puzzles, and cook for them, but cook fun things like biscotti and cookies. It was a promise she made to herself and intended on keeping forever. She would tell her children every day how much they meant to her and that she loved them. She would tell them how much she valued them. If she didn't think she could make these promises, she'd never have them. It was what they deserved. It was that simple. Children didn't ask to be born, but when they were here, they deserved everything you could give them.

In the meantime, she would look for ways to integrate this kind of family bonding activity into other Stark International Hotels so that other families could make lovely memories during their holidays.

She stepped into the restaurant to have a word with her hostess, another college student with a desire to one day work in the hospitality industry. Meagan, a brunette, went to Oregon State University and seemed more mature than the ladies at the front desk, but Maria was trying her best not to play favorites.

"Good evening, Meagan."

"*Buonasera*, Maria," the girl replied with a shy smile.

"*Molto buono!* Meagan, you flatter me."

"I'm trying to learn a little Italian," the girl replied with a shy smile that told Maria she was very pleased with the compliment.

"*Prego*, you ever want to practice, you find me, and we will talk," Maria offered.

"You're serious?"

"Of course!"

The girl's face lit up. "That would be great!"

"So, how are we doing tonight?"

"We are short on the fresh Kokanee special."

"How many?" Maria asked.

"We only have five left last time I checked, with more guests wanting them."

"Free dessert for anyone who gets denied the fish."

"Thank you," Meagan said, with a smile, "That will ease

things a bit. We also have a lot of guests who wanted reservations at seven."

"Four parties that were turned down. I staggered them to seven-fifteen, seven-thirty, seven-forty-five, and eight. After a bit of discussion, they were okay, and they all have free appetizer vouchers signed by me," Maria offered.

"We just served one order of nachos with bison to the lobby. I didn't know that was your doing."

Maria still didn't like the nachos, but as long as her guests did, that was all that mattered.

"*Si, prego*. I'll be at the bar making the rounds if you need me. And don't hesitate. We do best when we get ahead of problems."

"Thank you, Maria! *Prego!*"

Maria spent the next hour chatting with the guests, hearing about their vacation adventures, and answering questions about the lodge and the surrounding park. Her shoes, which she used to think of as her 'conservative' heels at three inches of spiked heels, were pinching her feet. What had happened to her? She hadn't gained weight, but anything remotely resembling business attire felt tight, uncomfortable. She liked the shorts and t-shirts too much. Back home, she would only get away with wearing shorts or pants when she had a day off. She'd worn jeans with Spencer. She'd lost her fashion sense.

Wishing she could trade her heels in for her now-familiar hiking boots, she leaned against the beautifully polished mahogany bar and raised one of her feet to get it off the slate floor and ease some of her pain. Could she get away with taking her shoes off and walking barefoot? It was something to consider. After all, she wasn't in an urban area. Was she going to have to get... something else... like... flats? Just how old was she?

"Come here often, miss?" a man's voice she didn't at first recognize asked. Then, it clicked for her.

Turning toward the tall, handsome park ranger she'd met on her first day, she replied, "Good evening, Forest Ranger Peter."

"How are ya doing, Maria?"

He'd changed out of his park ranger uniform and was now sporting an evergreen cashmere sweater to ward off the evening chill and a pair of dark jeans. For an evening in the middle of Central Oregon, it was considered formal attire. It fit him well, but as nice as he looked, she wondered how Spencer would look sitting on the same barstool, wearing something similar. He'd look great, she decided. Peter was very nice, but he wasn't Spencer.

"I'm just resting my feet. I think I'm getting soft, getting used to my big, ugly hiking boots," she announced. "Now, every time I wear something with a little bit of style, something fashionable, they hurt my feet. I've gotten soft in this high mountain air. I'm very worried about my fashion sense when I return to Roma. My staff will make fun of me for getting soft."

He laughed, "How about I buy you a drink to ease your pain? Or would you like some nachos?"

He was a sweet, good-looking man, but she couldn't give him hope where none existed.

"Thank you, but I can't. I'm still on duty, and the nachos are not to my taste," she said, the smile fading from her face.

He winced and asked, "I see. Maria, let me be blunt. Is there someone else?"

"What are you asking about?" she asked, wishing the conversation was not going in this direction and trying her best to claim a language barrier confusion issue.

"You don't like me, do you?"

She felt horrible. "Of course, I do. You're very kind and helpful, but I think what you're asking is if there is another man in my life."

"Yes, I'm asking."

"So I was right. Thank you, I am so flattered. But there was something that happened before I came here. I'm not recovered from it yet. It is complicated, in a couple of different directions. My fiancé broke off our engagement, and then I met someone else. I think it might be very serious. I know it is complicated."

He paused and then asked, "Wait, let me get this straight. A man, your fiancé, let you walk away?"

"Oh yes, my ex-fiancé is a very scary man. Remember my black eye?"

"He did that?"

"Yes. I'm very thankful I didn't marry him."

"Maria—I had no idea."

"No, it is fine now. And the man who helped me to get away from him, we… well… that is to be determined." Her relationship with Spencer was new, but it was serious. Peter didn't need to know the details.

"So, the fiancé is gone, but there is someone else."

"Hopefully, just one now."

"Is it why you left Italy?" he asked.

"Yes. Of course, my ex-fiancé isn't someone who takes things lightly." She caught the bartender's attention, and he immediately appeared in front of her. "I'd like my usual red wine, please." Then she turned to Peter, "I've decided I'm no longer on duty and would like to join you in a cocktail. Maybe we can talk of other, more pleasant things. What would you like? It is my treat. I get a company discount."

Smiling broadly, Peter patted the barstool next to him and said, "I'm not sure I can let you do that, but let's get a bottle of whatever you're drinking."

"I think that having some wine is probably a good idea. I've had a hard day as they say," Maria said, promising not to drink too much with Mr. Tall Dark and Handsome Forest Ranger.

Over the next two hours, they enjoyed a bottle of Willamette Valley Pinot Noir, and Maria listened to Peter explain everything there was to know about being a forest ranger at Crater Lake.

Wanting to keep the focus on him, she'd asked question after question, not allowing him an opening into her background. She could respect his passion for his job, but it literally bored her to tears.

Turning the tables, he asked, "So, we've talked a lot about me. Are you sure you don't want to talk about what happened in Italy? The black eye? I have broad shoulders you could lean on. And I'm curious and not that complicated."

She smiled. "I'm sure I'd prefer to talk about the future, not my troubled past."

He studied her in subtle light. "Why do I get the feeling you're hiding? Coming out here from the hustle and bustle of an exotic city in Europe?"

"Because I am," she replied, finishing her glass of wine.

"So, he's still after you? Is he dangerous?" he asked, his voice taking on an ominous tone.

Thinking of how Pablo threatened her, she made the mistake of answering, "Yes, my ex-fiancé is dangerous, but he doesn't know where I am. The other man, the man who helped me get here, is working on my hotel in *Roma*, making necessary updates. I was supposed to be there helping him, but it got complicated. Now, I'm here, and my ex is in *Roma*, wondering where I went. That is all fine. I don't want him to know."

Peter straightened his shoulders, his face turning serious as he reassured her, "Don't worry. I'll protect you. Your ex won't get anywhere near you as long as I'm here. Once all the rangers know, we will protect you."

"That is not necessary." Maria looked at Peter's handsome face with his earnest brown eyes and said, "Peter, I'm sorry, I didn't mean to infer my ex-fiancé will come here. I was very clear, and he would never go to lengths like coming to Crater Lake. My brother and my friend are watching him. It will never happen." She could see by the way he bristled that he'd already made his own conclusions. He'd be on alert, and maybe that wasn't a bad thing.

A few minutes later, Maria walked him through the lobby to the front entrance, feeling guilty. "I'm sorry. I shouldn't have told you all of that. I speak too much, and it depresses you. It makes the evening heavy."

"Don't you worry, I had a wonderful time," he gently reprimanded. "But if this guy shows up at the park entrance, I'll be able to give you a warning."

She shook her head. Pablo would not be coming for her. It was Spencer who needed to be careful of Pablo.

"Thank you. I don't think that will be necessary, but I appreciate it."

"Look, I have no illusions about how I feel about you, but I understand you are kind of with someone. All in all, you probably shouldn't be romantic with anyone so close to your broken engagement. So how would you feel about being just friends?" he asked and extended his hand.

"I'd like that. Friends," she replied and shook his hand. "Thank you, Peter." Her relationship with Spencer was none of his business, and to lecture her about the timing just made her angry. What she had with Spencer could not, would not be ignored.

That night she dreamed of the Italian police, headed by Pablo's brother, raiding The Caldera Lodge and hauling her away. In her dream, Pablo was with them, pointing at her and telling them that she had ruined his political future.

Waking up in a cold sweat, her heart racing, she reminded herself where she was, what had happened, and that she was away from Pablo.

She checked her cellphone to see what time it was and saw that a miracle had happened. A text from Spencer was there. *I miss you. I love you. I'll see you soon.*

She was counting the minutes.

CHAPTER SEVENTEEN

"Are you going to be all right?" Spencer's father asked him as they sat around a smudged glass-topped table in the funeral home on a hot afternoon in Austin, Texas. A bouquet of dusty silk flowers in a color that did not exist in nature sat atop the coffee table. The air smelled musty, a mix of strong cleaning products, formaldehyde, and death. They were here because Ruby's parents had requested this funeral home, although all the places that processed the bodies of your loved ones were basically the same. Creepy. Ruby's parents sat with Spencer now, as did his parents in the strangely loud silence.

Without waiting for an answer, Spencer's mother gently rubbed his back as they waited for the funeral director to arrive. This was all wrong.

It wasn't supposed to be like this. He might have one day been at a funeral parlor planning for Ruby's final preparations, but that was supposed to be fifty or sixty years from now. Instead of being with their parents, he was supposed to be with their children, a boy who looked like him and a daughter with red hair like her mother. They were supposed to have a life together. He'd had almost three years to understand why this little fairy tale wouldn't happen, but all that time and reason was hard to find when events you always feared happening actually happened. This was just wrong. Spencer found he was angry all over again, but there was no outlet for his rage, no place to blame the unfairness of it all. His optimism was like a spoiled child, and now it didn't know what to do because it hadn't gotten its way.

"I wish I'd been here when it happened," he answered, the jetlag and the sorrow and grief all catching up with him. He hadn't seen Ruby in six weeks when she died. He'd been with Maria and in Rome. "She shouldn't have died alone."

They all murmured their arguments, but it was Ruby's father whose voice became his focus.

"Spencer, there was nothing any of us could do. Since the moment of her accident, Ruby was a ticking time bomb," Ruby's father said. "The Ruby we loved has been dead for three years. I finally feel like she has peace. There is joy in the freedom of her spirit. Please try to remember who she was and that she would never have wanted to be like she was these past years. She knew you loved her. She knew we all loved her. And she didn't die alone. There were caring people there with her."

Yeah, the best money could buy, Spencer thought.

"And you were there for her, more than she probably would have ever wanted. Do you know how many spouses would have walked away three years ago? You weren't even married, yet you stuck by her. We will never forget that. I have a feeling that wherever she is, Ruby knew," Ruby's mother said before she dabbed at her eyes with a tissue.

Two days ago, Spencer, who had been diligently working in Rome, updating the hotel and missing Maria, had gotten the news about his first love, a woman to whom a part of his heart would always belong—Ruby. As the doctors had always feared, she had a massive seizure and was rushed to the hospital, but she had died within an hour of arrival.

If he'd have been in Austin instead of Rome, if he hadn't moved her into the care facility three months ago, if she was still living in his home and if he had visited her that day…

Would he have been able to prolong her life? That wouldn't have been what she wanted. Did he think she would have had a moment of pure clarity and told Spencer she loved him and to go on with his life?

Nothing would be different. He knew that in his heart. But this kind of torture was nothing new and as familiar to him as shaving each morning.

The guilt had raised its ugly head again, and it was going to feel like this for a bit, he knew. He felt sad, but more than anything, he felt guilty. Ruby's potential death was always hanging over them, but doctors had told them it could be days or years.

Ruby wouldn't have wanted to live the way she had been for the last three years. For all intents and purposes, she had died three years ago. What had been left was a shell, a body that looked like Ruby, sounded like Ruby, but she wasn't the woman he'd fallen in love with six years earlier. She might have the same sweet smile, but the quick wit and humor were gone. Her intelligence—she was more brilliant than he'd ever be—would never return.

She wouldn't want him to feel like this. She wouldn't have wanted him to put his life on hold for her. Even their parents had told him this at every opportunity. Yet hadn't he done just that? Only when he started living again in the last couple of months had he realized all that he'd lost.

They all went to lunch after making final plans for Ruby, but none of them had much of an appetite. Picking out a coffin for a thirty-three-year-old woman had a way of putting everyone on the worst of all diet plans. Spencer would be surprised if he ever ate again.

"I think the black suit that she loved so much would be perfect for her to be buried in," Ruby's mother said as they all sipped sweet tea. They had been over this in the last hour, but Ruby's mother needed to process, so they let her talk on and on about the suit.

Spencer knew the suit. Ruby wore it several times with him, and he had thought with her red hair that the suit looked magnificent on her body. He liked it when she wore it for him, but having her buried in that suit tainted every memory he'd ever had of Ruby wearing it. Death tainted everything.

"Is there another outfit that you think would be better, Spencer? It is not too late. We can change it out."

Spencer shook his head, wished the iced tea had alcohol in it, and wondered why the hell they were acting like teetotalers on one of the worst days of their lives.

"She always loved that black suit," he said as he signaled the waitress. When she arrived at their table, he put an end to the dry, horrible lunch. "We'd like a round of Jack Daniels. In fact, why don't you just bring us a bottle and five glasses?" Turning to the others, he said, "Ruby wouldn't want us to feel like this. She'd want us to be happy that she was free of her miserable life."

"It is about damn time," Ruby's father said. "Thank you, son."

⁘ ⸻ ⸰❦⸰ ⸻ ⁘

Two days later, Spencer placed his luggage in the trunk of his black Mercedes-Benz GT, which was parked in front of his parent's large two-story ranch house. He hadn't wanted to stay at his own house just down the road. It held too many memories with Ruby. Maybe he'd have it bulldozed.

His parents had purchased the five-thousand-acre parcel of land that made up The W Ranch when they were first married. The Whitlows had been in Texas for five generations. Aside from his father's dalliance with Stark International Hotels, they'd been cattle farmers for years. His grandfather had struck liquid gold with a few well-placed oil wells in the 1930s, which was when the family had gone from being comfortable to really having money. Still producing, the oil wells continued to provide a comfortable income.

Aunt Vic, Spencer's favorite aunt, was a born and bred Texan. She reclaimed her southern accent when she visited the ranch several times a year, bemoaning the hustle and bustle of New York and Portland.

Now, Spencer had decided he liked the hotel business because it was far away from Texas. Most of the ranch was leased to other ranchers who worked the land with their cattle. The Whitlows didn't need any extra income, but they loved Texas. Spencer didn't feel the same way, not on the day he watched Ruby get buried.

Before the accident, they'd discussed building something that would rival his parents' house. A big, sprawling ranch that they would fill with children and dogs. It was a dream that wasn't going to happen.

Texas now held sad memories of dreams that would never come true. Ruby had died along with any last fiber of hope he might have for her recovery. He'd known the truth, but there was always a small part of his heart that couldn't give up hope for a miracle. Now that was gone, and he couldn't wait to leave.

His home was elsewhere. Maybe it had been for a while.

He hugged his mother in a tight, tearful goodbye. Ruby's funeral had been that morning, and Spencer didn't know how to feel. Alex, Rebecca, and Adam had all come, but he didn't have much to say to them. They knew what he was going through. Even his crusty, up-tight Aunt Victoria held his father's hand and cried with Ruby's family.

One thing he knew for sure, he couldn't spend one more minute in Austin. He couldn't think of Ruby's body, the body he'd once held and had held him, being in the ground. When he thought of the black suit she wore, he had to swallow down bile.

"Are you sure this is a good idea?" his mother asked. "It

seems rather rash to me. Wouldn't you like to spend some time with your family, ride your horse, eat some home-cooked meals, call up some of your old friends?"

"Who used to hang out with Ruby and me? No, thank you. I can't do that. I can't think of being here without her. I can't think of trying to pick up where I left off." And that was true, he suddenly needed to see someone else who'd become very special to him, and he wasn't feeling guilty in the least. He wanted to see his Italian princess—he needed his Maria. To spend a day without her seemed incredibly stupid.

"I need some time to myself. I need to drive. I need to think. If I go to Crater Lake, I can do it in four or five easy days. I need to see Maria. I need to hold her. I need her like I've never needed anyone in my life."

"Ruby would want you to be happy. You knew that, son. You just never allowed yourself to open up to someone else. You have too much love to give to live alone in this life," his father said. Always the man to add wisdom into a conversation—that or a dirty joke. What had Alex always called Spencer's dad? *The Fun Uncle.*

"Maria and Ruby would have liked each other," Spencer said. "They have the same edge, the same way of giving me shit. I must like women who see through my charms. You'll love her, I know it. She needs to know what it is like to be loved by parents."

"My sweet boy, you are perfection. Lucky is the woman whom you love," his mother said. "Of course, we'll love her."

"I think I'm lucky to have found such extraordinary women."

"I look forward to the day you bring your Maria home to meet us," his father said.

"I'm just worried about you being on the road that long," she said. "You could fly to Portland and borrow a car from Alex. I'd sure feel better about it."

"He needs this, Liza. Spencer needs time to come to terms

with what has happened. He will be fine," his father said, coming up behind his mother and slipping an arm around her waist.

"Will you call each day?" she asked.

"Yes, but only because I love you," he said.

CHAPTER EIGHTEEN

I
t was mid-July, and at the front desk, Jennifer and Ashley were at each other's throats, bickering nastily, oblivious to Maria's arrival. Maria still hadn't heard from Spencer in a few days, which was too long to not be in contact. He'd sent her the text: *I miss you. I love you. I'll see you soon.* Then nothing.

She was angry. Her anger was only made worse by her recent call to Alex, who told her Spencer was fine but on a special project and unreachable for a bit. If she found out later that he was in some Italian prison, she would kill her brother.

Maria placed a Mason jar full of purple wildflowers she'd picked earlier on the long walk she'd taken to calm down on the corner of the front desk and asked, "Ladies?" She'd purposefully lowered her voice, hoping they would follow suit. They did not comply.

"She overbooked us on one of the busiest weekends of the season," Ashley said accusingly.

"I thought you were taking a cancellation," Jennifer replied.

"For next weekend, duh. You shouldn't have been eavesdropping on my conversation. And you shouldn't have, like, made an assumption."

"How many rooms?" Maria asked to try to get the details, ignoring the quibbling as she began to form contingency plans and ignored the headache that had started pounding over her right eye.

"One, but that's enough. What will we tell the guests when

they arrive this evening? It's not like they can stay at the Holiday Inn down the street. Why did you, like, take the reservation before you checked with me?" Ashley asked.

"He had a lovely voice and was in a terrible hurry. I don't know. I just couldn't, like, say no to him." The girl was flustered, looking as though she might cry.

"Let's all calm down," Maria said. "Has anyone tried calling our guest back?"

"I must have, like, copied the number down wrong," Jennifer said, not meeting Maria's eyes.

"Okay, then we will handle it when this man's party arrives."

"I'm so sorry, Maria," Jennifer said. "I thought I heard Ashley say she was sorry they weren't coming tonight."

"Next Friday," Ashley corrected.

"Well, we can all work on our communication skills while I bunk with you ladies tonight," Maria announced.

"What?" Ashley asked.

"If we don't have any other cancellations, I'll give them my quarters for the evening. How long is this guest planning on staying?"

"Three nights," Jennifer replied meekly.

"Then, you have a new roommate for the next three nights," Maria said and thought of the old couch she knew adorned their cramped sleeping quarters. Ugh. Maybe she could think of other sleeping accommodations. She was tempted to drive to Klamath Falls and check into a Best Western with internet and cable.

"I'm so sorry...." Jennifer began.

"Shhh… we just won't let this kind of thing happen again. Communication—that's what we need to work on," Maria said and smiled. This crisis had been avoided.

Maria had her room cleaned and prepared for their overflow guests. She removed her personal items and packed her bags. She couldn't fault her summer employees. They were young, and mistakes were easily made. Having a flash of what she'd have done to her staff in Roma if they'd made the same mistake, she felt guilty. Whenever they made a mistake of this magnitude, she gave them a severe lecture. As she finished packing, she wondered if maybe the Oregon wilderness had mellowed her.

All those hard edges she'd needed to build her confidence and make her untouchable as a hotel manager at one of the best Stark Hotels in the fleet had all but disappeared. She no longer cared about being beyond reproach. These people didn't look at her as a waif from the orphanage. She was the strong, independent woman she'd always wanted to be. She just hadn't realized that by relaxing, she'd be more of herself. She even looked younger. She smiled more, and it brought a softness to her face she hadn't known for many years. Her body was fully healed, thank God, and she could do more hiking around the lake than her small Wilderness Walks.

Her staff back in Italy wouldn't recognize her. She hadn't worn her stilettos in weeks, had no idea if any of her designer suits would even fit her anymore, but she doubted it. Her hair hadn't been styled in almost two months. Now, she just pulled it back into a ponytail while it was still wet from the shower. Did she have split ends? No doubt, and she didn't care. Not like she might have once cared. Maria was very thrilled her genes allowed her zero grey hairs therefore her personal maintenance was light makeup of mascara and her favorite new shiny lip gloss that tasted of raspberries.

And shock of all shocks? Maria learned to like the taste of the nachos. The smoky bison was her favorite, though the chef changed it up for her and made some with the Kokanee, and those were to die for. In fact, she was thinking of adding them to the menu, Kokanee nachos. Next, she'd be eating hamburgers and French fries or something with American cheese in it.

A knock on her door pulled her from her reverie. Handsome Peter Finn, who she been told by the front desk ladies looked a little like the actor George Clooney (Maria saw the resemblance, a very faint one at that), was filling the doorframe, wearing his uniform, and looking like he was on official business. In the past few weeks, their friendship had flourished. Although she knew he'd be willing to be more, they had developed an easy camaraderie she enjoyed.

"I heard about the situation," he said seriously.

"My situation?" she asked curiously.

"Having to bunk with those two blondes for Thursday, Friday, and Saturday."

"Oh, yes… the overbooking. It happens even in the biggest of hotels, but we can usually arrange alternate accommodations, but that is only when there is another hotel in proximity. Out here, the best we can do is offer a sleeping bag on the floor of the lobby," she said with a smile.

"Well, that is where I come in. I think I can help," he announced, his broad smile transforming his serious face.

"Help?" she asked and gave a tentative smile. "What do you have in mind?"

"My cabin has a spare bedroom. Nothing fancy, as you know, but you'd have your own room, and it's only a couple of miles from here. That must sound better than being with those two."

She'd been to dinner at his cabin and knew it was a lot like him, nice and tidy. The thought of getting away from the lodge was very appealing. "I… I don't know what to say. I can't impose on you like that."

"Say yes, so I don't have to think of you sleeping on the floor," he said thoughtfully. "And it isn't an imposition. It is a treat to have a house guest."

"There is a couch in the ladies' quarters," she explained. "I'd planned on sleeping on that."

"Yes, but you'd still have to share space with those two Barbie dolls."

She laughed. "They're not so bad, and I don't want to put you out."

"You're not. I'd enjoy the company." Reading her unspoken thoughts, he added, "Don't worry... I won't try anything. I think of you as a friend." Then, he winked and reached for one of her bags.

She liked Peter and even wondered if she wasn't still in love with another man if something more might have been possible between them. She was just flattered that after all she'd been through, another man found her attractive. Especially not wearing all of her armor—that was something in itself and something she needed to take note of. People liked her for her, not her designer suits, shoes, makeup, manicures, or fancy hair-cuts. She was likable without what she'd thought of as a need for perfection. Not to say she didn't like looking her best, but the reasoning behind looking her best had changed. Maybe looking her best was when she looked her most natural.

The rest of the day was hectic. She met with the executive chef to discuss an idea she had for a reoccurring Sunday night spaghetti dinner. With the weather starting to show the first chill of fall, the heavier meal might be more appropriate. And even though it was only July, she was already feeling the cool fall weather trickle its way in during the hottest days. It was going to be an early winter. They were almost halfway done with the season.

But that didn't mean she didn't miss her beloved Italy. Even with the threat of Pablo, she missed her home country and the pasta and cheese, tomatoes, and other fresh vegetables. Maria vowed to herself she would find a reasonable home in the Italian countryside to experience the joys she'd found of the great outdoors. This experience was something she'd keep in her heart forever. She wouldn't tell Alex that, though; she hated to admit that he was right about something. Well, a lot of things, actually. Then she wondered what Spencer would think? He had a ranch. What was that like? When would he take her to see it?

Presenting the chef with a recipe she'd written from memory, she was flattered when he asked if she'd like to make it with him. Over the next couple of hours, she wasn't Maria Medici, hotel manager; she was Isabella Medici's adopted daughter, fussing over the perfect gravy for pasta. When the chef tasted it for the first time, when it still needed several hours to cook, she could see the happiness on his face. They had bonded over their love of food, but this was even better.

She'd almost forgotten about the overbooking until she returned to the front desk and found Ashley and Jennifer doing something they never did—not speaking to each other. Although she enjoyed a bit of the quiet, this could not go on. Guests would be able to sense the tension. This was a teaching moment.

"Ladies, what now?" she scolded from the small confines of her office. "I thought we'd gotten over this."

They both turned to look at her over their shoulders.

"You are friends," Maria prompted. "Forget about this morning and move on. For me, it is as if it never happened. I want to hear chitchat. Talk about boys. Talk about clothing and music. It is almost too quiet for me to think."

They smiled tentatively, and before long, the endless monologue on boys and fashion began as if it had never stopped. She hardly noticed when there was a brief pause. Then, Ashley announced, "He's mine."

"That's not fair, Ashley. He's not even out of his car yet," Jennifer sniped.

"Doesn't matter. I could see his profile through the window of the Mercedes."

Maria smiled as she looked down at her computer screen. A nice-looking guest must have arrived. Not caring to hear who won the argument, she stood up and stretched. "Okay, I think it is time I wish you both a goodnight."

Jennifer turned to her, sounding disappointed. "Wait, aren't you spending the night with us?"

"No," she said, shaking her head, "a good friend has offered me his spare bedroom."

"Go, Ranger Finn!" Ashley said with a little too much enthusiasm.

"It isn't like that, girls." Maria clarified—no one needed to get the wrong idea. She was still their boss. "He has an extra bedroom, so I'll have my own space. I will *not* be dating Ranger Finn."

"Yet," Jennifer said smugly.

"You should, like, totally go for it," Ashley encouraged her. "He's cute for an older guy."

"Girls, like, really," Maria chided, mimicking their slang as she shook her head in disapproval. "Gossip is toxic. Use this alone time to strengthen your friendship. Do each other's hair or something."

Walking out to the back patio, she decided to take the long way to the parking lot. She wouldn't be coming back for the dinner service. Peter had promised some sort of American Southwestern casserole for dinner and a chick flick movie afterward. She'd always been curious about casseroles and was looking forward to trying one over a good bottle of wine. What she really craved was to have a good conversation with an adult. And as long as the casserole didn't include a carcass shot within one hundred miles of their current location, she was happy.

Her thoughts went to Spencer for the hundredth time that day. He still hadn't called. He had been distant during their last phone call, and it bothered her. Despite what Alex had told her, what if Pablo had gotten to him and threatened him? He'd have told her, wouldn't he? She had the feeling something was going on, but she'd have to wait to find out what it was.

He needed to tell her about Ruby and his plans for New York, though the latter wasn't too much on her mind—he did say he wasn't going anywhere with her. But Ruby lay heavily on her mind. She wanted to understand where he was coming from after all that had happened to her. Until he did, she would feel this edge of unease.

She'd be damned if she would call him. She didn't have a good reason, and there was an old and fast rule that she had always lived by: Don't chase a man. Let them call you. Let them pursue. If they don't, they don't.

It was a hard rule to live by, but she had adopted it early in life, and it had served her well. The men who were in it to win her affections showed up.

CHAPTER NINETEEN

The casserole at Ranger Finn's was a new experience for Maria. It reminded her of one of her specialties, baked ziti, but with flavors and vegetables from Mexico instead of Italy. And thankfully, it did not include any exotic meat that Peter had shot.

They drank beer with it instead of wine, which matched the flavor of dinner perfectly. Peter had wanted to make margaritas, but Maria didn't like drinks that had so much salt around the rim. And she didn't like tequila after a horrible experience at university with a drinking game that made her sick the next day, all day.

Maria slept in and slept well in the guest room of Ranger Finn's, which was basic but nice and had a television which was a treat after being without even the basic news stations for the last seven weeks. Being away from the lodge gave her permission to be lazy for the first time in weeks. She was, as Americans say, "off the grid." She didn't jump each time the phone rang, thinking it was Spencer. She had taken the extraordinary step of leaving her phone back in her office. If the girls at the lodge needed her, they had Peter's number. Spencer couldn't reach her, and for one night, she was okay with the distance. She needed a little break from the worry. She knew he had more reliable internet than The Caldera Lodge, but the new relaxed Maria didn't care. If Spencer wanted her, he'd call, and after the non-communication, she was a little proud of herself for not being too easy to find.

She took her time leisurely getting ready. The sun was high and warm by the time she arrived at the lodge wearing her uniform with the light pink Polar Tech jacket tied around her waist. Sipping coffee from a mug that Peter insisted she borrow, which carried the slogan "Rangers do it in the Wilderness," she casually greeted Ashley and Jennifer.

The girls looked at each other and then back to her. They had a look of fear mixed with something else. It was something bad. They didn't need to say a word for her to know. She was immediately put on guard.

"What's wrong?" she asked, looking down at her green shirt and khaki shorts to make sure she hadn't spilled. Then she admitted, "I know I'm a little late. It was hard to get up this morning, and I trusted you both. See? That is progress."

The girls looked at each other again and then back to her. Finally, Jennifer spoke up. "A man, that overbooked guest, has been asking for you, like, all morning," she explained, her face unusually serious. "He is, like, obsessed with you or something."

"Do we know who he is or why he is asking for me?" Maria asked, immediately thinking of Pablo. He couldn't have found her. Everyone had been so careful. She looked around and started assessing which items could be used to fight off another one of his attacks. The fear was back with her, and in a moment, she felt hunted.

"No, he said you would know what it's about. I'm really sorry, but I think I made it much worse. At least he seemed to be really, like, really upset," Ashley added.

Maria frowned in confusion. There was more here than just fear of Pablo. Something had happened. "What is it, Ashley? I don't understand. Why are you sorry? What did you say? Why did he get angry?"

Jennifer explained, "Well, not at first, but then he looked angry. He wanted to know where you were, and she told him you were spending the night with your boyfriend, Peter."

Maria looked at the girls and shook her head. "Peter Finn is not my boyfriend. I've told you both that several times. Did you not listen to me?"

Jennifer cringed. "I tried to correct her, but it came out wrong, and I think it sounded more suspicious."

"Who is this person looking for me? What does he look like?" she asked as she set her mug on the front desk before she dropped it. Alex and Daisy were coming up the following weekend, so she knew it wasn't them. The only other possibility was Pablo. She felt a faint sweat break out on her brow.

Spencer wouldn't have flown over from Italy without calling her. There were days when all she wanted was for him to show up, but he wouldn't just do that. He'd call her first. He wasn't a man who surprised her, not after all she had been through. Besides, he wasn't getting closer; in fact, Maria feared he was pulling further away. The lack of phone calls was evidence of that.

Ashley looked at her computer printout. "He spent the night in your room. He's the overbooked guest. The one I talked to on the phone."

"The gorgeous one who drove up in a big black Mercedes. He's, like, so… hot," Jennifer added, making a soft chill creep along Maria's spine. Pablo was very good-looking. But she thought the girls would probably think he looked old—then again, anyone over twenty looked old to these two.

After Pablo had beat her, Maria could only see how ugly he was. His face lacked kindness. Unlike Spencer, he was kind. He had kind eyes, and when he smiled, he had crinkles around them that made his smile light up his entire face. At first glance, he looked like a beach bum, but on closer inspection, you could read the intelligence in his face. Maria loved the contradiction.

"A name please," she demanded softly, her voice taking on an impatient edge.

"Here it is," Ashley replied, her voice turning dreamy as she pronounced, "Spencer Whitlow. He sounds like he's from Texas. He has this sexy drawl. He's been by, like, three times this morning looking for you. Is he, like, an old boyfriend?"

Ignoring the question, Maria asked, frantically looking around the lobby, "Spencer! Oh my God. Where is he now?"

In response, both girls stared at her, their eyes widening as their mouths opened, but neither uttered a word.

The buttery soft voice came from behind her. "Maria, is that you?"

"Spencer, you're here," she said and flew into his open arms. Feeling his solid form, she pulled back just far enough to whisper, "Why didn't you tell me you were coming?"

"I wanted to surprise you," he said coolly, "But I think I'm the one who is surprised. You have a boyfriend?"

"No, no… of course not. Nothing has changed," she said, trying to meet his questioning blue eyes, then indicating the girls behind the desk. "They just like to make assumptions."

"Okay, then where were you last night?" Not waiting for an answer, he glanced pointedly at the cup she'd placed on the front desk. He added, "Nice mug."

"It belongs to a friend, my only real friend here."

"Really?" The question sounded like a growl.

Small children conspicuously began appearing in the lobby and looking anxiously in her direction. Her tour was supposed to start any minute. "I'm afraid we will have to continue this later today. My Wilderness Walk is supposed to start now. I'm glad you are here. I've missed you so much. Don't go anywhere." Maria didn't want to leave him like this. Was Spencer misunderstanding the situation—maybe even jealous? That would be ridiculous. He should know that she could never feel what she felt for him for someone else.

"I'm not sure I am glad I came yet. I didn't know what I'd find when I got here, certainly not Ranger Peter," he said, a small, tight smile appearing on his face.

Grabbing his arm, Maria assured him, "There is nothing between me and the forest ranger. I'll tell you all about it after the tour—"

"I signed up for your tour last night," Spencer said a little more than sarcastically. "Maybe we can discuss it on the trail."

She looked toward Ashley, who shrugged her shoulders in apology.

"You look a little older than the children I usually take on this walk. I don't usually let adults go on my children's walks. No one fifteen or older." Noticing a smirk appear on his face, Maria decided to tease him a bit. Once he realized how ridiculous he was being—good lord, he was jealous of Peter, seriously? Yes, it was time to have some fun.

"I'm a kid at heart," he said and leaned close to whisper, "Besides, I bribed one of the blondes at the front desk to let me join. They resisted at first, but I kept at it. A few C-notes later, more than they make working for you, they let me join."

"What?" Maria asked, looking at her front desk employees. They should never be accepting bribes. She'd have to deal with them later, even if it was Spencer.

"Go easy on them. I made refusal not an option. And now that you're finally back at the lodge and I can stop having a heart attack because no one could find you, I'm not going to let you out of my sight. So, you've got a bigger kid than normal on your tour." He broke away from her and meandered to the back of the pack, letting the small children get in front. The glint in his eyes made her feel more at ease. Maybe everything will be ok.

Maybe she could drag him behind a large tree on the trail and kiss him there. She had to get on with the tour.

Maria greeted each child and asked them for their name before leading them out to the back deck. Each time she looked in Spencer's direction, he met her gaze and held it—only in his blue eyes, which used to look at her with such kindness, did she see a barely contained fury? Or was it lust? If anyone had a right to be mad, it was her. He hadn't called for several days, and now he just shows up? Maybe it was for a special project for Alex? Regardless, he had no right to surprise her like this. Thank God he was here, but no way should he be upset.

Pausing by an outcropping that offered a spectacular view of the lake, she waited for the children to catch up. She smiled down at them, trying to get each child's attention as she spoke. "Crater Lake is the deepest lake in the United States and seventh deepest in the world. That is why it is so blue. If you were to drop something in the water, which none of you would do because we are very careful what goes into our lake, it would fall almost two thousand feet—one-third of a mile. Does anyone know how it became a lake?"

Several of the children looked puzzled. A particularly bright-looking little boy offered, "It was a volcano."

"You're right! Four hundred thousand years ago, Mount Mazama erupted."

She paused and watched the children register this information, then asked, "Who knows what happened next?"

A few children murmured different suggestions, but it was the big kid she knew in the back who offered, "A caldera basin formed, which means the volcano fell in on itself."

"Very good," she offered condescendingly. "You see, everyone, Mr. Whitlow has done his homework. The volcano was like a cake that falls in the oven… poof…."

Illustrating the action with her hands, she received chuckles from the children. After a few other facts that she knew the children would like, she moved on to a viewpoint at the top of the boat landing. Raising her hand, she asked how many of them were planning to go to Wizard Island. Half of the children raised their hands. "Take some snacks and something to drink. It is one mile to the boat from here and one mile back… all uphill. You will feel your lungs working harder because of the high elevation here. It will feel harder than it really is, but don't worry. Everyone feels that way."

Several of the children chimed in about their own experiences with the strenuous walk, making all the other children look at them as if they were warriors. Maria had yet to take a boat to Wizard Island. She'd promised herself she would but hadn't made the time. Someday, a child would ask her how she'd enjoyed her time on the island, and she would get caught.

"Excuse me, miss?"

Spencer. Again.

"What's Wizard Island like?" It was like he could read her mind. Why was he doing this? Couldn't he just observe and shut up?

"It is beautiful but rocky. You can see the entire lake from the top. The lodge looks beautiful from there but very small."

"What do you like to do when you visit the Island?" he asked.

"I don't get there as often as I'd like," she bluffed, and unfortunately, Spencer saw through it. "But it is a great place to have a picnic or hike around."

"Have you ever been to the Island?" he asked incredulously.

"Well, it has been a long time," she lied. He knew she was lying. She could see it in his eyes. He'd caught her in a trap. She almost laughed at his antics.

"Why do I think you've never been there, Wilderness Walk lady?" The mischief in his eyes was evident.

"I've been a little busy running the lodge," she replied, getting a little annoyed now with his persistence.

Glancing around, Maria thought some of the children looked at her as though she'd told them there wasn't a Santa Claus.

"You've never been there?" a little boy asked, scrunching up his face unpleasantly as he pointed at Wizard Island.

"I must be honest," she said, firing a dagger-laced glare at Spencer. This was not the kind of reunion she had pictured. "I haven't had a chance to go this season."

There was an immediate difference in the children. She could sense it. Her credibility was gone. By the time she led them to the area where the chipmunks were almost tame enough to eat from their hands, the children were rebelling. Several were complaining about being bored. She'd never had a group go sideways on her. She knew just who to thank for throwing her off her rhythm. As she handed out small bags of raw peanuts in the shell to each of the children, she feared her reputation for the Wilderness Walk would never be the same. She had no idea what she could do to save it.

"What? I don't get one?" Spencer complained, stepping toward her.

"Maybe I should give you the biggest one. With any luck, the chipmunk might take off the end of your finger and get you to leave the tour," she said in a low whisper meant only for him.

"The chipmunks bite?" a little girl asked, her voice laced with terror.

All the children jumped away from the timid animals, scaring a few of the creatures back into the bushes. Several high-pitched screams emanated from the younger children. One boy picked up a rock, ready to defend himself against the menacing chipmunks.

"There is no need to panic. Put down the rock. The chipmunks are sweet. Everything is fine. I was just teasing Mr. Whitlow because he gets scared easily and then jumps to the wrong conclusion," she explained pointedly, trying to soothe the scared faces. Damn it, how could he not trust her?

"It is okay. Here, watch me. We let the chipmunks feel comfortable by letting them take the peanuts from the ground." Taking a shelled peanut from a bag, she bent down, dropped the peanut, and waited for a small puffy-cheeked chipmunk to approach.

A little boy named Bobby, who looked like he might be nick-named Trouble, said in a thunderous voice, "Watch me, I can feed them out of my hand!"

"No, no, Bobby," Maria said as she ran to the little boy and grabbed the peanut out of his hand. Unfortunately, an industrious chipmunk had the same idea.

The chipmunk missed the nut and bit her finger instead, sinking its sharp, bucked teeth deep into the end of her finger. It took every ounce of her self-control not to react to the pain. It reminded her of the time she'd accidentally stapled her finger. She saw stars. The children did enough of the reacting for her as she calmly grabbed a tissue from her pocket and wrapped it around her finger once the chipmunk decided to let go of her.

"Cool!" Bobby yelled and smiled. "He bit you! Look at the blood! Do they have rabies?"

"I'm sorry about that," Spencer said gruffly, as the tour was cut short, and they all marched back to the lodge. The happy excitement was totally lost as the kids dragged their feet, not wanting to end the adventure. Maria glared at him. Looking down at her finger, now wrapped in several tissues to stop the bleeding, she tried to put her thoughts into words.

"I don't think you are. For some reason, you are mad at me when you shouldn't be. You are probably happy it bit me," she said.

"I wouldn't want to hurt you," he said. "You should know that after all we've been through."

"Then why didn't you call me when you came to the United States? What does that say to me? Don't you care about me any longer?" she asked, rounding on him.

"It has been a very difficult few days that are very hard to talk about, and I didn't know what to say to you of all people. Of course, I care. I'm just going through something personal I'm dealing with."

"Pablo?"

"No, I haven't seen him in days. Well, to be fair, I've been in the United States for almost a week. So, I haven't seen him in over a week."

"What? You've been here for over a week? Why? Where have you been?" she asked, seeing red and forgetting about the throbbing pain in her finger. How dare he be in the United States and not tell her? She added, "When you called last, you were in the United States?"

"Yes, it is a very long story. I had to go to Texas. It had to do with Ruby. I've told you a little bit about her."

"You didn't tell me much, but Rebecca and Daisy did before I came to The Lodge. She is the love of your life but currently injured." Maybe she had recovered.

He nodded but didn't respond. At least he hadn't argued with her, though the look on his face was one of pain. Something did indeed happen.

By now, they were entering The Caldera Lodge, the children running ahead to tell their parents about the violent chipmunk attack. Spencer and Maria were finally alone. "I cannot believe that you've been in this country and didn't tell me. What does that say about us?"

"I came to talk," he said sternly, his face serious. "I came here to tell you what has been happening with me. Hell, I only told Alex I was coming to see you yesterday. Texas wasn't easy."

"Great, everyone knows you are here but me," she retorted. Not only had Spencer lied to her, but Alex also had. "And now you've decided to grace me with your presence. Maybe you are a sewer rat after all."

"No, it isn't like that, Maria. It was awful. The last thing I wanted to do was to cut you out. You were on my mind—"

"But you did, you forgot me," Maria protested, trying to keep her voice low, knowing she was drawing the attention of several guests.

"No Maria, dammit—look, we need to get that taken care of first," he said, pointing to her finger. "We can talk in the car. We can talk for as long as you want."

"If you can wait, I'll get a band-aid," she said sarcastically. "Then, I suppose we can talk."

"You need a little more than that. I didn't come all this way to lose you to tetanus. We really should find out if there is a possibility of rabies. We'll get a doctor to look at it, get the shot, maybe stitches if you need them, and then we'll talk until you're satisfied," he announced. "Does that sound good?"

"Oh, I'm so glad you've planned it all out," she said, hands on hips.

He sighed loudly, trying to keep his cool. "I'm doing no such thing. As soon as you get the shot, we'll talk for as long as you want, wherever you want. I want us to discuss everything."

"What is tetanus?" she asked. Maria was sure it was similar to something in Italy, but the name was not familiar to her.

"The thing you get when you live out in the middle of nowhere and things bite you, or you step on a rusty nail. Haven't you ever had one?" he asked. "Is it a standard vaccine to get as a child in Italy?"

"I'm not sure," she said. Her records of shots were still with the nuns at her orphanage. "But I'm sure I'll be fine, thank you."

"I'm surprised you haven't already had one. We aren't taking any chances. You're going to get one today, a booster at least," he insisted, grabbing her arm and herding her to the front desk. His eyes never left her face as he asked the blondes, "Is there a doctor on call? She needs a tetanus shot."

Ashley and Jennifer noticed the hand clutching Maria's arm and then looked at each other. "No. The closest is, like, maybe Roseburg?"

"No, wait. I think that, like, Klamath Falls is closer," Ashley said.

"But, like, Roseburg is near the freeway," Jennifer argued.

"Like, I don't know, but, like, I think it is Klamath Falls," Ashley insisted.

Spencer looked like his head might explode as he listened to the two girls prattle on, sounding nervous and flustered.

He turned to Maria. "We're going to Klamath Falls."

Grabbing her arm once again, he half led, half drug her toward the front door of the lodge.

"I'm not going anywhere with you," Maria said quietly, not wanting to fight with him and create a scene. They already had the attention of several of the parents of the children who'd gone on the disastrous Wilderness Walk.

"Yes. You're coming with me to get checked out," he announced. "You don't ignore an animal bite."

"No, I'll get it looked at, but you aren't taking me anywhere," she protested and planted her feet solidly, refusing to move another inch. Bending close enough that she could smell his cologne, she whispered, "I still don't know why you are here. All I know is that you are mad, and I stay away from anyone who is mad."

His face just inches from hers, he said, "I've had a very bad few days, now I'm trying to take care of you and make sure you don't get lockjaw. I would never hurt you. How could you ever think that?"

"Lockjaw?" she asked, not understanding. "From the *colpo di tetano*? That is tetanus?"

"Excuse me," a strong voice interrupted. Ranger Peter stood before them, appearing out of nowhere, dressed in his uniform and Smokey the Bear ranger hat. Effectively blocking their path to the door, he asked, "What is going on here?"

"Something that isn't any of your concern," Spencer replied

coldly, looking down at Maria. "Great, now you suddenly understand tetanus."

"I'll be the judge of what is of my concern," Peter replied authoritatively, his hands on his hips. "Maria? Is this man bothering you? Do you need my help?"

She looked at Peter and back to Spencer, who was looking at her with murderous intent. "Peter, this is my boss, Spencer Whitlow. He's come all the way from Italy, unannounced. I've mentioned him. I don't know why he is here exactly, but I'm not going with him. We're fine."

Peter tensed and reached for the non-existent weapon on his belt. "Now look here, Whitlow; Maria isn't going anywhere with you. You can start by letting go of her. I think it would be best if you left before this turns unpleasant."

"Who the hell are you?" Spencer asked, directly addressing the other man for the first time.

"I'm a good friend of Maria's and the law in this area."

"Really?" Spencer asked and stifled a laugh, looking at Maria suspiciously.

"Really," she confirmed.

Spencer let go of Maria and shook his head. "This is the man you spent the night with last night?"

She didn't know what to say. Peter, the girls, and a handful of guests were watching them. "How many times do I need to tell you that nothing happened?"

Spencer leaned close to her ear and whispered, "Well, if it looks like a duck and quacks like a duck, it is probably a duck."

"What about the duck? Who is the duck?" she asked, not understanding.

"He is inferring that you're lying," Peter said.

She looked from Peter to Spencer.

"After all we shared, how dare you? And until you believe me, I don't want to see you. So, I guess this is goodbye, Mr. Whitlow."

Then she turned her back, nodded to Ranger Peter, and walked away from the man she loved but currently despised. Maria's Italian anger was flaring, and she couldn't get it under control. She was her own person now. She was to be respected, and never again will she let a man belittle her. Maybe she was overacting—whatever—she'd think about it later. All she could see was red.

An hour later, she was on a boat to Wizard Island. She didn't notice the mile hike down to the water's edge. She didn't know where she was going until she had gotten there. An hour later, she was sitting on a stump high up in the trees, looking across the lake to the lodge.

The view was incredible, but hard to see through her tears. When she'd heard Spencer's voice that morning, her first instinct had been to jump into his arms. She'd wanted to kiss him and be held by him. What a fool she'd been to believe he'd come back to the United States for her. He'd come back for Ruby, not her. Was the other woman better? Was that what he wanted to tell her? Was he going back to his first love, Ruby?

Boat after boat stopped at the dock below. Watching people get on and off, she wondered what Spencer was doing now. Was he calling Alex and complaining about her? Getting her fired from *Roma* and The Caldera Lodge? Could he even do that? She was a stockholder! He probably could get her fired from her position in *Roma* because he owned that hotel. She didn't care. Her whole life had been turned upside down. She would survive, and she would thrive, but whether Spencer would be in the picture was yet to be determined.

Would it have been so bad to go with Spencer for a tetanus shot? No, she needed the shot. She knew she needed to have the wound looked at by a doctor. Her temper, something that hadn't raised its ugly head in a while, had made her do something stupid, like get on a boat to an island in the middle of nowhere. Had she put her health at risk to make a point? Maybe. Well, Spencer needed to understand that she was her own person and not obedient to any man. If he still was her man. She wanted to be with him, but she wanted to be the only woman in his life. She wanted it the way it had been in Portland and on their trip to visit the other hotels, but something had changed. Whatever it was, she didn't want to hear it because it would be bad. Not after everything she had been through in the last two months.

Damn it, she couldn't lose Spencer. She loved him.

Now she was sitting on an island, looking at where, just a few hours ago, Spencer had been waiting for her. Was he still there? She should not have run away. As the sun dipped behind the lodge, she felt chilled and put on the jacket tied around her waist. She should head back and face him, face whatever he had to say, no matter how much it hurt her. She'd learned a lesson with Pablo. Secrets were bad. She wanted to talk to Spencer, to see him. He had driven up to The Caldera Lodge to see her. What had he been doing in Texas? When he called her last, and she'd thought he was in Roma, he'd lied to her. Ugh. Her thoughts were going in circles.

By the time she made her way to the dock, she felt uneasy. It was very quiet. She could no longer hear boats. When did the last boat stop at Wizard Island? Six p.m., if she remembered right, but surely it couldn't be that late. She glanced at her watch. It was seven. The last boat was always dispatched just to pick up stragglers like her, but it had come and gone. "*Merda*," she said aloud and shook her head. At least her Italian cursing vocabulary hadn't let her down.

Turning in a complete circle, she scanned the hill she'd just walked down and skimmed the water's edge looking for boats. Nothing. No one else lingered. She was alone on Wizard Island. It wasn't like there was a satellite phone available to call the lodge and arrange a pickup. This was a stupid mistake, and she was not a stupid person.

Panic. She hadn't felt panic since she left Italy, running from

Pablo. This was a new, different kind of panic. This was terror. The temperature at night dropped off rapidly. They had yet to have their first night of freezing temperatures, but she'd been told to expect it any day. If she didn't want to be a human icicle, she needed to get help or come up with a plan to survive a cold night on a deserted island. If only she had her phone with her. Why had she left it on her desk? Spencer. She'd been thinking about getting it, then she'd seen him and totally forgotten everything. Not that it would have worked, but she would have liked to have it with her.

Dread settling in, she looked for anything that might prove useful. Spotting a small shed, she felt a small measure of hope. Not like it would contain a satellite phone and a warm meal, but you never could tell. It might not be any warmer than the outdoors, but at the very least, it would shelter her from the elements. She didn't think there were any animals to worry about on the island, but better to be safe than sorry. What if there was a hungry bear or an angry cougar? Gingerly, she made her way up a slope of unstable volcanic rock to the shed and hoped the door wouldn't prove to be locked.

Happily, she pulled open the door to a small space, just big enough for her to sit down and stretch out her legs. Someone had left an old canvas tarp, neatly folded in a corner, and a pair of heavy cotton work gloves. For the first time since she realized she'd missed the boat, she relaxed a little. Not a satellite phone, but some assets, nonetheless. The canvas was heavy and smelled of mildew, but she didn't care. She wrapped herself in the canvas tarp giving special attention to her bare legs. Sinking to the floor, she curled into a fetal position.

Well, at least she could say she'd been to Wizard Island. For some reason, this made her laugh. She would never live this down. With any luck, she'd catch a boat back to the lodge early tomorrow morning, and no one would find out about this little experience. She would have to casually walk on the boat, maybe the second or third, so that they wouldn't ask any questions. She didn't want to have to explain this. It was outright embarrassing.

Her finger throbbed painfully when she put her hands in the work gloves. Why had she let her temper get the better of her? Perhaps, if she survived the night and had light to examine her finger, she'd find it was all black and shriveled. It would serve her right.

Her thoughts ran back to Spencer. She'd dreamed of him showing up at the lodge and their happy reunion. She thought of him in her bed. She had spent many of her waking hours thinking of him, hours when sleep wouldn't come and rescue her from the longing of him. Then, in the scope of one day, she'd lost any hope of having him in her life and then proceeded to endanger her life. All because of this one man. She should have known he was too good to be true. Would it be so horrible to be alone? Now that she had the Starks, maybe not—though she always wanted a family, children.

Oh, why couldn't she like someone like Ranger Peter? Well, that was easy to answer… because she was in love with Spencer.

Her stomach growled noisily. It was her own damn fault. If she was going to sleep in and only have coffee for breakfast, she had to suffer the consequences. Skipping lunch due to emotional distress was equally stupid. She remembered the chipmunk and thought of the peanuts. Fishing into the pocket of her fleece jacket, she found the rest of the package of nuts she'd meant to feed the little creature before the biting incident. Nothing had ever tasted as good as the ten peanuts she ate in that cold, dark shed on Wizard Island.

Chapter Twenty

Maria heard the voices before she was completely awake. Every muscle in her body ached, and her finger throbbed with pain. She managed to sit up in time to look through the small, dirty window of the shed to see Ranger Peter and several other forest rangers disembark from a boat at the dock. They were calling her name in the early dawn light. Thankfully, she was rescued, but if they had discovered she was missing, her thoughts of returning to the lodge undetected were gone. Oh well, she didn't care any longer. The need to get warm and eat something could erase a lot of embarrassment.

She stood stiffly and pushed open the shed door. She was so stiff she almost fell on her face when she tried to walk out of the small shed. So much for a graceful exit.

Waving her arms, she yelled, "*Io sono qui!*" It wasn't until they looked her way that she realized she'd spoken in Italian. Coughing, she tried again. "I'm over here!"

Several men made a beeline for her. Peter was the first to arrive and insisted on carrying her to the waiting boat. Midway down the dock, he faltered and almost dropped her in the water. Another ranger tried to take over for him, but she insisted on walking. If she were going to further embarrass herself by falling into the water, she'd do it by herself.

Eventually, they helped her into the boat, wrapped her in warm blankets, and gave her hot coffee.

"I'm so sorry," Peter said. "We didn't figure out that you were missing until this morning. We thought you just wanted to be by yourself after that guy showed up. But your room hadn't been slept in, and your car was still in the lot. If we hadn't found you here, we were going to call the police and start a ground search. One of the boat operators remembered seeing you yesterday."

"Do you think she needs an ambulance?" one of the men asked. "I could call ahead and ask for one from Klamath Falls."

"I'm fine, just a little cold and hungry. Do not call an ambulance," she interjected. "I'm glad you didn't start the ground search. I'm fine. Thank you for figuring it out."

"I think you should be checked out by a doctor," Peter said.

"Okay, but no ambulance. I can drive to Klamath Falls. And I'll get that shot. That *tatunass*," she said, not wanting to look at her finger still covered with the tissue that had dried to her skin.

"Tetanus?" Peter asked.

"*Si*, that's the one."

"Why do you need a tetanus shot?"

"A chipmunk bit me," she said, holding up her finger still wrapped in ragged tissues.

"On Wizard Island?" Peter asked.

"No, yesterday during my *vilderness valk*. I should have gotten it looked at yesterday, but I got mad and took the boat to *Vizard* Island to think about things. I'm sorry to have caused all the fuss."

One of the rangers scolded her. "Do you know how lucky you are to be alive? I bet it got below freezing last night. You could have gotten hypothermia or frostbite, not to mention how long it could have been before you were rescued. Lady, you were fortunate…."

Maria thought of the ice crystals she'd seen on the glass window in the shack. She knew she was lucky. Interrupting the tirade, she interjected, "*Si*. Thank you for rescuing me. You're my heroes. It is a dream to be rescued by so many handsome men." Then she smiled, which worked to silence the other man.

"Why didn't you get on the last boat?" Peter asked, sounding frustrated.

"I didn't know what time it was then realized I'd missed it," she answered honestly.

"You need to be more careful, Maria!" he shouted over the whir of the engine. "People have died out here. We could be taking your body back to the station and calling Alex."

"Oh, that is a horrible thought to fill in my head. I'm sorry, I didn't mean to cause a fuss. I didn't want to stay out all night."

"We should have counted her," another member of the rescue team chimed in.

"What?" she asked, recognizing the captain of her boat from the day before.

"We didn't count you because you are staff of The Caldera Lodge. We count park guests, but you were in uniform, so we didn't count you and didn't realize you were missing until this morning."

The rangers discussed the idea of tracking the staff as well as guests for the next fifteen minutes as the boat made its way back to the main dock. Maria was happy to no longer be the center of attention as they worked out a plan. By the time they'd arrived back at the dock by The Caldera Lodge, they had a tentative strategy, and she was warm for the first time in twelve hours.

Back inside the lodge, her staff swarmed around her. They hugged her and brought her food and seemed genuinely worried about her. It made her feel cared for in a way she'd never felt before. One thing was quite apparent. Spencer had left. He hadn't waited to talk to her. She'd told him goodbye, but she hadn't expected him to leave. She didn't know what Peter had said to him, but whatever it had been, it was enough for Spencer to leave. She wished she could rewind the last twenty-four hours and do everything differently.

She took a long, hot shower where she cried about Spencer.

How could he have just left? If he had cared, he wouldn't have given up so easily. Didn't that tell her all she needed to know?

When she got out of the shower and was completely dry, she discovered that Peter had returned her luggage. Knowing she needed to get checked out by the doctor, she ignored the allure of her tempting soft bed and dressed in her regular uniform of green polo and khaki shorts.

The tissue she'd wrapped around her finger fell off in the shower. The missing bandage exposed a swollen finger that was twice the size of her normal finger with two teeth marks where the bucktoothed chipmunk had penetrated her skin. She had been beaten up too much in the last few months, but animal bites were something new. It looked angry and by chance infected, but at least it wasn't black and shriveled, as she had feared.

An hour and a half later, a doctor in Klamath Falls confirmed her amateur diagnosis before giving her a tetanus booster and cleaning the wound. Thankfully, rabies wouldn't be an issue. She treated Peter, who'd insisted he drive, to lunch after they picked up her prescription for antibiotics.

"So, Spencer is the one," he offered casually.

"I thought he was," she said, but by the scowl on Peter's face, asked, "Wait. What do you mean?"

"The one who hurt you," he clarified.

"No, that was Pablo, my ex-fiancé. Spencer hurt me in a different way. I thought Spencer and I had something special. I thought we were in love."

"I thought he seemed hostile and threatening," Peter concluded. "I'd take him out again in a heartbeat. You know, Maria, once you date an abuser, you are attracted to abusers."

"Spencer is not abusive." She hadn't seen this side of Peter and didn't know what to think. He seemed to be a little too excited at the possibility of getting another run at Spencer. She asked, "Did he say anything to you as he was leaving?"

He seemed to reflect on this for a moment. "He didn't say a word. He seemed almost amused when I told him I'd have him arrested if he ever set foot in the park again. Within fifteen minutes, he had packed his big expensive car and was on his way. I escorted him to the edge of the park and watched him go. I'll tell you this if he ever sets foot in the park again; he's mine."

"Can you actually do that?" she asked, curious about the full extent of his power.

"What? Have him arrested?" he asked. "Sure. I'm the law."

"Well, I don't think he'll come back," she said regretfully. "But if he did, I'd want to talk to him before you did anything like arresting him. I should mention that he is cousins with the owner of The Caldera Lodge. You know, Alex. Spencer is a good guy."

Ignoring her wishes, Peter said, "Whatever you say, it doesn't matter. I neutralize threats at my discretion. Men who aren't respectful to women get what's coming to them. Maybe Alex doesn't have good taste in relatives. Maybe this person is Alex's opposite. You can't choose family."

"Spencer isn't abusive," Maria said, holding her arms up in frustration.

"I see what you don't," Peter said. "There is something dark about that guy."

"You're wrong, Peter." She resented his tone. No amount of reasoning with Peter seemed to work. Peter wasn't listening, and it was starting to annoy her. He was acting like a nean-derthal, and she was glad nothing else had developed between them. The last thing she needed was another controlling male in her life.

After they returned from Klamath Falls, she spent the rest of the day going over the reservations, noticing that her brother and sister-in-law had booked two of their largest rooms for the upcoming weekend. One suite was reserved under the name of Mr. and Mrs. Alexander Stark and another under the name of Mr. and Mrs. Mitchell Wilder. Alex and Daisy had somehow convinced Rebecca's family to come with them. She would get to spend more time with her sister and niece, not to mention seeing Lexy and meeting the new baby, Lily. The thought warmed her heart.

For the rest of the day, people sought her out to talk about her adventure on Wizard Island. It seemed that everyone knew, and rather than it being the embarrassment she thought it, everyone thought she was a hero for making it through. Tired of the attention, she escaped to her quarters. Thoughts of Spencer and the night she'd spent in the cold had taken a toll. She knew she should call Alex, but she wanted to rest up before talking to her big brother. He had a way of making her feel stupid if she wasn't on the top of her game. He'd have a few things to say to her about this misadventure. Well, she'd have a few things to say to him, too.

She was drained and fatigued, both emotionally and physically. By the time she opened the door to her room, she wanted another shower to stave off the chill she couldn't seem to shake. She climbed into bed early and fell asleep the moment her head touched the pillow.

A soft knock at her door awakened her from a lovely dream about Spencer a little after ten.

Wrapping herself in the pink chenille robe Daisy had insisted she buy to ward off the wilderness chill, Maria made her way to the door.

"Who is it?" she asked.

"It's me," the reply came, and she threw open the door.

Spencer was there. As real as he had ever been. She pulled him inside her room and wrapped her arms and legs around him. She should be mad at him, but she was too happy to see him.

"Spencer, damn it! They told me you left. Peter said he'd threatened you not to return."

"You told me to leave. That little asshat can go to hell. His attempt was more bravado than anything." He hesitated, gently grasping her jaw, so she looked directly into his eyes, "You are mine, Maria. We belong together. Don't ever forget that but do forget Peter for his safety's sake. Thank God he isn't armed."

She smiled at Spencer's words. "I didn't mean it, that you should actually leave."

He sighed, his face growing serious. "I was worried about you. I heard about your little adventure on Wizard Island—what were you thinking, my love? If I'd known you were out there in the cold, I would have commandeered a boat, helicopter, hell—something, and rescued you myself."

She wished he'd been the one to rescue her, too. "I would've liked that."

"I'm sorry about yesterday," he said. "I'm sorry about a lot of things. I wanted to see you. I wanted to be with you, that's why I came. I couldn't spend another day without you in my arms. I should have known your hot Italian blood would've made you do something crazy like run off to Wizard Island." She almost took offense to that when he asked so genuinely, "You are feeling better?"

"Yes, yes, and I've had that shot." Maria paused and said, "I went to the island to stop thinking about you because I missed you so much. I was hurt you hadn't told me you were in the United States and then coming to see me."

"How did that work out?" he asked coyly, nuzzling her earlobe. "Did you stop thinking about me?"

He knew the answer to that. Pushing him away from her ear so that she could look him in the eyes, she asked, "How did you get to the lodge? I thought Peter was making sure you never got into the park."

With a half-smile, he answered, "He is monitoring the gate. I bribed your wine distributor to let me ride in the back of the van. He delivers every week, and I happened to intercept him before he got to your boy scout."

"You bribed him?" she asked.

"He was cheaper than the girls at your front desk. Heck, I would have been here much earlier if your boyfriend, the boy scout, wasn't monitoring the park entrance. He told me he wouldn't let me back in when I tried to drive in with my car. Then I let him know that I was one of his bosses, and he'd better shut the fuck up, or I'd make sure he'd lose his job."

"No, Spencer, you were not so rude?"

"You're mine, Maria, never forget. I did try to get Alex to talk to him first, but he wouldn't do it. Sometimes cousins can be assholes. He told me to figure it out for myself. Alex said I went a couple of days without calling you, which upset you, and that was unacceptable. It was and that I need to explain." He said, his voice softening.

"Alex. He is a good big brother."

"He can be a jerk when he wants to be, but we all love him anyway," Spencer said.

"You should've called me," she said, trying to ignore the way his fingers were tracing patterns across her skin.

"Would you have let me in?" he asked seriously.

She ran her hand along his smooth back. "Maybe. Probably. Yes, damn it."

"Great, well, at least I figured something out."

"What did you figure out?" she asked.

"I am madly, passionately in love with you. I'm tired of missing you when I could be with you. Especially like this," he said, rubbing his body against hers. "Whatever I do next, I do it with you."

"That makes me feel good, but I think it is time you told me about Ruby," Maria said, feeling Spencer's body stiffen.

"Okay," he said and cleared his throat. "That is fair. You need to hear the whole story and how it ended in Texas, which is where I've been." They sat on the bed and then reached for each other, holding each other as Spencer let go of her to ease out of his jacket and let his shoes drop to the floor.

"I need to know. In order to move forward, I need to know."

Spencer pulled her into his arms, where Maria snuggled close.

"Okay, no more secrets."

"Thank you. Continue."

"We met six years ago. She was the builder's marketing assistant working for the company that built my house next to my parents. You know… she helped me pick out the finishes, colors, things like that. It felt like we were picking out the house details as a couple might. I fell for her, hard. She had long, curly, copper red hair and deep, cornflower blue eyes. You could see the humor in them. They danced when she was being mischievous, which she was often. I asked her out before the house was finished. We were inseparable after a month of dating. I asked her to marry me after a year, but she turned me down. She didn't want to commit to it yet, said she wanted to prove herself and make a career before getting married, then pregnant. She was thinking about getting a real estate license to sell on her own. She'd be thirty in a couple of years and rethink it then, she told me. So, we had fun. We traveled, hunted, fished, and explored Texas. She liked country music, so I liked country music. I won awards for my barbeque, so she stopped being a vegetarian and started eating my brisket. We already knew how it would be when we eventually decided to get hitched. Hell, she'd picked out the colors in our house.

"I won't lie, Maria. It frustrated me to no end. I knew what I wanted to do, but she wouldn't move forward. There were even times I threatened to break up with her over it, but she'd just laugh at me. She knew I'd never leave. And you know what, she was right. I was beyond smitten.

"She refused to live with me, but that didn't mean that she didn't spend most nights in my house, my bed. On Sunday night, she'd arrive with enough luggage to last the entire week as if I was a Hyatt she was visiting. Eventually, she left things at my place so she wouldn't need to keep the back and forth of the laundry and the bags coming and going. I thought it was a good sign.

"Hell, our parents didn't even give us any slack. They knew where I stood. I wanted to make an honest woman out of her. I wanted to marry her, but she was adamant. She didn't want to marry until she was thirty. She was firm, had dug in her heels.

"Then one Sunday night, she'd needed something from home, her home. She said she'd be back in a half-hour, but she didn't come back. I started worrying after an hour. She wasn't answering her cellphone. Then I got the knock at the door.

"It was a guy I'd gone to high school with, Jeremy Jones. He'd become a trooper or some sort of highway patrol. He told me there had been an accident, and Ruby had been hit by a second car. You see, the first hit hadn't hurt her at all. She'd gotten out of the car, and that is when the drunk hit her.

"She should have died. Her body was thrown, but she landed in a field. In retrospect, I wish she had left us that night. Instead, she had an injury that couldn't be fixed and would never get better. The vital, smart, funny woman who always had stars dancing in her eyes was gone. This shell, this body without a healthy brain remained."

Maria snuggled closer to Spencer; she didn't know what to say. She hurt for him. He was upset over another woman, but his pain was greater than any jealousy she'd ever have. She felt horrible for everything he'd been through and ashamed for the behavior she displayed and the worry she caused him. She was jealous of a woman who had lost everything.

"You brought her into your house?"

"Yes, when the hospital and rehab did all they could do, I brought her home. I let her have her favorite spaces, which she seemed to recognize, but she forgot me. In fact, overnight, she had become scared of any human that tried to get close to her. I presume it was from all the pain she had during recovery, but the doctors couldn't figure it out. I couldn't get near her, neither could her friends or parents. It was awful, but I could, during her better times, put one arm around her or hold her hand, wash her hair, but other than that, she had no one. Even when the nurse tried to help her bathe, it was a fight. It got so bad that I knew I couldn't keep her at my home, but I did for three years.

"Six months ago, we moved her to a place where they care for people with brain injuries. It was a place called Featherwoods. The price per month was astronomical, but I didn't care. I've got a lot of money. I'd just hoped to be spending it on her in a different way, a big engagement ring, an expensive new car as a wedding present, and an elaborate honeymoon to far-off locations. I had it all planned.

"The first few weeks at Featherwoods were rough. Then, she started to like it. When I visited every day, she'd smile. It wasn't the smile I was used to, but she hadn't smiled in so long that it was lovely to see. The nurses and aids told me she smiled a lot and seemed to enjoy the other patients. Ruby was dead, but the new person who lived in her body was thriving."

"But, she died," Maria surmised.

Spencer nodded, wiping away a lone tear that had appeared and taken a serpentine path down his tan cheek.

"We always knew it could happen. The doctors had warned us. And every month or two, she would have a seizure. Each time we'd rush her to the hospital, and they would always bring her back, well as far back as we could get with Ruby. It became almost routine. This was the third seizure she'd had at Featherwoods. Only, this time, it was different. It was massive, and it killed her."

"I'm so sorry," Maria said, wiping away her own tears.

"The odd thing is, I'm sad, but I'm relieved, too. I'm glad she is out of the prison that was her body. I've missed my Ruby for three years. I don't miss the shell she'd become. Maria, Ruby became a different person; the Ruby I knew died in the accident. I've grieved her for a long time." He hesitated then said, "I don't feel guilty wanting to go on with my life. I believe Ruby would've wanted that too—we even talked about mortality back in the day, the what-ifs. She'd want me to go on with my life."

"I would want the same if it were me," Maria said. "I'm sorry for you. I'm sorry for her."

"I stopped at her grave on the way out of town. I put some pretty sunflowers next to her headstone because they were her favorite. Then I talked to her. I told her how sorry I was, that I had a much different future planned for us. That I knew she'd finally found peace. I let her know that I'd be alright. And I told her about you. How strong and independent you are and how much you remind me of her. I told her that she'd like you. I told her I'd found someone who took the pain away."

He stopped then, choking up a little to the point he couldn't talk.

Maria kissed his cheek, pulled him closer, and felt the dampness on her cheek. She didn't know that she'd shed tears, moved as she was over his words. This is the type of man she wanted. She knew Spencer was special, and he was—even more than she realized.

"Now you know why my feelings for you are so strong," he said. "Why I'm so protective. Why I need to have you near me."

"Yes," she said and snuggled closer to him.

"I can't be without you," he said.

"You don't want to drop me off in some out-of-the-way place like your ranch or back in *Roma* while you move on to New York?" she asked.

He smiled, "New York was a conversation, not a decision. Tonight is about being honest about what is important to us. I love you, and you love me. That's enough for tonight."

Gently, he rolled onto his back, held out his hand, and whispered, "Come here, love."

Without thinking, she sat astride him. She looked down at her lover, the man who'd taken great lengths to get to her. They were together, and they were in love. For tonight, it was enough.

CHAPTER TWENTY-ONE

Waking to misty, gray clouds, Maria rolled over and reached for Spencer. Her bed was empty and cold. She couldn't believe he'd left. Not after the night they'd shared. They'd talked. They'd made love. They were in love. Where the hell was he?

Sitting up, she had the tortured feeling that she'd dreamed it all, dreamed every word he'd said. With a sinking feeling, she got out of bed and headed for the shower.

Was she losing her mind? Her muscles were sore, but why wouldn't they be? She'd spent the previous night sleeping in a shack covered with an old, ratty canvas cover. And last night in every contorted position possible—and loved it!

As she got dressed to look for her man, she tried to tamp down the uncertain feelings overcoming her. No, she would not worry—instead, Maria was ready to let Spencer know to never leave the bed without her.

She left her room and walked down the stairs to the main lobby. Everything felt different. Jennifer and Ashley were waiting behind the front desk, their faces wide-eyed and, if she wasn't mistaken, a bit frightened. Some other drama had definitely unfolded.

"What is wrong now?" she asked.

"You're, like, not going to believe it," Jennifer said.

"What? Try me," Maria asked, growing impatient.

"Ranger Peter and that man, that Spencer guy, they, like, got into a fight, right here in the lobby. Two other rangers had to break them up. Peter hauled Spencer off in handcuffs."

Shaking her head to clear the cobwebs and fully understand what they'd just told her, she asked, "What? When?"

"It was, like, I don't know... maybe two hours ago."

"Today? This morning?" Maria asked, her heart beating hard in her chest.

"Yeah, he said he was staying with you. He even tried to order room service. Can you imagine? That guy is, like, whacked in the head," Jennifer supplied.

"He's, like, your stalker. I was just, like, glad I thought to call Peter. He was here in, like, an instant," Ashley added.

Maria leaned wearily against the desk for support. "You called Peter?"

"Like, yeah... That dude left, like, last night, and then he showed up again. It was creepy. And, he was, like, totally saying he was Alex's cousin, which was so bullshit. He's not a Stark," Ashley said.

"Where did they take him?" Maria asked curtly.

Jennifer laughed, "He's so busted, no pass go, no collect $200, right to jail for him."

Not understanding, Maria asked, "Jail? Peter took Spencer to jail?"

"Well, like, after Peter showed up and grabbed him making a citizen's arrest, that, like, Spencer guy got Peter in, like, a head-lock so fast... then all these other rangers arrived and jumped on him. He was saying all sorts of things, like, he was part owner of the Stark Hotels. What a poser!"

"He does own part of the Stark International Hotels. He is Alex Stark's cousin. Is Spencer alright? Where is the jail?" Maria demanded, pounding her fist on the wooden ledge of the massive front desk, causing both girls' eyes to widen.

"OMG, like, we didn't know. Did they say, like, Klamath Falls?"

"I think. I wasn't paying attention. I was trying to get the camera to work on my phone to make another YouTube video." Ashley announced. "I cannot wait to upload this to Insta and YouTube. I've got a big following from my videos this summer."

"Did you make a video of Mr. Whitlow getting arrested?" Maria asked, throwing the lid off the bottled anger she'd learned to control so carefully since arriving at the lodge.

"Yeah, here, take a look. I was just getting ready to upload it. I've been, like, documenting my summer here at The Caldera, and the response has been amazing. This video is, like, going to be epic."

The video showed Spencer calmly standing by one of the large windows that looked out at the lake, then Peter ran up behind him and tackled him to the ground, screaming "Citizen's arrest" at the top of his lungs. When Spencer flipped the ranger and got the upper hand, he was tackled by two more rangers. He'd been ganged up on by the overzealous rangers. Maria saw him go down, hoping he hadn't been hurt. She knew firsthand how it felt to be battered. Spencer was tackled, *her Spencer…*

Maria unleashed her full fury on her staff. "You shouldn't have called the ranger. That wasn't your call. I run this hotel. I'm the manager. You should have called me. And, if I find out that you've posted that video online or YouTube or whatever, I'll fire you on the spot, or Spencer or Alex will, and you can forget your summer bonus or any job references. Do you understand me?"

Reacting to her tone, both girls nodded, the blood draining from their faces.

Maria grabbed the phone out of Ashley's hand.

"Hey! I owe my audience a video a day."

"You'll get it back later. You can rough it without a phone for the day," Maria replied, pocketing the phone. "I'm speechless. You just had your boss's partner arrested by an idiot park ranger acting like an out-of-control boy scout."

She didn't wait for their response. In truth, she didn't blame them; she blamed herself. Everything had gotten out of hand, she should have told the staff who Spencer was in the first place, so they could treat him like a VIP. Not that there had been a free moment for that. *Damn.* Racing up the stairs back to her room, she grabbed her purse, pausing when she saw Spencer's duffle sitting in the corner. She found his wallet, placed it in her purse, and ran for her car.

At the Ranger Station, she inquired as to where they'd taken Spencer and got the directions to the jail in Klamath Falls. As soon as she had cell service, she called her brother, Alex.

When he wouldn't stop laughing, her anger took over. "Alex, this isn't funny! Spencer is in jail. What if he's hurt? What if they put him away?"

"Calm down, Maria. Everything will be fine," he reassured her. "If you can't get him out, I'll call our lawyers and get someone over there. I own the hotel for fucksake. They can't haul him away without my blessing. This is some funny shit."

"Damn it! You need to stop laughing. This isn't funny."

"Yes, it is. He's been here for what? A week? He finally pulls his head out of his ass, and now he's in jail for stalking you and assaulting a forest ranger. It's ironic. Are you sure you just don't want to leave him there for a few days?" he asked. "Maybe he needs a little time to assess his priorities."

She hung up on him after swearing at him in Italian. Arriving at the jail, she got confirmation that Spencer was on the third floor in a holding cell. When the elevator opened, she stepped out, intending to go to the front desk and ask to see Spencer when she almost ran into Peter.

"It's okay," he said, placing his hands on her shoulders reassuringly. "I got him. They arrested him on enough charges to get him put away for a long time. You don't have to be scared anymore. Heck, you might not need to testify at his trial. The other rangers will back me up. He assaulted me."

Maria shook her head. Peter had let his testosterone get the better of him. There wasn't much excitement in Crater Lake, so obviously, Peter and the rangers needed to create some. And he hadn't listened to a word she'd said about Spencer. She wanted to assault Peter herself.

"There's been a big misunderstanding," she explained and looked him over. "You look fine. I don't see a hair out of place. Spencer had better be fine, or it is your ass."

"What? You can drop the act. You don't have to worry, sweetheart," Peter said. "You're safe now."

Her eyes burned with anger. "Stop that kind of talk! Listen to me. You've got to get Spencer released. He isn't an abuser."

"Maria! Is that you? Get me out of here! Call Alex! Have him get me an attorney!" Spencer yelled from somewhere down the hall, his voice echoing against the cinder block walls.

She yelled back, "It is alright, Spencer, I've already called Alex, and I'll be right there."

"What are you doing?" Peter asked with disgust as he firmed his grip on her. "That guy is abusive. You left Italy because of him."

"No, you aren't listening. I'm starting to get very pissed off! He's not the one who hurt me. How many times do I tell you this? That man is Pablo Tino. Spencer saved me," she said and added, "The only one who is acting abusive is you. Did you ever think of getting the story verified? What kind of justice exists in this Klamath Falls? I'm beginning to think it is a big joke." At her words, Peter let go of her.

She tried to explain. "Look, that man that you locked up helped me get away from my ex. He isn't the man who beat me up. Spencer escorted me to the United States. He and Alex, my brother, agreed on The Caldera Lodge as a safe place for me. Well, until you decided to make everything your business, butting in where you don't belong. If you get out of this without getting fired, I'll be surprised."

"I love you, Maria!" Spencer yelled from somewhere back in the jail.

Peter threw up his hands. "You're so complicated. I didn't like the way I saw him talking to you. And, I don't know if I believe you. Victims never want their abusers to get in trouble."

"I love Spencer. Pablo is the abuser. Did you not listen to me?"

"Here I try to help you, and this is the thanks I get. You know what? I think you two deserve each other."

"I think you're right," she agreed. "Now, go away."

Two hours later, after several phone calls to Alex's lawyer and the video captured on Ashley's phone had been played again, and again, Spencer was released.

Spencer and Maria sat silently in the Land Rover, still in the parking lot of the police station. Maria started to turn the key but hesitated.

"What?" he asked dejectedly.

"What is ironic?" she asked, breaking the silence.

"Why are you asking?"

"Alex was saying this whole thing is ironic. I want to know what he meant."

"Us," Spencer replied with an indifferent shrug. "Please start the car. I want to get as far away from the jail as possible."

"Why?" she asked, her hand pausing on the key.

"Because," he said, his mouth set in a fine, angry line, "I don't want the cops to change their minds."

"What does ironic mean?" she repeated, turning the key in the ignition.

Sighing, he rubbed his temples before replying. "It is ironic that I tried to protect you, and I got arrested for being a threat to you. But what is really ironic is that when I finally tell you how I feel, I'm the one who gets arrested for stalking you and assaulting a forty-year-old boy scout, and I'm the one who got assaulted. That son of a bitch said one of the employees called him? I think Barney Fife just wanted to get back at me—little does the fucker know I could get his ass canned."

She refrained from saying anything. Instead, she giggled. The giggles turned to laughter, and before long, Spencer joined her. They looked at each other, and he said with a wry smile, "Thanks for bailing me out."

"Anytime," she replied. Smiling wickedly, she added, "It is ironic that I'm in love with a lawbreaker."

He drawled, "You catch on fast, green eyes."

<hr />

The rangers looked menacingly at Spencer as Maria stopped briefly at the Ranger Station at the park entrance. They all recognized her, but it didn't prevent them from being slow to open the gate and allow her access.

"Hello, boys, this is Spencer. He owns The Caldera Lodge with my brother Alex," she said and watched as they grumbled and shuffled their feet. "I'd suggest that if you want to keep your jobs, you'll give him respect and never, ever arrest him again. He is a VIP, understand?" Head nods and grumbles followed this declaration.

"Word travels fast in a small town," Spencer muttered as they drove away.

"I guess I should find their protection comforting," Maria added.

"Or smothering," Spencer added. "You know Alex owns this particular hotel. I'm just his partner in Stark International Hotels, as are you. We have influence. We are shareholders, but still, Alex has a soft spot for this hotel and everyone around it. I don't own it."

"So, I misled them a little. That is okay," she said.

Pulling into the lodge parking lot, she put the Land Rover in the space next to a familiar black Mercedes.

"I get arrested when I park in this lot."

"Well, you did show up unannounced," she said as she opened her door and stepped from the Land Rover, slamming the door behind her.

He caught up with her on the steps to the lodge.

"I need a drink, and I'm starving."

They found a quiet table by the window in the bar. The bartender arrived and took their order, a bottle of Pinot for Maria and a vodka neat for Spencer, plus two club sandwiches with fries.

"I can't drink the whole bottle," she protested after the bartender left.

"After I finish with the vodka, I'll drink it with you," he said.

Maria nodded and waited.

"Maria, I'm sorry. I can't mess up what we have. I feel I almost did."

"I would agree with that," Maria said.

"When Ruby died, I came back right away to help her parents with her funeral. I needed some time to deal with that. I should have told you, but I didn't know what to say. Are we okay now?"

Maria looked thoughtful and asked, "Do you still love me after spending time in jail?"

"Hell yes. More than ever," Spencer said.

"Then we are okay."

Chapter Twenty-Two

J ennifer and Ashley stared as Spencer followed Maria out of the bar and into the lobby. She paused to grab his arm and say, "This way."

She walked him right up to the front desk. They had spent the last hour discussing Spencer's time in Texas. She learned about his parents, his upbringing, and his friends. His childhood was vastly different than her own as it was filled with nurturing parents, family, and encouragement. But they'd both lost and had to look to new futures, but fortunately, they decided to find it together. She was more in love with this man than she ever thought possible.

"Ladies stop staring, it is unbecoming, and I'm tired of it," Maria chided, placing Ashley's phone on the desk. Without skipping a beat, she announced, "Let's try this again. And let's use our listening ears this time. I'd like you to meet Mr. Spencer Whitlow. He is one of the owners of Stark Corporation. He should be considered a VIP. Understand? Mr. Whitlow, this is Miss Jennifer Stevens and Miss Ashley Carter. They are front desk staff for the summer, and up until you arrived, they've been model employees. They usually think on their feet and don't accept bribes."

Extending his hand to each of them, he offered, "Ladies, we meet again."

Ashley found her voice first. "Will you be staying on with us, sir?"

"Yes," he replied.

A panicked look crossed between the two women. "Will you need accommodations?" Jennifer asked nervously.

"No," he answered with a half-smile and looked toward Maria. The light bulbs went on at the same time for the young women. They both smiled and looked down, embarrassed by their thoughts.

"That right," he said. "I'm your boss's main squeeze."

"Spencer!" Maria chided.

Without looking at Spencer or Maria, Jennifer placed a set of keys in front of Spencer.

"Thank you," he said and reached for the keys.

"I took the liberty of having it brought here. It wasn't hard to find," Maria said. "Thank you, Jennifer."

"No, thank you, Maria. It was a blast to drive," she replied with a grin.

Suspiciously, Spencer examined his keys and gave one last look to each of the women before turning to Maria and saying, "I'm going to go get my luggage out of the trunk."

"I need to do a little work in my office. I'll be back to the room in a few minutes, and I'll meet you there," she said, her eyes never leaving Jennifer and Ashley.

They had talked about a nap to sleep off the alcohol they had just drunk. However, Maria needed a little time to digest the events of the last few days and decided to play a little hard to find in order to get some time alone.

"I want to shower off the jail," Spencer said.

"I'll join you in a few minutes," she repeated.

When he was gone, she looked at the front desk staff and shook her head, "Bribes? Videos?"

They both spoke at once, but Maria silenced them by holding up a hand.

"I'm willing to forget all this if you remember who Mr.

Whitlow is to this company and treat him with respect." They both nodded, and Maria gave them a serious look.

As Spencer showered and got dressed in her room, she worked in her office. When he finished, he reappeared and inspected the lodge and seemed to be everywhere she needed to be. As the sky darkened and she retreated to her room to change for dinner, he appeared just as she was placing her keycard in the lock. He followed her in without saying a word. When he tried to help her undress, she gave him a look that could freeze boiling water.

"You're a very complex woman," he observed.

When he was close enough to reach out and touch her, he said, "I'm sorry. I behaved like a jerk. I should have told you why I was in Texas."

"It wasn't an easy thing. I wish I had been there for you," she said, wishing she could have been there yet understanding that wouldn't have been proper. Then Maria asked, "I need to ask you, are you really okay? How do you feel today?"

"A mix of remorse and oddly relief too. But mostly now, just anxious to make love to you."

She leaned into him, snuggled against the curve of his neck, inhaling the scent of him. "I'm sorry," she whispered, her lips puckering to place fat kisses against his cheek. Without answering, his hand slipped under the clasp of her bra and gently released it.

"You're the only woman I've been with since her accident. It took me years to get over feeling guilty. These feelings for you hit me like a tidal wave. I didn't know if I should be happy and live life again when Ruby was struggling to find her new normal."

"If the situation were reversed, you'd want her to go on living. Falling in love."

"I would."

"What we have doesn't take away what you had with Ruby; it is just something different."

"I know that, and I need to get there. I'm almost there. I love you, Maria. That isn't going to change."

Maria nodded but wondered if Spencer had his heart fully to give. As she was thinking this, he asked, "What about you—you've been through a lot these past few months. Do you think you're ready for something more? Something long-term with me?"

She circled her arms around his shoulders, answering him with all the emotion she could muster, "I only think of you, Spencer. It's as if nothing, no one, was before you. A future with you is what I hope for." She knew this time with him would be most memorable.

"You know, this white ensemble against your tan skin is the sexiest thing I've ever seen you wear," he whispered wickedly in her ear.

"I'll have to thank the American designer, Jockey. He makes very comfortable lingerie."

They were late for dinner, arriving when the restaurant was packed, people milling about in the lobby waiting for their reservations. Feeling unusually relaxed and sexy under Spencer's appreciative scrutiny, she worked the room with her usual flair, handing out complimentary glasses of wine to guests waiting for their tables. Spencer followed behind her, carrying two bottles, one red and one white, to refill glasses.

By the time they sat down in a quiet corner to enjoy their dinner, it was late, the dining room quiet with soft piano music playing in the background. Spencer took her hand across the table and held it. She thought momentarily about pulling away from his grasp. She wasn't used to public displays of affection. They weren't in Roma. They were in her hotel, surrounded by her staff.

"Don't pull away," he ordered gently.

"I'm not," she said, forcing herself to leave her hand in his as she casually took a sip of wine. "Eat your dinner. It has been a long day."

After the dishes had been cleared and they were both enjoying a slightly warmed cognac, he smiled at her as he swirled the liquid in the glass. He announced, "I'm not going back to Italy without you."

"Well, I don't know when or if I'm going back," she said vaguely, quietly meeting his blue eyes. "There are other factors to consider. There is a lot to discuss, and although I haven't been bothered by Pablo, he could be waiting for me. I don't want him hurting you, and I still feel like he is a threat. I love you, Spencer."

"Marry me."

"What?" she asked, putting her glass down with a large thud.

"I want you to marry me," he said softly, "Will you marry me, Maria Medici?"

She sat back and tried to make sense of his words.

"You just want me to marry you to send a message to Pablo."

"That is an added benefit, but it is one hundred percent that I'm madly in love with you and want you to be my wife. I don't want you to wonder how I feel about you, ever. We will figure out the rest, but I know that I can't be without you. And I damn sure don't want you with anyone else—in particular Barney Fife."

He pulled a black velvet box from his jacket pocket and slowly opened it, the antique hinges making a creaking sound. Inside, nestled in velvet, was a large, oval diamond on a platinum band laced with delicate filigree. "It was my Grandmother Whitlow's. If you don't like it, we can find something else. It will not hurt my feelings."

"But… "

"Ruby never saw or wore this ring. It wasn't her style, and so

I never even thought to give it to her." Maria saw the love and sincerity in his eyes. "But I see it on your finger. It belongs there."

"Yes," she managed. "I would love to be your wife, Spencer."

He carefully took the ring in his hand and looked at her, his blue eyes warm, the lids crinkled at the corners framing his dimples. She knew it would most definitely hurt his feelings if she didn't like the ring. It was a good thing that she loved it. It was so much more her style than the emerald Pablo had given her. He picked up her left hand and gently slipped the cool metal on her finger. The ring fit perfectly. Its heaviness was foreign to her usually unadorned finger.

"Perfect fit," he observed, more to himself than to her.

The stone was vibrant, sparkling wildly in the candlelight. She leaned toward him, and he closed the distance, kissing her in a way that made the other diners envious.

"Wait until Alex hears of this," she said, her eyes never leaving the sparkling, mesmerizing ring on her finger. "What do you think he'll say?"

"I think he suspects, though I've not told him. We've been talking about the hotels, and the options are open to us—we can even live here or in Italy. We can go to New York or Dubai like Alex wants. I don't care. I have a cattle ranch in Texas. With your new appreciation of the outdoors, I think you'd love it there if you want a break from hotel life," he said, indicating the lodge. "But it can just be a place we visit so I can see my parents a couple of times a year. You decide what is important to you, and I will follow you. I've been given a second chance at love. I will never take you or it for granted. I never want there to be unsaid words between us. I want to marry you. I want to be your husband, and I'm willing to wait until you tell me I can be. You set the date."

He reached out and took her hand in his, gently picking it up to kiss the ring on her finger.

The smile never left his face, but a small flutter in his eyes told more than his words ever could.

She looked away as tears started to bubble in her eyes.

He picked up his cloth napkin and gently dabbed at her eyes.

Unable to speak, Maria felt the tears streak down her cheeks. Spencer was here to stay, and they were together, but there was something that held her back.

"Could we wait a day or two to tell everyone?" she asked. "I just want to have it be ours to savor. A lot has happened to us both in the last few weeks. A lot has happened today. I want just us to enjoy it for a couple of days. Tell them when they are all here this weekend?"

"That sounds fine. I know I want you in my life. If you want it to be our little secret for a day or two, that is okay."

She nodded and gave Spencer a small smile. "Please."

Spencer nodded and grabbed her hand.

"Wear the ring. I want you to look at it and know how much you mean to me that you are wearing it."

"Spencer," she said, wishing it were a month from now, a month from Ruby's death, her ghost no longer so close. A month from all the drama that had played out between them in the last several days.

"No, it is yours. Wear it, try it on for size. You'll be Mrs. Spencer Whitlow or Maria Medici Whitlow, whatever you'd like. The family is going to be beside themselves."

CHAPTER TWENTY-THREE

Having three young nieces enchanted Maria. If she wasn't holding Lexy or Lexy's new sister Lily, she was having in-depth conversations with the ever curious and intelligent Emily. Her niece wanted to know everything about Maria and her life in Italy. She hung on Maria's every word. Maria loved it. Emily would always be special to her.

Although Maria had always wanted to be a mother, she never thought she would be one. But now, with Spencer, inevitably, they would have children. However, she hadn't seen the role model of a good mother and sadly didn't know how a proper mother acted.

Her adopted mother wasn't a mother in the sense of what a mother is. She wasn't protective and didn't necessarily care about Maria as if she were her own.

By seeing Rebecca and Daisy interact with their children, Maria now had siblings to share her future family with. Even though everyone was exhausted when they arrived the night before, there was still an element of excitement as the children ran from room to room and had fun before bedtime while the adults enjoyed cocktails and the conversation of family.

At the lodge, some of her favorite walks were with the children. She'd grown attached to quite a few of them and knew in her heart of hearts she wanted a daughter of her own.

She liked being an aunt to these young, sweet girls who were now part of her life. The need to let them know how special they were to her came naturally. She always wanted to be there for them. She would step in if they needed another maternal figure who would always love them unconditionally.

"You're a natural," Daisy said as Maria cradled Lily in her arms.

"I don't know about that. I like the idea that I can hand her back to you," Maria said with a teasing smile. "But I want to protect them. I want to be there for them if they ever need me."

"Think of how much stronger that feeling becomes when it is your own kid. It changes; just wait and see," Daisy said, but Maria continued to shake her head. "And if someone tried to harm one of my children, you'd be there to fight them off."

"Of course! I would never let anything happen to them," Maria said, horrified.

"Trust me, you're a natural," Daisy repeated and patted Maria affectionately on the leg.

"Thank you. It all sounds good, but I just worry. I worry about being a good wife someday, and I worry about being a good mother."

"Well," Daisy said, "Love is messy. It usually doesn't come with a sign that points to the right one. You have to figure it out a bit for yourself. You can do it. I believe in you."

"It was messy when you thought I was Alex's mistress instead of his sister when you first met me," Maria said with a laugh.

"Hey, I figured it out."

Maria laughed, looking down at the empty finger that had just held her engagement ring. They wanted to surprise everyone when the time was right, so Maria had taken it off for a few days, "Eventually."

"Yeah, I know I'm never going to live that down," Daisy said with a shake of her head.

"Something has changed," Rebecca observed, and Maria looked away.

"Really?" Daisy said and nodded. "I agree. Something has changed."

"He's the one," Maria confided to her sister and sister-in-law.

"Is it official yet?" Rebecca asked, her smile contagious.

"It is Spencer's story to tell, but I'm very happy."

⚬

After they had looked at the lovely photos from cousin Adam and his wife Laura's Fourth of July wedding that Alex and Daisy had attended, Maria could picture herself walking down the aisle with Spencer. It had only been four days since his proposal, but she was ready to tell the family.

Maria walked hand in hand with her niece Emily who wanted her own private Wilderness Walk. Who was she to deny her precious niece anything? She had started wearing the engagement ring Spencer had given her. She had slipped it on the last time she went to their room to find her sunglasses. It was time to tell the family.

When she and Emily had left the rest of the family for the walk, she'd held out her hand to the child, and it was the one wearing Spencer's ring on the third finger. A quick glance at Spencer confirmed that he had noticed. She'd seen his eyes go large, and the subtle smile adorn his sweet face. She gave a slight nod, and his smile got bigger. When she got back from the walk, they would tell the family.

They talked as they walked. She loved this child. Someday, maybe she and Spencer would have a sweet little girl like Emily. Maria couldn't wait to dress her in pretty dresses like the ones that Emily wore and explore the world with her and discover new things. Maria's future was full of possibilities, and she smiled at the thought of all she had to look forward to.

The blow came from out of nowhere. One minute she and Emily were talking about the chipmunks, walking along the path, and the next moment she was on the ground, lying on her back, her body slammed into the hard earth. Not only had the wind been knocked out of her, but her temple also throbbed, and all she could see were fuzzy stars and bright light until one menacing figure blocked out the sun.

Emily screamed, and then all Maria could see was Pablo's angry face, sweat dripping from his brow as his large hands pushed aside her hair and went around her neck. They felt large and vice-like as he squeezed on her tender flesh and screamed obscenities at her in Italian. He was going to kill her with his bare hands.

The back veranda was quiet and peaceful on that Saturday afternoon. Spencer only wished Maria was with them, but Emily had asked Maria for a Wilderness Walk, and Maria was completely in love with her little niece. He had noticed that she was wearing his engagement ring. He wanted her to say the words, but he couldn't help smiling to himself. They were going to tell everyone.

When she got back, he would pull her to the side and kiss her. He loved her, and he really didn't want to go another day without everyone knowing. They would all celebrate together.

A bottle of champagne could wait until they were back from the private Wilderness Walk, but it would be hard. This family time was wonderful, and he would miss it after he and Maria went back to Italy.

"When will Italy be ready?" Alex asked.

"By the end of the month. However, I've got to be honest. If

Maria isn't happy with anything I've done, we have to get her to be okay with it. If she wants changes, I'm making changes. I want her to be happy."

"She looks pretty happy wearing Grandmother Whitlow's diamond," Alex said, to several gasps and congratulations. Spencer responded, "Wait until she gets back. We wanted to tell all of you at the same time. Don't ruin the surprise!"

"Rebecca and I guessed," Daisy said as she handed Lily to Alex.

"Fine, so much for waiting," Spencer retorted. "I'm in love with Maria. And she loves me."

"I'm glad you want her to be happy. I hope you always strive to keep her that way," Alex replied as he held his new baby daughter, looked down at her, and smiled.

"I will. That is a promise," Spencer said.

Rebecca laughed and said, "Mom is going to shit a brick."

"Why?" Spencer asked, having momentarily forgotten the ring's history.

"The ring on Maria's finger. That was Mom's mother's ring."

"Yeah, oh shit," Spencer said, having been left the ring as the only Whitlow male. "Well, I hope Aunt Vic can see Maria as my wife instead of your half-sister."

"We will work on her for you," Alex said.

"Your family is so complicated," Daisy remarked. "You'll be cousins and brother's-in-law."

"Could we not talk about it, please?" Alex said.

"When is the next one?" Rebecca asked Daisy, interrupting the man-to-man Spencer and Alex were having. Daisy smiled and said, "I think two years, then we will have another. But in the meantime—"

"We practice," Alex said and smiled at Daisy.

"We start in less than a week when I get the okay from my doctor next Tuesday," Daisy said.

"You know, I'm your sister, brain-bleach, please! Could you two knock it off?" Rebecca asked.

They all were still laughing when the door to the deck popped open, slamming against the wall of the lodge, causing all the windows to shake, and Emily appeared, breathless and upset, tears streaking her dirt-covered face. Very, very frightened, her eyes were huge, and there was dirt covering her pink gingham dress that she'd been so proud of earlier in the day.

She yelled, "He's hurting Maria! I tried to get him off, but he pushed me away, and I fell! He hit her, she fell, and then he put his hands around her neck."

Emily ran directly to her father first, but it was Spencer who instinctively stood when he took one look at the little girl's face.

"Daddy, we have to help her," Emily said, pointing toward the front door of The Caldera Lodge. "He's hurting her! He's so big. She was hitting him, but nothing was happening."

"Can you take us to where them?" Spencer asked as his heart thundered. He only hoped they already weren't too late. His mind flashed to Ruby. Once healthy, then injured. What if the same thing happened to Maria?

"Yes, it was by the bend in the trail. He was waiting there. He talked funny. I couldn't understand him, and then he grabbed Maria."

"Okay, okay. We will help her," Mitch reassured Emily and then looked up at Spencer.

"It sounds like Pablo. We're following you, Emily," Spencer ordered as Emily took off at a run with her father, Spencer, and Alex, who had also witnessed the exchange, trailing after her.

Spencer yelled over his shoulder to Rebecca and Daisy, "Have the girls at the front desk call that forest ranger and an ambulance. We need help."

"What is his name?" Rebecca called back.

"Smokey, fuck, I don't know!" Spencer replied.

They ran by the chef and asked him to watch the parking lot

and yell if Maria or Pablo appeared. They followed Emily's little feet as she ran. At one point, Mitch dropped to his knees and scooped her up, then he said, "Direct me, honey. I'll follow your orders."

After what felt like an hour, they rounded the bend of the path and almost ran directly into Pablo.

Spencer, worried out of his mind for what they would find when they got to Maria, stopped Pablo with his fist. The blow hit Pablo square in the face, with the sounds of bones breaking.

The man crumpled before them, his face red and his breathing sounding more than just labored, but potentially very wrong.

"Stay with him," Spencer ordered and started running in search of Maria.

Mitch stayed, but Alex joined Spencer as dread filled him. What had Pablo done to her? Had he killed her? Had he left her for dead? Was she injured? Panic seized his heart.

•❦•

Maria lay in the dirt, tried to get her breath, and swallowed; her throat felt like she had eaten broken glass. It had all happened so fast. She hurt, but she was alive. She was going to be okay.

Looking at the bear spray in her hand, she silently thanked Rebecca and Daisy for thinking of all the "just in case" items. When Pablo knocked her down and started strangling her, she knew she was dead. Her hands were powerless to fight him. It was only when she stopped and touched the ground that she found the bear spray canister that had rolled out of her pocket but was next to her body. With the flick of her finger, she armed it, then lifted it, and sprayed it into his left eye. It wasn't a direct hit, but he immediately let go of her neck. Before he could grab the bottle from her hand, she sprayed him again, bettering her aim as she gasped for breath. She only partially hit him again, but it was enough. Pablo quickly stood and started running away from her.

Grabbing the pepper spray, she held it in both hands and waited for Pablo to return. When she was sure he was gone, she wearily sat up and leaned against the nearest tree. She had survived. Without the pepper spray, she didn't think she would have. She was dizzy and disoriented, but she had to get back on the path. She needed to stop him. Pablo needed to suffer.

"Maria!" Spencer yelled when he saw her staggering on the path. She needed to get to Pablo and hold him until the authorities arrived. But Spencer was there, in front of her, and she fell into his arms and savored the feel of him, his clean cotton scent that she could never get enough of.

Roughly, he pulled her to him then pushed her away to inspect her for injuries.

"I'm okay," she said in a voice that sounded more like a croak, but he was already shaking his head.

"I can see his finger marks on your neck, and you have a goose egg on your temple, probably a concussion," he said and then pulled her to him, wrapping her so tightly he almost hurt her.

"He tried to kill me," Maria managed, "But I…" She held up the bear spray.

"I'll kill him," Spencer announced, his own breath coming out in spurts.

"No, don't leave me," she said. "I thought I'd never see you again. You're here. Don't leave me. I love you."

"He will never, ever hurt you again. I love you," Spencer said as Alex hugged Maria and added, "Police are on their way, but we still have time to kill him and toss his body in the lake."

Maria couldn't help it; she smiled at these men, her protectors. And the thing was, she wasn't sure Alex was making a joke.

"Stop him before he leaves the park. This time I press the charges," she said.

———————— ⋅⊙⋅⊙⋅ ————————

Slowly, they retraced their steps on the path, Spencer and Alex all but carrying Maria as they heard the man before they saw him.

Pablo rolled on the ground, a mix of blood and snot pouring from his nose as he cried like a wounded animal.

"I hit him," Spencer admitted as they got closer. "Only wish I'd had a gun."

Alex nodded in agreement and added, "Me too."

Pablo had tried to kill Maria. There were not enough hours in the day to articulate all that he wanted to do to this man, but it was his Maria who said it best.

Maria tapped Pablo with the toe of her hiking boot. "If I were you now, do you know what I'd do? I'd kick as hard as I could in the ribs, not once, but twice, and then a third time to make sure you were listening. Maybe I'd make sure to crack a few ribs. Then, I'd try to strangle you. Should I do that now?"

"I'm sorry, I was upset then. I couldn't believe you'd lied to me," Pablo managed between sobs. "I didn't mean to. I just wanted to be with you again. I was so angry, I... I... Please, some water, please, Maria."

"You're begging me for water?"

"Yes, I beg your forgiveness, and I beg for water for my eyes. Everything burns."

"You came all the way from Italy to beg me for forgiveness, but you tried to kill me?" she asked, ignoring his request, then she asked, "How did you find me?"

"Some American girl who works here, she posts daily videos on Instagram about life in the middle of nowhere."

"How did you know to look?" Maria asked.

"I asked my people to find you, they were looking for any mention of Stark hotels, and they saw you. Something about hashtags. Italian Transplant."

Damn those girls, filming her and linking videos to Instagram!

"When did they see me?"

"Last week."

Maria shook her head. She hated social media. "You did all that, having people look for me just to apologize and beg me to return?"

He nodded.

"Then why did you call me all of those filthy names and hit me? You didn't want to beg for forgiveness. You wanted to hurt me again."

"Maria, what do you want me to say?"

"I don't think anything you say will ever be enough after what you did to me," she said and bent close to whisper, "Do you know what it feels like to have someone try to kill you? You said you loved me. I thought you were my protector, yet I need to be protected from you. Your protector is the person you are always to feel safest with."

"Maria, please—"

"The asshole deserves anything that you could dole out to him, but what did you do to overcome him?" Alex asked, looking down at the man who was now foaming at the mouth and sobbing as snot poured from his nose.

"I remembered the bear spray Daisy and Rebecca got me just in case of emergency from the REI. This seemed like an emergency."

Pablo groaned and carried on, even as Alex poured bottled water on his face. When Pablo could speak again, he began swearing at Maria, telling her all the bad things he was going to do to her, calling her a host of horrible names.

Alex held up his cellphone, and after Pablo's declaration,

Alex added the time, date, and location to the recording he'd done.

"I didn't give you permission to record me," Pablo said, just as Peter Finn arrived at the bend in the trail.

"I heard you give permission," Peter said, and added, "Hey Alex, congratulations on becoming a father again."

"Thank you! This man tried to kill my sister. Look at the marks on her neck. It isn't the first time he has done so or been abusive. We will all press charges. He scared the hell out of my little niece and deserves all the law will give him. Can you haul him away?" Alex asked.

"Yeah, take him to the jail where you held me," Spencer said.

"Don't let him out," Maria said. "He deserves to be locked up."

"I'll take care of it," Peter said. "Are you alright?"

Maria recounted how Pablo had jumped out in front of her and Emily and assaulted Maria.

"It was awful, and I do not regret defending myself," she said.

"Good. I'm glad you could fight him off. We are taking him to the hospital before jail," Peter said.

"He deserved it," Maria added.

Later, in the privacy of their room, as Spencer puller her close as soon as the door was shut, wrapping his arms around her, he said, "I'm very proud of you for what you did today. I don't think I've ever been more frightened in my life. I was so worried that I'd lost you."

He inspected the area where the ice had been held to her temple. A doctor had checked her out, and aside from the bruising, she was going to be fine. Thankfully, she didn't have a concussion.

"He deserved it and more, but it was enough for me," she said. America, Spencer, her life since Pablo, she was a different person, a kinder, gentler person. "I couldn't think of a different outcome. We have too much to do. We have our lives ahead of us."

"He deserved more, I agree, but it is a nice start."

"I didn't want him to interrupt our happiness."

"I like seeing the ring on your finger," he said.

"I love your ring," she replied, her eyes gazing at it as she felt the warmth of Spencer's skin against her own.

"Your ring now. Do you know what they need? I mean the family. They need something to get their minds off this unpleasantness," he said with a shy smile.

"Maybe announce something?" she teased.

"Yeah, like an engagement."

"I think some of them already guessed," she answered.

His heart seemed to beat double-time as she listened to his chest, her cheek against his heart.

"Yes, I got that feeling."

"I want to be married to you," she said.

She felt him smile, the curve of his lips against her forehead.

"You do, huh?" he asked with a chuckle.

"Yes, do you still want to be married to me?" she asked.

He pushed away from her to look into her eyes. "Every minute of every day."

Chapter Twenty-Four

Maria and Spencer arrived back in Roma a week later, turning down Alex's offer of the family jet and taking a commercial flight where they held hands in the first-class cabin and tried not to steal glances at each other.

Pablo had a plethora of attorneys, but he was still detained in the United States, and it didn't look like he'd be returning anytime soon.

"Your place or the executive suite at the hotel?" Spencer asked.

"My place, tomorrow a thorough tour of my hotel."

"Yes, ma'am."

"Don't call me ma'am, I'm not eighty-five, but when I am, you can call me that," Maria said and looked out the window at the rising sun that they would chase during their entire flight to Roma.

"How about, my Maria?"

"I like that," she replied.

A limo from the hotel awaited them at the airport. As they sped off to her apartment, Maria worried about what she would find when she got there. Had Pablo had one of his people destroy everything she'd left behind? She wouldn't put anything past him, not after what he'd done.

They walked up the narrow stairs like Maria had done so often in the past three years. At her door, she noticed not one but two new locks, which looked very imposing. Questioning the new hardware, she looked to Spencer, who shrugged and said, "I didn't want anyone to try and get in while you were gone."

Her apartment was much as she remembered it, but now it felt small and exposed. She realized she liked the space and distance of being at the lodge. It was so noisy, and she wondered how she had ever slept. It was a little like visiting the apartment of someone else. It felt stuck in time, held there. She wasn't sure she could ever live there again, which was good because she had a sense that Spencer would want to live in the corporate suite. Maria wasn't the same person who had left over two months ago, terrified for her life. She'd found her peace, her place in the world, and her love. All of which gave her the inner peace she had been searching for her entire life.

Spencer sat on the couch and said, "We have some decisions to make."

"Like what?" Maria asked, but she knew.

"Where do we go from here? Do we stay in Roma, or do we move on to another adventure? Where is home going to be for us? We have many options open to us. It is just a matter of deciding."

"Home is wherever you are. What do you want to do?" she asked, the first time she had ever asked him, but now she wanted to know what he thought. Living without him was no longer an option.

"I want to talk about the wedding."

"I do too," she said, "Someplace beautiful and in nature."

"The Caldera Lodge next summer?" he asked.

"Perfect," she said. "Now, your turn. What would you like to do next?"

"Ideally? I'd like us to finish up here until you are satisfied with everything, and then I'd like to move on to New York. When it is finished, I'd like to take a month off and visit my family in Texas. I'd like them to meet you before the wedding; I've told them all about you, and they want to schedule a Zoom call in the interim whenever you're ready."

"Oh Spencer, I would love that too." She said, observing that his boyish grin was adorable bordering on conniving.

"Good." He said, then pondered his next words. "I know there is some bad blood over the fact that my father and Victoria Stark are brother and sister. I know that you are a reminder to her that her husband was unfaithful, but we can't turn back time. We need to make peace. My family is willing, so are Alex and Rebecca. We need to do everything in our power to mend this rift. Vic is very special to me. She is my favorite aunt, and I want her to know that when we marry, that won't change. If she can't find peace about what happened in her own marriage, that's fine. But she can love you for being the love of my life, my wife. If she can't, I won't subject you to her scorn."

"Thank you, Spencer. She's never given us the opportunity to know one another. I feel horrible for what her husband did; I have complicated feelings about my father. But she is a blood relative who doesn't approve of me, and I don't know that we can change that," Maria said. "It is up to her, yes?"

"Losing her would be hard, but I can't see spending my life without you. It is time for her to move on, and if she can't, then we will. You will always come first to me. Always."

It was the first time anyone had held her in such a high position, and at that moment, she could not speak, so she leaned over and kissed him.

◆————— ◦⊙◦ —————◆

The next day, Maria had a hard time recognizing the hotel she had left two months earlier. The once traditional lobby that had been awash in red and white was now elegantly demure. Soft colors of sage, burnt umber, and dark red accented the space, along with new furniture and a fresh, modern look that still managed to be classic and high-end.

Maria touched the arm of one of the new dark red chairs, the fabric still stiff and new under her touch.

"What do you think?" Spencer asked, his voice carrying an edge of unease.

"I don't mind it," she said, secretly pleased. She had worried he would do something much more extreme. She could live with this. In fact, she liked it.

"Wait until you see the rooms."

Spencer nearly jogged to the front desk, was handed a keycard, and returned to where Maria waited. She had already greeted many of the staff and was treated like a celebrity with hugs and well wishes. She hadn't realized how much her team meant to her or how much she meant to them. It was humbling. When she told them she'd been overseeing a hotel in America, a hush went over the group, and several nodded as if this was the next logical step in her career.

"Ah, but of course," her assistant manager, Jacque, said and then leaned close conspiratorially. "Mr. Whitlow isn't a great manager. I had to take care of most of the day-to-day activities without him. I think he cost us a lot of business."

"He should have been thankful to have you," she said as Spencer rejoined her.

She regarded Spencer and smiled. "Jacque was saying nice things about you. You know, he should interview to be the next Villa Roma manager. I think he'd be fabulous."

"I couldn't have done this without him, and I agree," Spencer said. "Jacque, you're looking good for a promotion."

Jacque was overcome and couldn't stop smiling.

"Thank you, that makes me happy," she replied and added, "So, show me this shower in the room." The quicker they got this over with, the better. For the first time in the last year, her hotel didn't feel like it was hers anymore. She didn't feel like the manager anymore, so maybe it was a fair trade.

Spencer took her to the third floor and paused by one of the guest rooms.

"Before I show this to you, I have to say a couple of things."

Maria nodded and waited. He leaned forward and kissed her, then he said, "First, just to reiterate, I only did one floor in this modern theme. The other floors have been updated, but I wanted to be respectful to what you were telling me about returning guests. And I gave you my word when we visited Bellevue."

Maria smiled and said, "I love you." Then, she pushed him against the closed door and kissed him until the room no longer mattered.

"There is a method to my madness," he said when they finally broke apart.

"Tell me," she whispered.

"I don't want to talk business. I want to drag you inside and find the bed."

"No, talk fast. Then we get out of here and go back to my apartment." They had enjoyed her little wrought iron double bed a lot in the last twenty-four hours since they'd returned to Roma.

He kissed her quickly and muttered, "Fine. I wanted our hotel to be the first of its kind, multi-generational. I think this kind of marketing will be wonderful. A place for the whole family. The kids can stay in one of our voyeur shower rooms with their hook-up buddies, while Mom and Dad keep it clean upstairs in the better view rooms with the lovely louvered doors that look out over Rome."

"Nicely done, Mr. Whitlow."

The hotel room was part grunge, part modern, and entirely hip. The shower was in the middle of the room. Maria extended one perfectly manicured red nail to the red leather headboard and shook her head.

"Okay, I know it is edgy."

"Yes, the color scheme is nauseating, but not as nauseating as Bellevue was because you went red instead of magenta, and I can see some balance in design, but it is still raw and crude. It looks cheap. I have to ask, who would want to stay here?"

"We've fully booked out for March through June."

Maria sighed and raised her hands in surrender, "Americans."

Spencer started laughing and put his hand on her butt. "Well, some of us know a good thing when we see it."

She backed into his palm and smiled at him. "Good thing I like Americans. I think I've seen enough for today. Let's go back to my apartment."

"And nap?" Spencer asked.

"Sure, I'm always up for a nap," she said with a smile.

Spencer's phone buzzed, and he glanced at the caller ID, then jerked up his head and said, "Crap." Then, he tapped the screen and started talking.

"Hey, Mom," Spencer said, murmuring under his breath before saying, "Where exactly are you and Dad?"

Maria smiled. His parents had told him they wanted to meet her. Something told her that they had decided they were tired of waiting. Were they in Roma? Well, the corporate suite was available, considering Spencer was staying with her in her little apartment. They planned to pack it up and ship anything she wanted to their next project, New York.

"And Aunt Vic? Did she come along with you? Really?"

Maria felt the blood drain from her face. Meeting Spencer's parents was one thing but meeting them with Rebecca and Alex's mother, who had previously shunned her, was another scenario that made her start shaking.

"Well, okay, as long as we all are happy to be in Rome. Are

we all happy to be in Rome?" Spencer asked, meeting Maria's gaze. She could hear the fear in his voice. This was bad. Then, Spencer shut his eyes and said, "Well, good. We are up looking at the remodeled rooms, and we'll be down shortly."

Maria felt her mouth fall open, but no sound came from her lips. Were they in the hotel? How could she sneak out and not be found? Service elevator to the basement. Out the back steps, taxi to her apartment.

He ended the call and looked at Maria.

"*Merda*, are they in the lobby?" she asked.

"Yes, and they brought my Aunt Vic with them."

"You are just as scared as I am," Maria said as she held up her engagement ring. "And I'm wearing your grandmother's ring. Your Aunt Vic's mother's ring. So, the lovechild of her husband has not only been acknowledged by her children, but she is also marrying her favorite nephew."

"Yeah, that about sums it up," Spencer said, looking as nervous as she felt.

"Why did I have to fall in love with you?"

"Because," he said, wrapping her in his arms, "My dimples are damned irresistible."

⊹────── ·◦✲◦· ──────⊹

Hand in hand, Maria and Spencer appeared at the top of the stairs, having decided that they might as well make a grand entrance to the lobby. The Whitlows turned toward them as they started descending.

Maria stopped short at the sight of Victoria Stark in all her grandeur. She wore a designer suit in deep purple with matching amethyst jewelry. Maybe they did have a little more in common than she'd imagined. Victoria was an elegant, beautiful woman who'd been married to a hotel baron and given birth to two wonderful children who happened to be powerhouses. And luckily for Maria, her half-siblings.

The matriarch of the Stark family was flanked by the couple who smiled at her, and, without a moment's hesitation, she knew they were Spencer's parents, Robert and Liza Whitlow. Robert and Victoria looked alike. Not for the first time, she realized that if she married Spencer, Victoria Stark, the wife of her father, who he had betrayed with her mother, would be her Aunt-in-law. This family tree was more messed up than an oak getting strangled by the ivy. It didn't take a genius to figure out who the ivy was in this scenario.

Spencer squeezed her hand and called out to his family, "Here she is, my Maria. Isn't she gorgeous?"

His parents and Aunt Victoria all nodded, and Maria had a hard time meeting the other woman's eyes as she descended the stairway.

"Well," Maria said, "Isn't this a surprise? I'm so glad to finally meet you all." She only hoped Victoria Stark wouldn't slap her or worse.

"We had to fly over when Spencer told us the news," Liza said and stepped forward to embrace Maria. "Thank you for making my son so happy."

Robert Whitlow was the next to join in, kissing her cheek and proclaiming, "You are just as gorgeous as Spencer told us you were. Well, we did have a preview; we saw you dancing with Spencer at the anniversary party in Portland. Welcome to this side of the family."

Victoria Stark was the last to join in. She gave a tight-lipped smile.

They ended up dining at a little restaurant Maria and Alex always enjoyed when he came to town. There were prosciuttos hanging from the ceiling, and the wine was a family vintage that came in a jug, not a bottle.

During three courses of antipasti, pasta, and main course,

the Whitlows satisfied every curiosity they had about her.

"I can't believe how difficult that must have been, being in an orphanage," Liza Whitlow said. "It has no doubt affected your entire life."

Maria thought of how to respond. She was only in an orphanage because of the fact her mother had an affair, and her father refused to acknowledge her. If fate had handled that pivotal moment differently, Victoria Stark might have been asked to accept Maria into her household.

"It built character," Maria admitted. "I have no family now, except for the olive branches extended by Alex and Rebecca. It has built character, and for that, I'm happy. It is my hope that now that Spencer and I have found each other, we can be a family and grow a family together because that would be the ultimate for me, for us to have children."

"Another Whitlow and Stark merger," Robert muttered and looked to his sister, who nodded but said nothing.

Spencer held Maria's hand on the rough-hewn tabletop and smiled at her. She smiled back and almost felt like crying. She was speaking her truth, which had not come easily or without much reflection.

"I love you," she said, looking at Spencer as a tear rolled down her cheek. He kissed it away and said, "I love you, too."

Maria felt another hand touch the one that was held by Spencer. His Aunt Vic had placed her hand on top of theirs. Maria glanced up and met Victoria Stark's gaze. "You look like my Rebecca. I'm sorry we didn't get to know you earlier. I'm very glad to see my favorite nephew happy. He deserves this more than anyone I know. My mother's ring looks very beautiful on your finger."

"Thank you. I promise to make him happy," Maria said as she looked at Spencer.

Spencer kissed her, and this time it wasn't on the cheek. "We are going to have a happy life, Ms. Medici."

EPILOGUE

Three Years Later

Spencer held his newborn son to his bare chest so that the baby would have skin-to-skin contact as Maria watched from the hospital bed with a contented look, tears streaming down her cheeks. She finally had created the family she had always wanted.

Spencer smiled as he met her eyes, his cheeks wet with tears. "This is the most beautiful baby I've ever seen."

"He is," Maria managed before Spencer carefully bent and kissed her.

"I love you," he said.

"I love you too," she said easily and meant it. The words hadn't come as easily before they were married, but now they quickly flowed from her lips.

"I've thought of a name," she said and smiled.

"Okay, something with a little touch of Italian, maybe?" he asked.

Feeling the exhaustion take over, Maria said, "No, something to honor your family, especially the baby's handsome father. How about Spencer Alexander Whitlow?"

"I'm flattered," Spencer smiled, looked at his son, and said, "How do you feel about Alexander Spencer Whitlow?"

"Okay, that was something I was considering, and my

brother will be thrilled—another Alex. *Merda.* We will have to watch him," Maria said.

"Yeah, he's going to be a handful," Spencer said and smiled down at his beautiful child. "You know the family is going to want to visit. They like the Texas hospitality and my brisket."

"We have the room," she said and smiled. She liked it when the family visited.

Spencer was right. The family quickly made plans. Thankfully, Spencer's parents, Robert and Liza, organized a family reunion in two weeks at the Whitlow family ranch to meet the youngest addition to the family.

❖──────── ⊹⊱✾⊰⊹ ────────❖

"How did you happen to plan that?" Alex asked Spencer as they stood in Spencer and Maria's impressive Italian marble kitchen and assembled drink trays. Spencer's parents, who were their next-door neighbors, were visible out the picture window preparing a Texas-sized barbeque for that night's festivities, including ribs, tri-tip, and lots of steak. Tomorrow, Spencer would be making brisket.

"Lucky, I guess," Spencer said with a crooked smile. Their son had been born on his and Maria's second wedding anniversary, August 12th. It was a lucky day. On their first anniversary, they'd heard the news that Pablo had been arrested for punching a police officer, his brother, who had pressed charges in Roma. Pablo was currently in jail and would be for several more years. Unfortunately, the resulting scandal had ruined his future political ambitions.

The Stark and Whitlow families had flown in from all parts of the globe to attend this quickly-planned family reunion. Luckily, between Spencer's parents and the house he and Maria had built the year before, far away from the one he'd lived with Ruby that was now rented out to a nice family, they had the room for all the aunts and uncles, cousins, brothers, sisters, spouses, and expanding brood of children.

"How does it feel to be back home?" Spencer asked. Alex and Daisy had been in Dubai for the past two and a half years running the Stark Corporations's crown jewel.

"I think I'm happier to be home than Daisy," he said. "But she wanted to return to Portland before Lexy starts kindergarten, and it is nice to be back. I like working with Adam. The family business is large enough that we need two leaders, and we work the same way and feel the same way about our hotels. And it gives me more time to hang out with my wife and children, same for Adam. By the way, if you ever have the desire, we could easily make room for you too. Portland is a lovely city. And we finally have some capable managers in place to run some of our hotels, so it is nice to have the family power back in one location like when we were kids."

"I'll think about it. Maria wanted to be home in Texas for little Alex's birth, so I'm not sure I'll be able to get her to do anything until she gets bored with Texas. Then we will think about Dubai, but I think it is a long shot. I'll suggest Portland to her."

It was an inside joke. Maria and Spencer had spent a year in New York after Rome, but surprisingly Maria loved the ranch life in Texas. Spencer had even taught her how to ride a horse and then gifted her with Buttercup, a sweet bay, which Maria referred to as her first child. The fiery Italian was still part of Maria, but being married to Spencer, she'd mellowed a bit to a lovely hot ember.

Out on the expansive back deck with a stunning view of land that belonged to the Whitlow family as far as the eye could see, Daisy and Rebecca folded their arms and regarded Maria.

"It is unbelievable," Daisy muttered.

"Yeah," Rebecca said as she looked at her sister. "It is kind of unreal, and I kinda hate you, but I still love you."

"What?" Maria asked with a chuckle as she held her two-week-old baby in her arms. Alexander Spencer Whitlow cooed in his mother's arms. He looked like his father as a baby at the same age but already had his mother's coloring, and it looked like his eyes were turning the beginning shade of emerald. He was going to be a heartthrob when he grew up.

"They are jealous because you look better than they did after having babies," Spencer said, setting a tray of lowball glasses, a bucket of ice, and a bottle of Jack Daniels on one of the low wicker tables for the non-lactating or pregnant members of the family. Then he wrapped his arms around his wife and hugged her from behind as he nuzzled her neck. "Would you like more iced tea, my Maria, darlin'? Or maybe something else, whatever you want or need, I'll get it for you."

"Hey Spencer," Rebecca said, heavily pregnant with her second child, a little sister for Emily, "Fuck you, and I'd say it if I weren't pregnant."

"Um, I know my Daisy won't say it because she is the mother of three beautiful children, and she is classy, so on her behalf, I say, fuck you, Spencer," Alex said. His eighteen-month-old son, Jasper, chased one of Spencer and Maria's Vizsla dogs around the vast lawn with Emily, Lily, and Lexy following close behind the girls in their pretty pastel summer dresses.

"Really? Where did I go wrong? Vulgar language around my impressionable grandchildren. I raised you better," Aunt Victoria announced as she joined her children and her favorite niece-in-law and nephew on the deck with a pitcher of iced tea in her hand. Looking toward Rebecca and Alex, she said, "Yes, Maria looks wonderful, but she always was stunningly beautiful, so it shouldn't surprise you. Shame on you both for using such language. It is as if rats raised you at the docks or at a truck stop."

A commotion at the front of the house drew everyone's attention before Alex or Rebecca could reply. A moment later, a little boy of almost four who bore a striking resemblance to Alex and his father, their cousin Adam, ran through the house.

"We're here!" young Sam Stark yelled at the top of his lungs as he saw the dogs and his cousins in the backyard and made a beeline for them as he yelled, "Dogs!"

His father, Adam Stark, was right behind him. He bent, scooped Sam into his arms and held him upside down as the child laughed, and announced, "Hello family. In case you hadn't heard, the other Starks have arrived."

"About time," Alex said, then asked, "Where is Laura?" A beautiful watercolor of Roman ruins, Maria's favorite spot in Rome, hung over the fireplace in Maria and Spencer's living room, which had been a gift from Laura.

"She is rounding up the twins," Adam said as he smiled at Maria and the baby in her arms and said, "Congratulations, you really look great, cousin. Motherhood agrees with you."

Adam released Sam gently onto the lawn just as Laura came onto the deck, a son holding her left hand and a daughter holding her right. Their twins, a little over two, were still shy around people they perceived to be strangers. Tabitha, Adam and Laura's daughter, broke away from her mother to hide behind her father's legs, while young Jack looked fascinated at the dogs romping in the yard.

"Great," Adam said, "The kids love dogs. Scooter Two hides under our bed most days. Your hounds will sleep well tonight after we release these children on them."

"It takes a lot to wear out three Vizslas, trust me," Spencer said as he hugged Adam and then Laura. "Hey Adam, where are your parents?"

"They are attending a sunset tequila tasting in Puerto Vallarta. They and their hangovers are arriving tomorrow," Adam said with a smile as he looked to his wife.

Laura and Adam were hugged by other relatives and then offered refreshments when Laura announced, "Guess what? We were going to wait until tomorrow, but I don't want you wondering why I'm not drinking. I'm preggers again. We've decided to have a fourth child because the first three worked out well."

Adam pulled Laura to him and kissed her. His second chance at love had turned out better than any of his family could have hoped for. His love for his wife and children was evident for everyone to see.

He looked at his wife and said, "The best is yet to come."

"Four, wow," Rebecca said. "I'm very happy for you two. It took us a long time to get the second one on the agenda, but then we've never done anything by the book." Her husband winked at her and added, "You love it that way and have from the first moment."

"Yeah," Rebecca said shyly. "Each day is an adventure."

"I just remember how Dad wanted to kill Mitch," Alex said.

"Really?" Daisy asked as Laura and Maria looked up at the mention of Garrison Stark.

"Another story for another day," Rebecca said with a wink. "So, Adam, Laura, going for a fifth after this one?"

"This is our last," Laura said. "Adam already has his hands full, what with keeping me, the kids, and the dog happy." Instead of answering, Adam put his arms around his wife and held her to him.

"I haven't decided," Daisy said, "But I'm leaning toward one more."

Alex smiled, "I'm always up for any job my wife has for me. Spencer?"

"One or two more," Maria answered for her husband.

"Six grandchildren and counting, and Adam and Laura's children," Victoria said with a shake of her head. "My Christmas list gets bigger when any of you just look at your spouses. I think I love it."

Maria noticed that baby Alex was included in the group that

Victoria called "grandchildren," and she couldn't help but smile. Victoria noticed and said conspiratorially, "You know, Maria, I think you are the only one of the Stark children with class and decorum. Spencer is a lucky man."

"And I'm a lucky woman. Thank you, Aunt Vic," Maria said and watched Alex and Rebecca roll their eyes as they grinned.

"You've come a long way, my Maria," Spencer whispered to his wife. "Welcome officially to the family."

"Thank you," Maria said. She had the family she always wanted. Meeting her husband's eye, Maria smiled brightly. She'd finally found love.

The End

About the Author

Mary Oldham is an award winning author, and three-time Golden Heart Finalist with the Romance Writers of America in the areas of Contemporary Romance and Romantic Suspense. When she is not sitting on her deck and looking at the Pacific in Yachats, Oregon—Gem of the Oregon Coast—Mary lives in Portland, Oregon.

Also by Mary Oldham

Don't miss any of Mary Oldham's other books, available on Print or Digital at Amazon or Barnes and Noble:

Stand Alone Titles

The Silver Linings Wedding Dress Auction, October 2021

Crush, Available May 2022

The Hotel Baron's Series

A Paris Affair, November 2021

A Summer Affair, December 2021

A Roman Affair, April 2022

A Hungarian Affair, Available December 2022 (Tentative Title)

Audiobooks

The Silver Linings Wedding Dress Auction, Available April 2022

Narrated by Gildart Jackson

Mary loves to hear from her readers! You can email her to sign up for her newsletter at www.maryoldham.com.

.

Acknowledgments

I wrote this book in a month as a challenge when I turned 40. It has been on the shelf for a few years. When Sue and I started discussing it, I told her it wasn't one of my favorites, so we did a complete rewrite. The end was rewritten three times just to show Maria's strength. I love that we get to see some of the people we've met in the series from previous books.

A huge thank you to Sue Grimshaw for encouraging and loving this story. I could not have done it without your talent and support. You bring out the best in me and keep me going.

To my beta readers, Lorinda Pratt and Maile Hammond, thank you for the suggestions and for loving this series.

Thank you,
Mary

Printed in Great Britain
by Amazon

22570385R00165